IN FRANKLIN'S HOUSE

IN FRANKLIN'S HOUSE

by
Beverly Lauderdale

Oak Tree Press   Taylorville, IL

Oak Tree Press

Oak Tree Press books may be purchased for educational, business or sales promotional purposes. Contact Publisher for quantity discounts

First Edition, February 2010

Cover by MickADesign.com

ISBN 978-1-892343-62-8

LCCN 2010921957

For my dad, "Doc" Shelgren
(1915 - 2008)

CHAPTER ONE | FEBRUARY

*T*oward evening the wind switched to a minor key to send depression like a living thing scuttling over packing boxes sealed with tape. I looked at the living room with its smoke-stained fireplace, window frames splintered and hungry for paint, and a twelve-foot high ceiling scarred by fissures that formed abstract patterns. The formal dining room that lay beyond a connecting archway was vacant except for a cabinet with glass doors and a chandelier minus pendants.

I gazed down at my tennis shoes stained with soil from my garden 2000 miles away. Beside rows of zinnias, asters, peonies, bleeding hearts and lily-of-the-valley sat my ranch-style home where living room walls were painted blue and—

"Enough wallowing," I said aloud and walked to one end of the couch to rip open another cardboard box. If I'd been organized when we moved, I'd have printed contents on the side or at least in large letters have labeled "Kitchen," "Bedroom," but years had passed between moves and I'd forgotten such basics. That first move had not been cross-county with couches, a television, beds, tables, and pieces from a united past tossed into a truck. In that other move there'd been no child to leave behind, no compulsion to pack fast and start immediately for California, a state as foreign as another country.

In dimming daylight I tugged at the cardboard flap. Backed by the room's emptiness and the rising wind, it gave a satisfactory crack, exposing band aids, Merthiolate, Vaseline, aspirin. . . What an assortment. I didn't remember dumping the medicine chest contents atop towels and wash cloths. If my daughter pulled a stunt like that, I'd lecture her. "But Molly does not live here," an inner voice whispered.

With sudden anger I yanked at the box, moving it across unwaxed floors toward the bathroom where I groped for the light switch; then groaned. Impossible to squeeze the box through this narrow doorway. At home the bathroom was big, modern, clean. Here a bare bulb dangled from a black cord, and a wavery mirror hung off-center above a basin. Faucets groaned before they spit water into the pitted bowl. Floor tiles curled, a shower head flopped from the head of the tub, and it was all too much.

I flipped off the switch and in the darkened hallway breathed deeply. What to do? I knew no one in this town where for the last two days I'd been alone. Around me the house creaked and sighed, so I moved toward the bedroom, but the furniture was a set Dan had picked out and bought some years ago. Not wanting to think of my husband, I retraced my steps but instead of stopping in the living room, I turned sharply to climb stairs that led to a pair of rooms tucked beneath the eaves. Within the northern room, warmth touched me, as it had when Dan and I toured the house last month. It was this room that prompted me to tell the realtor, "We'll take it."

And Dan, resentful and silent, simply followed me to the rental car after my announcement, and there said, "Kate, you want that place? It's a mess."

"It's about the only one we can afford, isn't it?"

"We could have checked around some more in other towns."

I shook my head, for in contrast to the neighboring towns with their Spanish-style names, Madison sounded reassuring, closest to my Midwestern yesterdays. And by California standards, Madison was small with a population of 20,000. Bordered on the north by the Carquinez Strait and ringed by hills in all other directions, its center rested in a valley. Madison did not sprawl. Madison had definition.

As we sped westward toward San Francisco and the plane which would take us Home for the last time, Dan pointed out negatives about a house constructed a hundred years ago. "Plus, it's on top that hill, not even the better hill either from what the realtor implied. Those on the opposite hill have views of the Strait. All we have is a view of the downtown. No neighbors. We'll be sitting up there cut off." And I'd thought, *he doesn't want to be isolated with me.*

"You didn't notice there are houses directly below us on the next street?"

"There's something wrong with a property that has sat vacant for so long. If it's such a good deal, why hasn't someone bought it?" he said.

"The realtor explained about the widow, how long it took to settle the estate."

"But buyers aren't lining up. I'm sure there are termites and that south side will have to be jacked up. Plumbing's going to—"

"Fine, Dan, don't buy it. Find someplace you like. But it's far different than anything we've ever owned. It's a different setting and if we're going to start over—"

He sighed. "You're going to be spending most of the time there. I'll be commuting, so guess it doesn't matter."

Yet that fast final week in Iowa while we packed and told people goodbye, while I swallowed sobs and paced the floors, the appeal of that upstairs room faded. And four days ago when we arrived in Madison with February rain graying our lives and future, the town appeared forbidding and solemn as did the house.

I'd driven our Chevy behind Dan's truck up the steep hill, pulled on the emergency brake and stared upwards. Charm had vanished. Instead I saw twenty-seven steps that rose abruptly to the front porch. On each side of them bushes and plants prevented dirt slides. There would never be a sloping lawn. There would never be grass.

Without speaking we shuffled upwards. Too spent to care, I let rain wet my hair and dampen my tweed coat. As Dan experimented with an unfamiliar key in an unfamiliar lock, I noticed a sag in the front porch. On the third attempt he forced the lock, and we crossed into an entry hall. Our footfalls ricocheted from barren rooms, and I closed my eyes to shut out emptiness.

Without comment we continued through the bottom level. To the left of the entryway was a small room, the purpose of which baffled the realtor. Miniature den? Study?

To the right of the entry lay the living room that merged into a dining room where a swinging door opened onto the kitchen. To the dining room's left, a hallway connected the bathroom and bedroom.

"Only one bathroom, you realize," Dan said as his first words.

I propped open the swinging door and walked into the kitchen, the antithesis of the one I'd loved in Iowa. The back wall held the patio door that opened onto a covered area where rain drummed upon the roof. The backyard was a tangled thicket, but the jungle effect was pleasing, for it spoke of mystery, of secret enclosures where rain drops splashed upon leaves. It hinted of coolness on hot days, of wild flowers. Even the scent of decaying vegetation which had fallen for unknown seasons suggested a rich texture of—

"While there's still daylight, Kate, I'm going to that gas station we passed and try to hire some guys to help unload."

I re-entered the house and listened to its silence. In the distance I heard the engine catch; heard the brakes protest as the truck rumbled down the hill. How frigid this place. I'd naively pictured California as sunny, but the chill gnawed. I buttoned my coat and began to haul items from the car.

The next morning Dan left in a downpour for San Francisco and his first day at a new job. Since he'd returned the rental truck, he took the Chevy, so I fought wind and rain as I hiked down the hillside to the phone company, to Pacific Gas and Power, to the garbage company, and then hiked back up the hill with a sack of groceries. Drenched, miserable, I'd grappled with despair.

I'd scrubbed and deodorized sinks, shelves, the toilet, the tub. Hour after hour with the rhythm of the rain I'd not thought to go upstairs. I simply knew I must keep busy, and when Dan came in long after dark muttering about confusing freeways and impossible traffic, I was so tired I could barely nod.

"Know what?" He gave a short laugh. "This is truly unbelievable, but Old Jer wants me to go to San Diego—tomorrow. A West Coast Independent Insurance Agents' Conference. Says it's necessary I learn about the region, that I—"

"Dan."

"It's just for a couple days. My plane doesn't leave until noon. Drive me in, keep the car. Don't worry. The house will wait." Before I could speak or ask questions, he laughed and with forced enthusiasm launched into describing the agency. He'd hit it off with the fellows. Friendly they were, not cold, sophisticated as he'd imagined.

Stunned by Dan's trip, by this false gaiety, by unasked questions (was there actually a trip? was it really for several days? could he be meeting Her?) I crawled into bed weighted by an exhaustion that lodged deep in my bones.

Fog horns woke me before the alarm. It took a second to identify those eerie sounds. I padded to the bedroom window to see an ash-colored garden and from the living room stared at the identical color which hid the valley. Horns moaning from the Strait, fog severing me from Madison, the fact that Dan would soon leave, the sight of rooms demanding attention, furniture and piled containers dulled my senses. The dullness persisted as we left town to join commute traffic. With detachment I watched road signs and memorized how to get back, for the Bay Area was a giant maze.

Late afternoon I returned to Madison, because after leaving Dan at SFO, I'd gotten lost. Even though fog by then had lifted, gray still draped buildings. In a house not mine, I attacked boxes. The telephone's ring, announcing it was connected, proved the sole interruption.

I longed to call Molly. No, I'd save that call for night, a treat for getting through the day. Thus when night smeared window panes, I punched in the ten digits and visualized the Hawkins' living room. I imagined Molly seated in the Hawkins's vinyl lounger. With long strides she'd clear the coffee table and the ceramic animals that Irma Hawkins had painted. In her eagerness, Molly might brush against the sofa dislodging the orange and green afghan Irma finished for Christmas. Now Molly would veer away from the needle-pointed footstool and clear the corner to the wall phone. She'd not glance at Irma's plate collection nor notice the sampler. She'd curl her toes into the braided rug beneath her feet, for Molly disliked shoes.

"Hello." A woman's voice.

"Irma? It's Kate."

"Why, Kate. Dexter," and my neighbor—former neighbor—called to her husband. "Kate Andrews." Her volume increased, "How you doing out there in California? Getting a sun tan?"

"Not yet. It's raining. Everything fine there?"

"Hunky dorey. Molly's out with Steve tonight. Basketball game. What a darling. Course I needn't tell you that. She's always been like a daughter to me. As I've told you a million times, if I'd ever had a child I'd have wanted a girl just like Molly."

On that spot where Irma stood to chat on the phone, she'd be running her free hand over the assorted plates, her fingers tracking a single dust grain. "Long distance costs, so I won't keep blabbing. I'll tell Molly you phoned, and she can get back to you."

As I heard Irma's closing speech and saw, as if I were there, the interior of the house, a throbbing began. Before my voice broke, before I might ask how strangers were caring for my Home, before I might ask if Molly missed me, I hung up and returned to boxes and mounds of torn newspapers in which I'd wrapped vases, figurines, and pictures. I'd tidy up, burn the mess in the fireplace whether it was environmentally correct or not. After I checked the damper I wadded papers, ripped off box flaps and piled them on the grate; then watched as a struck match tip nibbled at the corner of a sports' page. The blaze caught. If Dan were around he'd mention the need for kindling and logs or offer advice. "You'll probably have to fan it."

As the fire grew, advanced, and hissed, I sat before it. The heat felt good, relaxing, and I stretched out flat before the skyline of flames. It would be nice to have someone—no, not someone, but a man—who would see with me an architecture created by flames. I smiled. What would it be like to have a man—might as well make him younger and desirable—beside me? I'd go one step farther. This man would want only to please me, would share my interests, would never consider unfaithfulness. Why, he'd be so captivated by my inner beauty, so in love with my laughter that he'd gaze with spellbound eyes, soulful ones, naturally, that promised, why not? eternal love.

The paper fire sputtered and retreated, but with additional cardboard and packing material I kept it and the fantasy alive. This man would treasure deep conversations so that after love making we'd trade ideas or read aloud to each other. When I was inspired by some profundity, he'd take my hand and murmur, "As you said that, you looked particularly . . .breathtaking. . . enchanting."

With a laugh I ripped more paper. We two would debate, discuss. He would never think I was lesser. My hands slowed on the inky newsprint. With this man I would never be second. I would be equal.

Now, however, almost twenty-four hours later, I sank upon a smooth wood floor near the north room windows and looked down on lights in Madison's downtown. Trees bent and swayed. The wind was obviously intensifying, but within these walls tranquility reigned.

Strange this room's power, that it by itself could soothe, for in Harding, Iowa, in my six-room, two bath, one-story that would forever be Home, each room claimed me because on them I'd put my stamp. In the form of colors and arrangements I'd brought myself to every inch. With Dan and Molly we'd webbed emotions—mostly positive—across cushions, books, prints, curtains, floor lamps, the silver tray honoring our tenth anniversary, the family portrait centered around a three-year-old Molly.

These bare walls, black with night's handprint, were simply walls. The one to the north was plain without windows, the eastern one was broken by a closet, the one to the south was cut by the door, and the one facing west, by me, held adjoining windows. Yes, just a room, and yet—

In here I'd place my desk. It would become more than a repository for bills, clippings, receipts, and letters. Maybe I'd reclaim the nearly-forgotten satisfaction of linking syllables across a blank sheet and would respond to the sensation of a pen etching white paper.

In childhood winters I'd retreated to my room to compose stories about sunny lands with princesses. Animals were soft and woolly; fruits and flowers sweet. For princesses the sole problem was deciding which suitor offered the purest love. My parents, hopeful I'd outgrow this phase, practiced patience. Occasionally, however, Dad—a county road maintenance employee—furrowed his forehead. "Such fairy lands don't really exist. You do know that, Kate."

I overheard him question Mom. "Is such imagination healthy? Shouldn't she be concentrating on something more practical?"

Several grade school teachers shared his sentiments, for they demanded reports on Liverpool or on the manufacture of steel. Stories about princesses with streaming hair entwined with garlands didn't please them. Even in high school, the English teacher urged me to plot fiction around contemporary social problems and to "write in a modern vein." After marrying Dan, when I'd infrequently experimented with verse, he'd joked about a wife and her "never-never land." Molly, a realist since toddler days, never cared for limericks about mystical beasts. Thus, gradually the writing impulse weakened and collapsed beneath meal preparation and housecleaning.

Once more I surveyed the room's stark face and the closet door where white painted wood shimmered in the gloom. Impetuously I rose and grasped the enameled knob. A glass knob might be under the enamel. I could sand and polish the handle, could decorate the entire room in turn-of-the-century décor, honoring the house's original era.

The knob spun effortlessly, and the scent of moth balls and age floated out. I groped for the dangling light cord and a muted yellow that erased the night illuminated a high empty shelf over a clothes rod. But the closet contained something intangible, indefinable, like an indistinct melody or a memory on the borderline of capture. Whatever this almost-force, it seemed to lure me closer to the shelf. I raised my right arm. Fingers scattered dust collected on the wide board, bumped against a bobby pin, a couple candles, stick matches, but I couldn't reach the back. A chair? I hurried down stairs and into the kitchen; then blanched when the phone rang. As I lifted the receiver I heard an angry wind knocking at the windows and patio door, a wind not heard in the north room.

"Hey, Mom, Irma said you'd called last night, but it was late when—"

"Oh, honey, it's so good to hear your voice, so good."

"Just a second. Steve, record that song. Yah, that's the one. Okay, Mom."

"Steve's there? Where are Irma and Dexter?"

"Don't start doing the chaperone bit, okay? They're square dancing."

Back off, Kate, I thought. *Don't resume the old war with Molly.*

"So, how's everything going?"

"Fantastic. The Hawkins are neat—well, after all these years you wouldn't expect them to turn into ogres or something. I've got my room totally fixed. There's a pretty good chance I can work weekends this spring at the drug store because Annette plans to quit and she's recommending me."

"That's—that's great, but don't let your studies go."

"Moth-er, I'll graduate. But, no way will I do well. You know that, I know that, but I'm making it. Come May, I'll be in cap and gown, no sweat. Don't worry about a thing, Mom, everything's going better than it ever has."

What do you expect, Kate? I thought. *An eighteen-year-old is supposed to perform a miracle? Is supposed to say, "Oh, Mom, I should have moved with you. I miss you. Can't sleep at nights. It was wrong to stay with Irma and Dexter so I could finish my senior year. . . .and I promise I won't make love with Steve"?*

"I'm here alone," I suddenly blurted.

"Where's Dad?"

I explained and listened to the ensuing stillness, until aware that her mother might require something more, Molly asked, "What do you think of the house?"

"It needs lots of repair."

"Dad's going through a mid-life crisis. I mean practically overnight he quits his job, gets a new one, buys a wrecked-up old house. Cindy's father started jogging, getting the bod in shape when he hit male menopause."

This fell short of the sympathy for which I longed. Molly's statements skirted close to the hidden reasons for our precipitate change.

Steve's mumbled undertone intruded, and it brought into bold relief his jeans stretched across hard thighs, his shirt taut over an expanding chest. And then Molly laughed, "Oh, Moth-er. Write. Love ya."

I backed away from thinking. I'd get something to eat, but an image of Molly pressed in Steve's arms walked beside me as I brought a cottage cheese carton to the sink where curtain-free windows exposed the valley town. It would never be mine. Mine sat on flat farm land where the population varied little. Twenty years ago after Dan and I married and he and his friend Hank rented a loft over the drugstore for their insurance agency office, we purchased the just-finished house at 905 Howlett Street. Surrounded through merging seasons by neighbors and school activities, by clubs, and Dan's business functions, I'd spent decades with the same faces. On this lonely hill, minus the passport of children, how could one start over? And could I start over with Dan? Like a swirling mass of album pages scattered by a retrospective breeze, stray snapshots from the last three months revolved.

Scrap one: I'd left Dan's birthday party for the bathroom when from the corner of my eye some blurred movement farther down the hallway snagged my attention. Movement emerged as two figures—Dan and Hank's wife Sheila. Sheila, with long, gorgeous legs, and tawny golden hair that always fell just right, wore clothing with a fashion model's ease. Since Hank and Dan had had their partnership, I had been in awe of her. Not only was I often forced into her presence because of the insurance agency, but her oldest son, Caleb, was in Molly's class.

"Needed a brush from my purse," Sheila said in tandem with Dan's, "Wanted to show her the chest of drawers."

They laughed and Sheila darted toward the safety of guests in the living room. Although it made no sense, it seemed unimportant, so with a vague smile I closed the bathroom door.

Scrap two: Dan creased his forehead and sighed when on that early December evening I asked about accepting the Hawkins' invitation for dinner next weekend. "A pot luck. The Stevensons are going and—"

"Oh, hon, that's a rough one. There's a possibility the agency'll be audited, so I'll be spending more nights at the office."

"Dan, I—"

He raised a hand to stem worry. "No problem. No problem. We'll do just fine, and it may be a false alarm but don't book obligations for us. Why don't you go?"

"Without you?"

Scrap three: Hank, his overcoat flapping in tempo with his stride, came toward me across a snow-crusted sidewalk. "Hey, Kate. Getting set for the holidays?"

Juggling packages, I nodded and because I'd never felt at ease with Dan's partner blurted, "Any news on the audit?"

"What?"

"Dan says you might be audited. That's why he's been working late."

"Well," Hank shrugged, "better check into that one, Katie. He must be pulling your leg so he can slip out for bowling, drinks, or a little whatever. There's no audit."

When I mentioned this to Dan, he chuckled. "Honey, Hank doesn't know. I didn't want to upset him. He's such an excitable guy."

Then scraps overlap on Christmas Day. . . before the tree that morning Dan handing me furry bedroom slippers and Molly giggling as I unwrapped her gift, a book entitled *A Romantic's View of Today*. . .Molly's hugs and excitement because Steve would join us for the meal. . .a brown-glazed turkey. . .Dan answering the phone and saying, "Be right back," before disappearing out the back door.

Then the face of Christmas Day grew a beard.

By mid-afternoon Steve, Molly, and I had eaten turkey dried from long warming in the oven and vegetables that resembled puree. Then they'd gone to Steve's home. After that each time the phone rang with holiday wishes, I fought disappointment that it wasn't Dan's voice.

When the Hawkins crossed the porch I'd feigned an expectant smile when I saw it wasn't Dan. When the Knightsen children knocked on the back door, hope momentarily flared. Then dusk concealed mounded snow. I lit candles in the front window and pushed my nose against the frosted pane. Erratic headlights pierced misting flakes. Car tires beat a Midwestern winter cadence upon the pavement, but no car carved a path into our driveway slowly filling with snow. I thought of death, injury, sickness, of Dan's face contorted as an angina attack lessened his grip upon the steering wheel. I imagined the car nosing into a culvert, and, crazily, wondered if Christmas ever after would hold impressions of waiting alone by a window.

Molly called. "I'm staying for supper with Steve's family," and the house and I again were quiet. It was 9:03, because I was watching clock hands measure time, when Dan walked inside.

"Did he call here?"

"Who? Where have you been? What's going on?"

He slung his coat across the couch and for once I didn't protest. As if separating himself so that in no way we could share a seat, he sank upon the footstool.

"Kate," and I saw how pale he was. "Stricken," Molly would have said, using her current favorite dramatic term. "I don't know. I don't know." He clapped his hands, repeated the motion but avoided my eyes.

"I'm almost hysterical with worry. What is it? Tell me."

He stared at the fire, at the waning flames, and I thought, *he's going to comment for the thousandth time on my inability to build a proper fire.* Instead he breathed deeply, exhaled, blew cheeks out in a cherubic fashion before he faced me. "This is it," and he clapped palms together in a decisive gesture. "For the last few months—" He faltered and raised a shaking hand to cover his face.

"Is it money, Dan? Embezzlement? Bankruptcy?"

He cleared his throat, once, twice. "Since fall—I didn't want you to know. Never wanted to hurt you. Believe me. But today Hank found out. That's why Sheila called. That's where I've been, going over it with both of them."

"Found out? Who? What?"

"Stupid me. I gave her earrings. Diamond earrings. For Christmas. Hank asked. She admitted."

Idiotically I said, "You gave me bedroom slippers," before the impact hit. "You mean, you can't. You've been with her?"

He buried his face in his hands.

My mouth dried as my heartbeat slowed, raced, and sought a stable rhythm. As if from a distance I heard him repeating, "I never wanted to hurt you. Never. Never. And Hank demands we end the partnership." Words began to swallow words and continued for the rest of that night. I must, however, have behaved normally because when Molly breezed in, tousled and suspiciously radiant, she just said, "You guys still up? See you tomorrow afternoon. No school. I'm sleeping in."

Like a parenthetical expression, Molly's intrusion seemed set apart from Dan's constant monologue of how he couldn't remain in town, how he was sorry, how he never intended to injure me, how Hank had become unglued.

Once I asked, "Why?" and he said nothing.

When I persisted, asking if he loved her, he studied the slumbering coals before he shut his eyes and nodded.

We both heard the sharp intake of my breath, and he said, "I didn't want to love her. I'm sorry, sorry." Then he stood. "Let's not go over it anymore tonight. We're beat. In the morning. . .." And he walked toward the guest bedroom.

I stared at his overcoat, tossed like an eviscerated form across the couch. It presented a mirror image, for I had no strength to rise, to think, to prevent a calliope of disconnected phrases, pictures, and questions from circling through my mind. Dan walking toward me on the college campus when we first fell in love. . .*how will I live?*. . .Dan and Molly making snow angels. . .*what did Sheila offer that I didn't?*. . .Dan cradling me after the first miscarriage and saying after miscarriage number two, "I've never loved you more". . .*I've never been alone*. . .Dan's laughter when we impulsively rode the Tilt-a-Wheel at the county fair. . .*Is she better in bed?*

The clock read just after 3:00, the fire had gone out, and the living room was cold, when I roused myself and automatically headed toward the bedroom, but I couldn't sleep in our bed. Once I'd read that sleeping beside someone is more intimate than sex, for throughout the night bodies conform, often turning in tandem as if alerted by some magnetic attraction. He'd say, "Put your cold feet against my calf," and heat from his skin would warm much more than the soles of my feet.

On the couch I pulled his coat over me for warmth. The fabric smelled of Dan—a toothpaste/outdoors/paper scent. *My life with him is as interwoven as the smells in this coat*, I thought. *I can not face life without him. Molly graduates in May. Then it will be just Dan and me. Now, just me?*

I cried into his coat collar until my eyes were swollen. Sleep was impossible. I slipped on the coat and went into the kitchen. From the refrigerator I removed the pumpkin pie, shook the Instant Whip can, and covered the surface. Then I sat in my usual place. After Dan left would I always sit in my customary spot? I dug into the pie. But he couldn't leave. What was the future for me by myself? The pie had no taste, but I couldn't stop eating. In robot fashion I chewed bite after bite as I tried to sort my thoughts.

When I dumped crumbs into the garbage disposal, I checked the clock. Nearly six a.m., nearly time for Dan's alarm, but he was in the guest room. Would he even go to the office today?

At the guest room entrance, I paused, aware of his regulated breathing. How could he sleep? How could he simply turn off what was the most challenging event of our marriage?

"Dan." When I neared the bed, he instantly opened his eyes. "It's almost six."

He frowned. "Why are you wearing my coat?"

"I got cold."

He scooted over a couple inches, leaving space for me to sit on the mattress edge. That familiar motion brought more tears, and in one non-stop movement, I threw myself across his chest. "Dan, don't. Please don't leave me." When had I ever begged? How demeaning and yet the words continued. "I beg you. I'll do anything, but stay with me."

"Kate, stop."

Even though I felt his revulsion, even though he made no effort to comfort me, I couldn't quit. I made wild promises, offered strange compromises. When Dan attempted to extricate himself and move further to the left, he managed to dislodge me and, incredibly, I was on the floor, kneeling, sobbing.

"Kate, you're going to wake Molly. Pull yourself together."

I dashed hands across my cheeks and looked up at him, seated on the bed.

"Yes, Molly," I said. "What about her? What about Hank and Sheila's children?"

Again, he closed his eyes. "Yes. We've talked of them. I—I don't know. I've never been more confused." He gave a short laugh. "Not that I expect any sympathy from you. I've made this mess."

Silence ringed us until carpet strands bit into my knees. To steady myself, I placed my right hand against the floor and Dan stood to help me up. For a second we stared at each other. He seemed, now, like a different man. Perhaps I, too, looked different to him.

"We'll have to see," he said.

"I'm taking a mini-vacation," Dan told Molly when she wandered out for lunch. "It's a slow time of year."

Engulfed in some private world with Steve, she simply grinned and nodded.

Dan paced from room to room as I alternated between anger and wretchedness, betrayal and grief. I spent long periods gazing out at the snow until I felt ice creep beneath the weather stripping and enter my veins, freezing emotions, and blunting questions when I heard him murmur into the phone or when he left the house without explanation.

For five days we assumed our typical roles in Molly's presence, and for five days we rewound sound tracks that basically consisted of, "I don't want to hurt you, but I love Sheila," contrasted with, "If you don't want to hurt me, you should be willing to try again with our marriage."

The rewind ended, when Dan said abruptly, "We can't stay in Harding. If you want to give this," (and he shrugged as if offering nothing) "another shot, we'll move. Old Jer in San Francisco will probably hire me."

Relief—the first emotion in days—brought a flush of hope. I could forgive. I could try. I could make this work. Yet, while Dan chatted on the phone with Old Jer, I picked up a woman's magazine. An article, "When Trouble Comes," advised readers to talk over problems, but in whom could I confide?

My women friends discussed breast feeding and how to decorate for banquets. They packaged cookies for bake sales and applauded at school programs but did not speak of private lives. True, they joked about good looking men and gossiped about others but never revealed their secrets.

Take Irma. If I told of Dan's affair, she'd compress her lips and announce, "If a man did that to me, it would be 'goodbye, Charlie'." She'd not advocate forgiveness. "Kate," she'd say, "If you stay with him, you're a fool."

But impossible to consider divorce. Life was husband, child, home. I knew nothing else, had nothing else. I would hang on. So I hung on while Dan told Molly and friends, "It's time for a change. Now there's no one anywhere better than Hank. He's been a hell of a partner, but, you know, twenty years is, well—heh, heh—twenty years. I'm not far from fifty. If I'm ever going to find those greener pastures it better be pretty damned soon."

Friends said, "How marvelous," "How exciting," and so I hung on when Dan flew to California and met with Old Jer. And I hung on when Hank phoned one night.

"Kate," he said, "it's all I knew to do, dissolve the partnership."

"You did the right thing, I'm sure."

"I know you're suffering, and because of you, Molly, and my kids, I'll never tell anyone the reason Dan and I split up."

During the month of January I mechanically baked a cake for Molly's eighteenth birthday, mechanically sorted through closets and the garage. And mechanically I shared our queen-sized bed with Dan every night. We each kept religiously to his/her side. In the middle of the night I would awake and feel that he, also, wasn't asleep. But we didn't talk. Much—probably too much—had already been said. As one-dimensional beings, we passed each day. Only at rare instances when I bumped into an acquaintance at the store or on the street and the person said, "Sorry that you're moving," did I want to cry.

With the house listed we arranged for Molly to room with the Hawkins after she, with amazing ferocity, said, "No way am I not going to graduate from Harding High. Take off if you have to, but I'm staying. I'm an adult, you know."

I assured myself that she'd come to California after graduation, that in but a few months we'd again be a family. So I'd flown with Dan to the West Coast, met Old Jer, taken a frenzied East Bay tour, signed papers for the house on the hill in Madison and returned Home to leave it.

In random fashion, I packed. Dan delivered loads to the Methodist Thrift Station and the dump, dragged in empty packing boxes, and paid bills. I did not ask if he'd seen Sheila. As much as possible I avoided farewell parties and vowed not to stare at Molly to record her expressions.

One night I woke and prowled through rooms in transition, yet didn't linger at Molly's door to eavesdrop on her breathing, because the sound—one to which I'd been accustomed most of my adult nights—would bring tears. In the living room I plugged my mouth to keep cries from waking Molly.

Toward evening on the last day in Harding, with everything boxed and minutes ticking off the hours before our morning departure, Dan eased out the back door.

"Don't go to her," I said.

He halted, kept his back to me, but I saw him stiffen. "At least give me this," he said. How much he must love Sheila. Had he ever loved me that completely? The door closed.

In a denuded house, I wandered through the rooms. By the kitchen cupboard Molly's high chair once sat, before the stove we'd placed a shoe box and nursed a sick bunny, on that wall a bulletin board had diagrammed seasons with PTA notices, crayon drawings, class photos.

I forced myself to change clothes as Irma and Dexter were treating us to dinner. There I pretended that it was a normal meal, that Dan hadn't walked in late. I concentrated on Irma's dilemma: enroll in tole painting or in antique doll reproduction at Leisure Service. Whichever she chose, I would not be around to see the results.

Before dawn we left. Dan drove a rental truck since we couldn't afford a moving van company. Behind him in the family car I blinked back wet goodbyes to Molly, to Harding, to everything.

It was a miserable start, a miserable trip with snow and ice across Iowa and Nebraska. Radio station played mournful country music, and no beauty livened the landscape. Sporadic dead cornstalks poked through white fields. Sometimes orange dots of snowplows moved along country lanes.

Finally in a desolate Nevada motel, while wind knocked at the door and rattled loose boards, I moved close to Dan, starved for contact, sympathy. But our eventual sex did not melt the ice, for I was unsure it was to me he made love.

Wind bearing rain hit the kitchen window and shocked me back to the present, to an exterior as bleak as scenes I'd just replayed. I left the cottage cheese carton by the sink and bumped a kitchen chair. Chair. That's why I'd come downstairs. With it I could investigate the closet shelf in that northern room.

Back upstairs I closed the door. No storm noises menaced; only peacefulness existed. Even the chair's squeak as I scooted it near the shelf was subdued. On the chair I stood eye level with the shelf, and then the feeling came from somewhere, somewhere beyond me. As if guided, my left hand reached to the rear of the board, across wood grain and grit to the smooth wall against which the shelf abutted. But this—this friendly power urged my fingers to the wall. Ignoring black-tinged cobwebs, I pushed and met resistance. Although feeling ridiculous, like an amateur detective from a murder story or a heroine in search of a secret passage, I tapped knuckles along the wall, listened to the resounding hardness of solid wood and then heard the hollow echo of—of emptiness. I leaned forward and thumped again. The muffled empty sound repeated itself. Now I banged my fist against the thin spot. Despite the sting of bruised knuckles, I banged once more, but the wall didn't budge.

I ran downstairs and grabbed a hammer from the tool box. On the third blow the wall cracked. I pounded until a jagged circle angled from the impact. Cautiously I poked two fingers into the opening where they bumped a small hard object. With the hammer I beat the weakened boards into a larger hole and plunged in my hand to extract—a necklace.

From a delicate silver chain dangled a carved rose bud, ceramic—a bisque, I believed. I laid it across my palm. What intricate layers, a pink tint; pale green leaves. Exquisite. Perhaps it was an omen that in this house an untarnished loveliness waited, one for which I must search. I extended my right foot toward the floor but stopped. Something told me to probe once more inside the opening. My hand brushed rough studs, braces, dust, and paper, for in a triangular joint, my fingers traced the shape of a book. In the closet's light I noticed first the black cover. Leather? The spine was broken and feeble threads laced the few remaining pages to the binding.

Seated on the chair, I stroked the cover and the faint gilded word, "Diary." Spidery penmanship had faded to a violet brown, while the paper smell had surrendered to mustiness.

"February 11, 1906. Tonight Franklin is with me in our room, crossing and re-crossing the rug. I wait at his desk ready to write what he tells me, like before."

Did this person, presumably a woman, mean this room? Who was Franklin? Why did he cross the rug? What was to be written?

"June 18, 1906. Today I made a mistake. When my sister asked why the house looked so nice, how I managed the yard because Franklin has been dead six months, I told her he appears whenever I wear the necklace, his wedding gift. Particularly he treasures evenings when he dictates his poetry. 'You are crazed with grief,' my sister answered and would hear no more."

"December 4, 1906. I am moving all my possessions into the north room, for it is free of winter chill and only vaguely can I hear friends and family who sometimes beat upon the front door."

"January 1, 1907. What a glorious beginning to the new year. Tonight Franklin's poetry reached a pinnacle although, as usual, he is dissatisfied and insisted I burn it. Someday people *will* appreciate him."

"February 6, 1907. I am so weak. My head hurts—"

There it ended. On the upper right hand corner of the back cover in the same handwriting was the name, Amy Elliott. Amy. Again I read the pages and studied the rose bud necklace.

Well, Amy, I thought, *you had one great imagination. But this Franklin you invented who entered this room six months after dying gave you a lovely necklace, and you're right about the sound proofing. Winter chill doesn't creep in.*

I'm glad you and your phantom husband enjoyed this room, for it is definitely a creative place.

Pleased that some long ago recluse had appreciated the room and feeling oddly satisfied, I set the diary and the necklace back on the shelf. I could return now to the living room, to the wind's screech, and the thankless task of unpacking and cleaning. But as I stepped forward something crunched beneath my shoe. A fragment of paper, having fallen, I guessed, from the diary, lay on the floor. I picked it up and saw a single line. From one of Franklin's poems? And although I read the phrase but once, it imprinted itself: "I shall be with you in a secret time."

CHAPTER TWO

Sunlight slanted across rumpled sheets and the blue quilt. As I pushed a strand of black hair from my forehead I watched dust motes filter sun's rays, and I smiled. For the first time in weeks—from the monochromatic Midwest to gray California—nature appeared conciliatory.

Ceiling cracks suggested islands and continents. The brown wallpaper's 1940s floral pattern looked less ugly. Upon that paper I'd paste a print design. Although Dan nor I had done much redecorating at Home, if we worked on this house, mightn't it help recapture love, provide a basis upon which to generate a second life?

I glanced at Dan's side of the bed, empty this morning. When did we assume this sleeping arrangement? Whether in motels or in other bedrooms, Dan bunched the pillow like a half-risen loaf of bread, stuck it beneath his head, and claimed the right half. With Her—with Sheila—had he lain thus after. . .

No. On a day that spelled hope I'd not go there, would bar the wondering that tiptoed in at unguarded moments of why Dan hadn't called from San Diego, the wondering if he was even there, the wondering if She could have joined him, the wondering of how much he missed Her.

I retreated to the north room to stare through its windows. At the base of the hill the road swung right into the older business section. Drawn in proper blocks it contrasted to the spread-out shopping center, some four miles away to which the realtor had proudly pointed. Brick buildings anchored this hill; the post office, a bank, the phone company and utilities offices. The library claimed a corner.

I shifted attention to the room, deciding I'd put my desk along the south wall. On bare feet, for I'd trashed Dan's Christmas slippers, I outlined a square and announced, "I *will* write."

And then I reread the diary entries that began in 1906, a credible date, for, according to the realtor, the house was finished in 1905. Amy spoke of Franklin and of a rug. I imagined it as gray. Then Amy mentioned a desk. Had a desk occupied the spot I'd selected? Did some enduring vibration lead me to that area?

"Don't be silly, Kate," and I turned the brittle sheet to summer's puzzling entry. In the same precise script, which showed no evidence of strain or incoherence, this passage told of Amy's widowhood and of Franklin's presence when she wore the necklace.

I re-examined the jewelry. It would be easy to hypnotize oneself. If Amy had focused intently on this bud ready to unfurl, she might have mesmerized herself, seen her dead husband's features, heard his voice. I flipped to the diary's February entry where a deceased Franklin appeared to Amy. In June he helped in the yard? Impossible. Amy could hallucinate and with inner ears hear his poetry, but just who did the yard work?

I returned to the window, noted again Madison's logical downtown arrangement. Logical. Be logical. Amy hired someone to maintain the house and clear the garden. Because of her grief and unbalanced state, she blocked it out, mistook the employee for her husband. Yet why tell her sister that Franklin came?

According to the December page, Amy moved her possessions to the north room, and although conscious of family members, she'd obviously lost contact with reality. Her fantasy with a poet husband dominated everything. Yes. The January paragraph spoke about beginnings and utter devotion to Franklin. Then what? Did she fall ill? Die? Where were the missing pages? Had other residents in this house read them, or was I the first? What urgency prompted me to discover them?

Throughout the morning as I cleaned, compiled lists, and paused for coffee, I speculated about Amy. Likely petite with a porcelain complexion, she'd choose ruffles and cameos. Through doe-like eyes, she worshipped Franklin and—I put the cup down. What if Amy had never married? What if she were a spinster who'd dreamed a husband? Or what if someone fabricated Amy and created this diary?

I opened the patio door to walk across the concrete slab. Greenness shimmered. Waist-high geraniums scattered water drops on my slacks as I wandered into foliage scented with over-ripeness. A gazebo with collapsed roof and a missing latticed side stood partially concealed by ivy and wisteria.

On languorous summer afternoons lovers might have rested on the warped benches. I touched a supporting pillar, then turned to study the rear of the house. If Amy and Franklin did indeed once live there, their story could be documented. I'd inquire first at the library.

Once inside the library doors, the fragrance of books rekindled early memories. I'd plough through snow-drifted lanes to clump up the Carnegie Library's concrete stairs. I'd remove my boots and line them with others and their melted snow puddles under the coat rack. I'd stack my returned books bound in newspapers onto the high desk before Miss French's pinched face.

However, the woman behind this desk bore no resemblance to Miss French or to later librarians—blue-haired ladies wearing sensible dresses. Dan would call this one "a hippie" in her jeans and tight green sweater that emphasized breasts and nipples. Her hair hung thick and straight below a bandana scarf, but her eyes danced, and when she parted lips devoid of lipstick they exposed perfectly aligned teeth.

"I need information about Madison's history," I said, "about individuals who lived here around 1900."

"Don't have much. We're a small library branch with a limited local collection. Mostly we've books on state and county history," but she showed me a shelf and handed over three volumes. I sat at a table to search indexes but found only statistics and dry facts about Madison; nothing about the house nor an Amy and a Franklin.

"Any luck?" The woman leaned across the table.

"No. I'm hunting for references to an Elliott family or their home. My husband and I just bought a house in which they might have lived." I nodded behind me toward the hill.

"Oh, on the eastern side. Neat property. I've walked by it. Been vacant for some while, or at least most of the time I've lived here. Tied up in an estate sale?"

"Well, a widow—"

"Why not try the historical society museum? Know where it is? If you can wait about ten minutes, I'm off work for today. I'll show you. I pass it going home."

We left the library for an afternoon courting spring. The woman, Lorraine, slung a pea jacket over her arm as we neared a gingerbread Victorian house with its hand-lettered museum sign.

"I'll go in with you. It's interesting, and Neal Parker, the director, is one sweet man."

We stepped into an entryway free from anticipated clutter—only a fern on an occasional table and a single picture on the wall, a water color of Madison (circa 1880) as viewed from a waterfront filled with tall-masted ships.

"Nice and neat, huh?" Lorraine said. "Neal's made this museum into a work of art."

We moved into what once had been a living room and instead of glass display cases or miscellaneous collections, the room held but one glass case. Lamps, sofas, fainting couches, small tables, were clustered to simulate conversation centers from various decades.

"Check out the discreet little plaques," Lorraine said, and I glanced at neat handwritten cards marking each object: "Antimacassar, 1879. Donated by Judge and Mrs. Tilman," "Chesterfield, 1901. Donated by the Arthur Whitson Family."

"Afternoon," and I turned when the male voice spoke. For a heavy set man he had approached quietly.

"Hey, Neal. Brought in a new resident, Kate Andrews."

"Welcome," and as he extended his hand, his left hand, I noticed the empty right sleeve. As I awkwardly extended my left hand I wondered what had happened and if he had carefully inked each of the informative cards with that left hand.

"Kate and husband bought the old house on the hill, the one long vacant."

"Ah." His smile broadened, and his large brown eyes—that impressed me with a hidden sadness—lighted up. "The Elliott House."

"Then there really was an Amy Elliott?"

"Definitely. Part of a romantic, tragic story. But come along," and he led us through a former dining room—organized similarly to the one we'd left. "Her maiden name was Bennett."

"She married Franklin Elliott?" I asked his back.

He nodded. "That's the romantic, tragic part. Franklin, apparently quite handsome, was a banker's son. The bank's still standing." He moved to the dining room windows and swept back the lace curtains. "Down there, that tan building used to be the Elliott bank. Today, remodeled, it's a savings and loan office. Well, Mr. J.P. Elliott had this one son. Good looking, as I've said, but a dreamer. Franklin, the son, never got the hang of the bank." Neal dropped the curtain. "When J.P. died, Franklin built his house and married Amy. They weren't married long when he was killed, thrown from a horse. Amy became a recluse, a bit, one might say, peculiar. Finally her family broke down the doors to get her, but, by then, she was near death. Pneumonia, I believe."

"Did Franklin write poetry?"

"That he did. To my knowledge he never published any, but he called himself a poet." He smiled and I felt warmed by it. Interesting the variety of smiles—the clenched teeth variety; the faked grin; the genuine but self-involved example; and the one that insisted you return the delight. "Come into the next room, the study. There's a photo." Neal, the one sleeve swinging free, strode through an archway. "It was taken some ten years after the house was completed and after the Elliott's deaths, of course, but still you can get an idea of what it looked like when relatively new."

The black and white framed picture showed the hill, scanty foliage, and the house, proud, regal, isolated.

"When were the other houses built at the foot of the hill?"

"During the 1920s and trees were set out at the same time. That hill, though, was never overbuilt as was the western hill with its view of the Strait. I could make you a copy of the print."

"That would be wonderful," and in my enthusiasm I reached out, catching the vacant sleeve. "Sorry."

Again the smile. "I like your enthusiasm because the Bennett-Elliott story has a special meaning for me. Amy was my great-aunt. Never knew her, naturally, but I grew up hearing about her, and I have a bit more information at home."

The floor behind us creaked as Lorraine moved and the noise, an intrusion, broke the moment.

"Stop by in a couple days and the print will be ready." He escorted us back through connecting rooms, and when on the porch, Lorraine said, "I'm starved. Like to come home with me for lunch?"

"Love to," and as we continued northward I asked about Neal Parker.

"A private man. I don't know much about him except he runs a quality museum and is a gentle giant. Unmarried. Not sure if he's ever been married. Lived here all his life. Don't know what happened to his right arm."

Next I explained about the diary and the necklace, about my interest in the Elliotts but said nothing about the force which had propelled me toward the objects. We neared the end of the block, passed two more. Ahead lay a railroad station, a road that curved, and in the distance a boat harbor that jutted into the Strait.

Lorraine continued across the railroad tracks, but I slowed.

"Hey, this way. I live on a boat."

Years ago, during a camping adventure, I'd nervously gripped sides of a canoe, and in a row boat a high school boy stopped rowing long enough to kiss me, but those equaled my nautical experiences.

"What kind?"

"Thirty-four foot ketch."

Lorraine's shoes crunched gravel as she crossed a dual set of tracks. Silently I tagged along wondering if a ketch were a kind of tugboat.

The roadway formed a semi-circle before it dead ended by a bait shop and harbor office. From a jacket pocket, Lorraine extracted a key and headed up a wooden rampway to unlock the pier gate. On each side, and along the T-shaped far end, boats tugged against ropes and nuzzled tires dangling from berth side—like inmates in padded cells or infants in cribs. But imagery fled before the sting of salty wind upon my cheeks and the sight of gaps between wide planks, of knotholes, of missing railings, and of the cold dark water that slapped against pilings. Lorraine hopped aboard a sailboat.

"Step on over this life line." With her shoe tip she bent a top strand and ignored my clumsy entanglement with the line.

She shoved the hatch forward and as she descended called, "Come on." I inched across the few feet of deck, tested the solidity of the first ladder rung, hunted for the next, the next, and cracked my head against the hatch.

At the bottom I clutched the ladder sides, a constant against the floor's subtle roll. I breathed in a strangely pleasant odor reminiscent of a locked country church, as I took in a stove beside me, dishes, and a play-house-sized sink. Ahead was a wooden table with a leaf that extended into a narrow hall, and matching bunks. On one of these Lorraine sat to untie her shoes.

"Take a look forward." I moved in the direction of that casual wave, bumping a knee against a closet door that was opposite a cramped bathroom. Beyond this, twin berths joined to form a V. They held an assortment of slickers, ropes, and lamps. In these claustrophobic quarters I felt big and displaced. I regarded the portholes through which streamed diluted sunlight. Was being on this ship any more alien than deserting Iowa? Than confronting Dan's infidelity? Than abandoning Molly?

"Not your standard suburban tract house," Lorraine said as I returned to the main cabin and perched on the other bunk. She poked through contents of a chest-type ice box, cut suspicious spots from a block of cheese, broke off chunks of French bread, divided a brown banana, and pulled out a gallon bottle of what she called, "cheap red."

With efficiency borne from functioning in a limited space, she set the meal on the table and dropped back down on her bunk.

"No, it's hardly typical." I quit reading book titles—*Primer of Navigation, Celestial Navigation, Sea Boating Almanac*—from the built-in shelves over the bunk.

"Minimal housekeeping." She bit into the yellow cheese. "Rent's cheap."

"Utilities?"

"I pay for electricity but burn wood in the stove, use ice in the chest and don't have a phone. With part-time work at the library, I just about break even."

I lifted the jelly jar with its "cheap red," which tasted heavy and acrid. *This is the first lunch at which I've ever drunk wine,* I thought. *Wine's reserved for nights, for daring.* I raised the jar for another drink.

Lorraine said, "I've lived here about a year. Came out last spring with a guy from Chicago." She drained her jar. "His buddy had this boat so we moved in with him."

Three adults in such confinement?

"It didn't work. The guy from Chicago, Rich, resented the 'friendship' I developed with Adam, the boat owner, so Rich went back to Chicago. I lived with Adam here on *The Eden* through spring and summer. Magnificent sailing, some good people, but in the fall Adam said he needed space and took off for a ranch in Oregon."

"And you have *The Eden*?"

She nodded. "I simply pay monthly berth fees."

"When Adam comes back?"

Lorraine wrinkled her nose and crossed her legs, yoga fashion. "Have to see. In the meantime there's Peter. However, the future with Peter is grim. He's married."

I unpeeled the banana. Never had I leapt into such frankness, for revelations among my Harding friends evolved slowly. We gathered levels of meaning from random conversations, arrived at conclusions from disparate information. And never had I talked knowingly with—with a—mistress.

"It doesn't bother you that he's—" Unfaithful, disloyal, cheating, sounded archaic "What about his wife? Ever consider her?"

"No." Lorraine poured more wine into our jars.

Unexpectedly, bitterness, fear, and the circumstances that forced our swift move from Harding burst out in the form of disjointed sentences. I mixed Sheila's name with selling the house and leaving Molly. Ragtag phrases fit no pattern, but when I spoke of Dan, I cried.

Lorraine's callused hand grazed mine as she gave me a cloth, but when I pressed it to my face, I breathed in kerosene fumes. Sputtering I threw the red rag.

"Oh, my God. Sorry," she apologized. "That was the dirty one. Somewhere there's a clean one." Like a strip-search cop, she patted coat pockets in the closet, and simultaneously we laughed, for I had with Lorraine's vision seen the scene: a weeping, spitting, throwing Kate.

"Hey, this is positive." She settled back further into the bunk. "I mean Dan's affair got you out of the Midwest. On the West Coast there's freedom, and you're overdue for some."

"I'm not after 'freedom.' I only want my husband, Harding, and Molly." My voice thickened.

"Well, it's time to let her go. Jesus, at eighteen I was on my own and I've been on my own ever since."

"You never married?"

Lorraine's laugh pealed free, poking back the musty corners of the boat. "No, I've lived the life I've wanted. Was in and out of several colleges and almost graduated with a library of science degree. Thus, I'm an excellent clerk. You're out of wine."

The dark liquid glubbed from the bottle.

"Now, Kate, if the fact that Dan had an affair really upsets you, have one yourself. Balance it."

"That's ridiculous."

"Why? And don't give me any morality crap, any trust-and-commitment stuff."

"Suppose you wouldn't accept that I don't care to sleep with anyone else?"

She grinned. "I won't accept that because I'd bet you never have. You don't have to know what you're missing. Come on, give me one reason not to have an affair besides STD."

"A reason? I'm forty-seven and not attractive."

"Bullshit. Since when does attractive have anything to do with affairs? If I had a full-length mirror on this boat—and you notice I don't—I could get terminally depressed about drooping hips and drooping boobs. But if you like yourself, if you like sex, you'll find a guy."

I banged the jar onto the table's varnished surface, slopping a red stain. Undoubtedly I was, as Dan would put it, "feeling no pain."

Telling Lorraine that I must get back, I made the deck on unsteady legs, astonished to see a westering sun. "Didn't mean to stay so long."

"Next time, stay longer. We'll go sailing."

With one leg on deck and the other suspended above the pier I asked, "Out there?"

"Sure, I handle her by myself. In a couple weeks we'll have some nice days. You and I can go out in the Strait. If tides are with us, we'll make the Bay."

Bolstered by wine, companionship, and with both feet on the dock, I said, "Sure, why not?"

I retraced the road and crossed the tracks to move past the Victorian museum, shuttered and prim looking. Neal must have locked up for the day. Nice man. Where did he live? What was his story? Now advancing evening sheathed the downtown with a mellowness and some bleakness dissipated. It was amazing what a hint of friendship could do. Tired but exhilarated, I entered the quiet house. Unable to face eating dinner in the lonely kitchen I carried a sandwich, salad, and milk upstairs.

Like a fairy-tale princess from one of my earlier writings, I surveyed my new realm, Madison's downtown, from the north room windows. Could I use a fairy-tale princess in a poem, a modern Rapunzel wrenched from her castle? Too dopey, romantic. As I munched on the bologna (bad) but in wheat bread (good), I considered Lorraine's revelation. Yes, I concluded, I had lived an insular life, but I'd liked the limitations, liked marriage, a family, and plans to age with a husband who would treasure grandchildren. I'd been content in my cocoon.

Night fell over Madison as I wondered how many others shared my dreams. Was I really an exception, as Lorraine hinted, or did most other women want more? Didn't they compromise to have a stable existence? Didn't they see what they chose to see, believe what they needed to believe? Didn't they have a world they'd fight to keep intact?

Surely there were clues to Dan's affair. Some part of my mind must have suspected but denied suspicions. At this moment, for instance, clues dotted the landscape that Molly slept with Steve. Still I'd ignored them, unwilling to accept my daughter's sexuality. How do others cope? Do they confront issues? Avoid them? I sighed. As Lorraine had emphasized, a move could alter one's thinking. Possibly I could explore the topic of moves—physical and emotional—on paper. When I carried my plate downstairs I searched for a notepad.

In a suitcase I found an envelope, spread it open to form a jagged sheet and sat at the kitchen table; yet nothing happened. No inspiration. The wind's volume deepened. The house seemed adrift. I pictured storm clouds above the Strait, thought of Lorraine snug in her bunk on *The Eden* as wind whistled through the rigging. So soon this climate reverses itself, not like Iowa with generally more predictable weather. Sometimes individuals aren't predictable. Maybe I should write about that, but not at this table.

In the north room I sat on the floor and my pencil scratched against the envelope. "When princesses walk the earth." Stupid. "Their voices sing a future song." Bad. It had been too long since I'd tried to write. Irritated, I rose and walked back and forth, annoyed at my sophomoric efforts.

Through the window panes I could see flailing tree branches and noticed lights blink out in one section of town. As I reversed direction, I recalled Amy's description of Franklin's pacing. I rescued the diary from the closet shelf. Tonight it held an added significance for Neal, the museum director, had verified this couple's existence. Yes, the first passage mentioned that Franklin re-crossed the rug. I replaced the diary to pick up the necklace. The dim closet light bulb tinged the rosebud with an ivory hue. I fingered the fine links and hung it around my neck. The rosebud nestled in the cleft between my breasts and warmed my skin.

Outside the closet I switched off the lights and returned to the windows, observing violence minus a sound track. In this aerie, the storm lost malice. Then, as I scanned the night, the remaining downtown lights blinked out. The valley was completely black.

Was this how it had looked at night in 1905-06? Had there been electricity? Had—There came a creak and I stiffened. Every inch of my body was alert. My throat tensed as across my back I felt a breeze and smelled stagnant air. The closet door *couldn't* be opening. But like a solid shadow behind me I sensed a something—a someone. Unable to breathe, to swallow, I was paralyzed, pinned by these windows.

A bump as if a door knob collided with a wall. My lungs ached and I gulped. Mustn't panic. The storm had forced the closet door open. I didn't close it tightly.

"I'm in my room, my favorite room," I silently affirmed, while my body told me that I wasn't alone.

My shallow breathing grated upon the air. It/He, Whatever, must hear my ragged breathing, must realize my terror. I'd read that if a rapist or mugger sensed the victim's fear, the victim was lost, for it must be a rapist or mugger who stood, simply stood behind me with no hoarse breathing, with no movement signaling his advance. Somehow this afternoon while I was out, he'd broken into the house. "Think, Kate, think. He wasn't in the closet seconds ago. The stairway door is closed. Think."

"Please," the voice was soft, melodic. "Don't be frightened. I've brought the candles from the closet, and I'll light them."

"Dear, God," I prayed, "help me."

A match rasped. Its flare was captured in the glass panes before me, and in an orange circle I saw a man's exaggerated figure.

"Oh, Kate, do turn around. It's only me, you know, Franklin."

I'm hallucinating, I thought. *That's it. Did Lorraine drop a drug in that horrible wine, so that on whatever kind of "trip" this is, I can't be hurt?*

I shut my eyes and reopened them upon the same reflected vision. All right, there must be a problem with the glass, some light refracted from some place. Yes, that was it, and if I turned around, blocking the window, I would find nothing. With fingers fused into fists, I forced my body on stiff legs to move.

The man stood in the middle of the room holding a lighted taper in each hand. Their glow wavered across his features, high cheekbones, broad forehead, finely chiseled nose and sensuous lips. I noted his hair was dark as I desperately gathered facts for if I weren't hallucinating, if he were indeed a trespasser, I must memorize every detail for a police report.

When he smiled, I thought, *He's not yet tried to hurt me. If I stay calm there's hope I can escape.*

He bent to set the candles on the floor. "I am sorry." His voice fell gently upon the room. "I assumed when you put on the necklace that you knew I'd materialize or that you wished me to. I don't want to scare you. I'm most eager to be your friend." He regarded me with serious eyes.

"I. Don't. Understand."

With the caressing tone one employees with a frightened animal or child, he said, "The necklace serves as a bridge from the other side to here." He gauged my reaction. "You don't believe me."

"No."

"Then I'll go." He smiled. "That is, if you'll release me. You must remove the necklace. You have the upper hand, Kate. By putting on the necklace, you summon me. It's the only way I can appear. By taking off the necklace, you release me. Therefore, if ever you care to call me, you know how."

None of it made sense, but I'd unclasp the necklace. Maybe that would satisfy him, make him leave. My hands shook, and I despaired of ever opening the tiny hook. He stood patiently watching me. There, there, the clasp opened, and the necklace dropped into my palm. Both candles sputtered. No man. Carefully I neared the closet. Empty. With uneven steps I reached the stairwell and leaned against the wall, a good solid wall, the same one I'd passed but a short while ago. Or was it a short while? Could I have fallen asleep? Dreamed this incredible sequence? In a dream state could I have entered the closet for the necklace?

I sank down onto the top step, clutching the necklace. I inhaled deeply and felt my heart regain its normal rhythm. Whether due to an ingredient in Lorraine's wine or due to a dream, I was no longer as terrified, no longer bent on calling the police. The invented man had been cordial and definitely handsome. His voice had been kind.

Once more I cautiously approached the north room's threshold. The scent of candle wax was strong. Then, as if from some far reaches, I heard a faint ringing—the phone. I felt my way down the blackened staircase and to the kitchen telephone.

"You all right, Kate?" Dan asked.

"What?"

"Are you all right. You sound, well, spacey."

Dan's term came close. "There's a bad storm," and I squinted at the opaqueness that disguised the kitchen. "The power's off."

"You afraid?"

"Not of the storm." Oh, no, the darkness wasn't upsetting, but tonight's bizarre episode had unnerved me. Was I losing my mind?

"Do you know where the fuse box is?" He explained about the circuit breaker, and that I must notify PGE if town lights came back on but ours didn't.

Next he asked if I'd heard from Molly and as I said, "Yes," the power resumed. Suddenly cupboards, sacks, cleaning supplies and even the antiquated sink appeared friendly. Such tangibles furnished the last necessary shove into life in this house in California. Again Dan sounded like the man I'd known for over twenty years, and as he spoke of Molly, an image of our daughter's face swam before me. During recent months Molly had furnished a favorite conversational subject, so I could follow Dan into that worn groove, questioning with him if she would ever attend college, affirming with him disappointment over the relationship with Steve.

"She better not be thinking of marriage," Dan said, a sentence that had become a litany.

"We should have insisted she move with us," I said.

"Insisted? As she pointed out, legally she's an adult."

Next we discussed Irma and Dexter as chaperones, Molly's borderline grades, and her tentative job. Apparently Dan felt, since we were of one accord, that he could slip into the purpose for his call. "I apologize about this, but if you're doing okay, and it sounds like you are, would you mind if I stayed a couple more days? Old Jer wants me to catch a seminar in L.A."

I paused. Had Sheila flown out? Was she with him at this moment? Was she arriving tomorrow? Would he/they go to Los Angeles together?

"Kate?"

Defeat nudged me as I said, "Let me know when you'll be back."

Okay, I'd fix myself a cup of tea, but as I reached for the kettle realized I still clutched the necklace. In the kitchen light it was lovely, a perfect work of art. How could anything threatening be associated with it? The upstairs room wasn't threatening either. What was that theory about getting back on the horse that threw you? I studied every petal on the flower. Only perfection. I climbed the stairs.

In the lighted room I experienced the familiar comfort, even though the scent of melted candle wax lingered, confirmation that something had happened tonight. For long minutes I debated, but with the ceiling light on, with lights on in the house, with lights outlining Madison, with the storm decreasing, with the assurance that I was awake, I fastened the necklace clasp.

He waited by the closet door and we looked at each other: then he smiled. "Shall we sit down?" He gestured toward the vacant floor and laughed. "We could pretend there are chairs."

I shook my head.

"Fair enough. I'll sit," and noiselessly he sank to the floor and crossed his long legs in impeccable black trousers. I listened to the thumping of my heart.

"I wish there were easy explanations, for, yes, this defies logic. But, oh, Kate, I have been waiting years." He pressed his lips together as if to prevent thoughts and words from making giant leaps, as I pressed my back against the sturdy southern wall.

"Let's say that for decades I've longed for a receptive soul. Back in the '20s, I had hope. The Del Montes had an artistic son, Bryan, but he didn't respond."

"Respond?" I whispered.

He tipped his head toward the closet. "I led Bryan to the shelf and Amy's diary. He read it; put it back, did nothing about it. Later his mother stored a heavy box on that shelf. She banged it with such force that a sharp corner gouged a hole in the wall. The diary tumbled down but caught on an angle brace with the necklace."

"The other pages?"

His fingers fluttered. "Down inside the walls. Before the Del Montes sold the property, they patched the hole, the one you broke open yesterday."

"And?" My voice stopped. This was crazy. A conversation with a—with a ghost?

"When you and your husband came through house hunting, I felt you were a writer, one who could help me, and I did my best to spread this room with appeal."

"I can't accept this. I can't."

He smiled. "I understand, but would you agree to give me time and a fair hearing? Allow me to talk to you, get to know you, and you, me."

I glanced away at the bare walls and windows. So many questions. Where to start, and so I started with something ridiculous, inconsequential. "If you've been dead all these years, have you just been hanging around watching people in this house?"

His smile was magnetic. "I've observed changes, but I've respected each resident's privacy."

"Yet you brought me to this room, this closet, the diary."

"You are impressionable. I felt that, so it wasn't difficult. Together we can write lasting poetry."

Dizzy, off balance, I put my hand to my forehead. Clammy.

"Accept what you can, when you can, but I beg you to put on the necklace again. We'll talk. I'll explain what I can." He stood up, I licked dry lips and pointed to the rosebud. "I just—"

He nodded. "Unclasp it."

With such a simple action I stood alone in the room. Slowly I wandered to the kitchen, drank my tea, and studied the necklace before I replaced it on the closet shelf. The north room was empty and tranquil.

At the door, before I left, I paused and let the indefinable atmosphere caress me. With a smile, I whispered, "Good night, Franklin."

CHAPTER THREE

*A*lthough the storm dwindled in the night, its mood lasted. Dawn brought but a tan version of gloom. Rain, like a veil, fell across the backyard's wild growth. How many rains had pelted plants, nourished weeds, washed the gazebo's latticed frame and crumpled roof? Had Franklin built it?

I leaned against the bed's walnut head board. In morning clarity, last evening's experience bore every earmark of an imagination as uncontrolled as the backyard's growth. Of course I'd been influenced by the diary, the museum visit, and subconsciously had accepted Lorraine's suggestion of another man. Add in hurt and anger at Dan, loneliness, the house setting, my desire to write. . .The elements fitted together.

Comforted by logic, I dressed, but in the kitchen—even before I poured milk on my raisin bran, the logic weakened. One "appearance" could be blamed on the elements I'd identified, but two? Could I have invented both and the information? Plus, Dan had definitely called for on the notepad I'd scribbled the revised flight number. If that were real, why wasn't the remainder of the evening "real"?

I couldn't eat. I climbed the stairs, felt the invisible comforting waves lap against me, and crossed to the front windows that framed a view of Madison. How could I explain this? A breakdown? Could Dan have hired someone to drive me crazy, a modern version of *Gas Light*? No, Dan was more direct. If he decided he couldn't stay married, he would walk off.

Carefully I examined the room. No sign of an intruder or of evil. I rested against the wall, succumbing to the serenity. At last, I moved to the closet for the necklace. Without materialization, light streaks, noises, chill winds or sulfurous odors, Franklin stood near the closet door. Dressed in black trousers and a white shirt, he looked as he had last night, except in morning light I saw more clearly his perfect features.

"Are we just going to stare at each other?" His question slipped into laughter.

"This is so improbable, what can I do but stare?"

"Yet you summoned me. That's the main thing."

I shook my head. "No, the main thing is figuring this out."

"Don't intellectualize." His voice, like the room's voice, flowed low, easy. "As a poet, an artist, you accept moments which defy explanation. Otherwise, how do you create? From some invisible source you draw worlds others don't see, characters that—"

"You're saying that you're part of me?"

His large brown eyes brightened. "I'm asking, regardless of your pragmatic side, to believe in me. Trust me. We can formulate fresh visions and—"

"You speak good lines." I crossed arms across my chest, aware on some level that my arms weren't shaking, that my tone and heartbeat were steady. "If I've invented you, I have a keener imagination than I realized."

"I'm not your second self. I've been around far longer than you have."

I tightened my grip on each upper arm as if that would help me select the best question, but when I said, "You're what? Late twenties?" he laughed heartily.

"Pharaoh, my horse, threw me three days after my twenty-ninth birthday, so that's how I appear, but through the years, right along with Madison, I've grown. I've seen the effects of war, have watched inventions and fashions change."

Franklin paused and looked toward the windows. "On second thought, perhaps I've not matured, because if one has to learn through actual experiences then I'm far behind."

"But is it necessary to live an event in order to feel it, to be affected? I think we can move through an episode with someone else and be impacted. We can read and empathize and—"

He spun around and laughed. "See, we are of one accord."

Such laughter quickened my heart, so its beat thudded against my ear drums. Too much was happening. I pressed my spine against the solid wall. "I'm totally baffled. Maybe I've made you up, maybe you exist. Maybe you're a neighbor or an enemy playing a trick. I don't know. At this moment I'm in shock, light headed."

He gestured toward the door. "Maybe you need some breakfast."

Food wasn't the answer, but perhaps if I left this room I'd see things differently. Alone, I descended the stairs, but as I neared the coffee pot in the kitchen, I saw him, propped against the wall by the phone. A shaft of thin sunlight angled across his shoulder and draped yellow along his forearm highlighting fine black hairs just below his rolled up shirt sleeve. He was as substantial as the stove, cabinets, sink.

"Do you eat?"

"Would rather drink, particularly wine," and laughter first spun in the north room brightened the kitchen.

All right, he could joke, but I'd eat my cereal. Vinyl upholstery wheezed as he settled on the chair beside mine. As I added sugar, he asked, "Do you like to cook?" and before I answered he said, "I think there are two categories of cooks. The naturals who don't need recipes or advance warnings. They enjoying preparing for unexpected guests. The non-naturals like an undisturbed kitchen, no one under foot to help and yet—"

"They usually get it."

"Right. Amy belonged to category two. It was hard for her when women—usually her sisters—gathered in the kitchen."

My mind felt disconnected from my body. I couldn't be discussing cooking with a ghost. To ground myself I whispered, "I am in the kitchen. This is a spoon. This is a napkin."

"More difficult in Amy's case was the fact that she was good."

My spoon clinked against the bowl. "Good?"

"Yes, good, eager to please. A product of her time, she believed that certain tasks were feminine, but when she arranged flowers, for example, or crocheted, it was a disaster. She was bothered about this but without any driving talent or passion she couldn't break free. So where could she go?"

"Where?" I echoed faintly as I chewed a raisin.

"Into my life. For me she was an ideal wife."

How would it have been to sleep beside that lean, shapely body, to make love to him, to gaze at that striking face, to record his phrases? How would it feel to be called "an ideal wife?"

"How long were you married?"

"Fourteen months. Then Pharaoh threw me." With a cracking noise, he sliced a hand across his windpipe.

"Instantly?"

"It's the best way to go when you must. But, of course, I've never completely gone." In one lithe movement he bounded from the chair, revolved it, and straddled the back. "So, I am grateful—eternally grateful— excuse the word play, that you've arrived to rescue me." He bent forward and covered my hand with his, a surprisingly strong cool hand.

My heart lurched. *I've gone over the edge,* I thought, *I'm getting turned on by a ghost, something unreal.*

"When I died, I was enraged. Such intensity touched Amy, made it easier for me to guide her to wear the necklace, my wedding gift to her. Charged with strong feeling, it worked well as a bridge. That is, until the pneumonia." He sighed. "Yet even Amy felt that was for the best, because her family's patience had run out as she refused to let them in. Definitely they would have institutionalized her."

With my tongue, I attempted to loosen a raisin skin that clung to a back molar, and I regarded Franklin. Earnest, sincere. How easy to believe that this was a normal, everyday conversation.

"You couldn't have visited her in an institution ?"

"No, I'm centered in this house," and his gaze traveled over the kitchen. "I built this place with money Father left me. I purchased land on a solitary hill and oversaw each bit of construction." His smile was wistful. "Since then, there have been modifications. The Richardsons, who bought it from Amy's family, lived here about nineteen years. They brought in electricity, installed a phone, removed the wood stove and put in gas."

"That's not the original?" I motioned to the huge black stove.

"Just before Pearl Harbor, the Samsons (they followed the Del Montes) found that stove somewhere. They also turned the back porch into a laundry room and enclosed it, leaving this side free for a patio entrance."

"The alterations bother you?"

He shrugged and the crisp, white shirt strained across his back. "They're minor. It remains my house, my only house, the one to which Amy and I came with such high hopes. I had Father's money to maintain it. I would write, but—"

"I know." With a click, I sawed my hand across my jugular vein and he laughed; then he sobered. "Now I have a second chance, a better chance. Over the years I've stored up ideas, waiting, waiting for a channel. Oh, Kate, you can offer suggestions, can see that my book is published. It's vital that my words be read, that I leave them as my legacy."

He captured both my hands with long, firm fingers that pressed mine with urgency. Quickly I rose, but he stood up to tower over me, as I protested. "This makes no sense."

"I promise I'll answer as many questions as possible, but it's going to take time. Also, there are some areas I won't ever be able to explain. Please, say you'll help. Please agree to write down as I dictate. At least, give it a trial run."

He grinned when I nodded. "You've got lots to do," he said. "I'll not insist, push, but whenever you have time, just summon me."

Yet I was reluctant to release him. "Is Amy with you?"

Franklin shook his head. "Her very goodness, her ability to follow rules and her lack of a compelling reason to hang around ensured that she'd go on. I fought to stay, and I'm glad I did." Flashing his infectious smile, he pointed at the necklace, which I unclasped.

Alone in the kitchen I watched the room reshape itself into a dark cave as fledgling sunlight had vanished. Rain splashed on tangled undergrowth and on the patio. With questions troubling me, unpacking and rearranging could wait.

Back in the north room I started to put the necklace back around my neck; then halted. I couldn't call him again like a celebrity-struck adolescent or a frustrated housewife. Yes, frustration undoubtedly accounted for my actions, because this Franklin had to be a product of my mind. If I left the house, might I gain a different perspective? At the library, Lorraine would connect me with Madison, with Now.

The mud styled its own geography upon the steep street: tributaries and peninsulas, plains and miniature mountains. When had the roadway been cut? Would it have been paved with gravel in Franklin's day? Against my umbrella, rain persisted in four/four time. The measures faltered only when I passed beneath tree limbs and branches spattered drops. Had he seen these trees planted? After Amy's death, did he observe growing branches from the north room windows? Did he resent additional houses at the bottom of his hill?

Enough, Kate, you're seeking perspective. Don't dwell on this bizarre happening.

Lorraine wasn't behind the library counter. Damn. Yet I lingered in the building, strolling among the stacks, for a library evokes sanity. Books lining shelves speak of reason and of humanity's efforts to gain meaning from contradiction. The rustle of newspapers, the flap of a magazine page from the reading section, where chairs forged a standard U-shape soothed me, reinforcing actuality. Ghosts did not exist. There couldn't be an other-worldly apparition known as Franklin. Kate Andrews, on the dark side of forty, slightly unhinged by traumas, had discovered solace in a fiction. As I turned toward the door, however, a title caught my eye, *Ghost Hunter's Guide to the Bay Area* by Jeff Dwyer.

At the oak reading table, I dragged a heavy chair back from its alignment and compressed my umbrella to fit beneath its rungs. As if illuminated, certain phrases, sentences, and passages rose from the text. "Ghosts may offer protection, guidance, even comfort. . ." Quite assuredly, Franklin offered comfort.

"Stop it," I scolded myself. "Don't agree with the book."

But the next page announced, "Full body apparitions are rare. The solidity of these images is highly variable." So someone, a ghost hunter, acknowledged the possibility of solid images. I rubbed a hand across my eyes. Weren't ghosts traditionally viewed as vaporish? Not solid? I skimmed ahead. "Most authorities agree that ghosts do not travel. . .They are held in a time and space by deep emotional ties to an event or place."

A coldness, a paralysis, gripped me. That's what Franklin had said. Slowly, I raised my head and concentrated on a figure at the end of my table. Full beard, red stocking cap, thrift-store vintage overcoat. Probably a homeless person sheltering in the library, but he was a *person*. I exhaled and thought, *Thank you, grubby man. You've grounded me.* But the subsequent passage reiterated the emotional attachments that a ghost had to a room, an activity, event, or building. Franklin loved the north room, stating it was where his creativity flourished.

I pushed up my sweater sleeves and rubbed my left hand upon my exposed forearm, proof that I was here, my body was here, and that I was reading improbable facts. I thumbed successive pages that dealt with locations where thin, wispy apparitions had been spotted, but when I read about a "kindly old man" who roamed the streets of a California town, I bit my lip. He "appears in work clothes. . .greets passersby in a clear voice and appears quite real as his dog sits at his side." Quite real. A clear voice.

The security alarm near the front door jangled, and I watched as the clerk signaled a patron with a tightly-permed head of blue hair to continue. "You've checked out the videos. Go ahead." Videos, perms and security systems were actual. I'd quit with this book, but not quite able to close the covers I read about a literature professor who arrived at the University of California Berkeley in 1890. For some twenty years, before his death, he lived in room 219 of the Faculty Club. "Many have seen his apparition sitting in a chair with a book on his lap. Some students, passing by his window, claim to have heard him recite poetry." Poetry? I jumped up, dropping the book to the floor.

I glanced around. No one had stirred. Red-hatted man, now bent over the table, slept. Fine, I'd retrieve the paperback, replace it on the shelf, but it had landed spread-eagled at an account concerning a Lady in Gray. Dressed in a gray Victorian gown, "she has carried on conversations with guests of the inn and burst into rooms searching for the children entrusted to her care." Enough. I needed fresh air. I left the book on the table and once outside welcomed the rain.

It bounced against my umbrella as I rested against the exterior library wall. I'd think no further, would survey the county courthouse across the street, would study that woman as she screamed at the man beside her as they halted on the fifth step. I'd count individuals huddled beneath umbrellas and laden with brief cases as they darted up the steps, and skirted the angry couple.

To my right, I analyzed architectural building styles and to my left, checked out additional buildings. Then I noticed through the gauzy scrim of rain the hill that rimmed the other side of Madison's valley. When weather improved I'd hike there, judge if that scenery surpassed ours. I could distinguish terraced houses and clumps of trees.

"On a pretty day you get a fine panorama of the Strait from that old cemetery. "A man had joined me.

As I turned, my umbrella spoke grazed a dangling raincoat sleeve. Neal was beside me. From a plastic conical hat that fell partly over his eyes, rain drops splotched against a matching transparent plastic rain coat, the kind that in a pouch accompanies the peculiar shaped hat. Molly would laugh, "Nerdy! Nerdy!" just as she did about Dexter's clip-on sun glasses. Yet I was inordinately glad to see Neal with his puppy dog expression, his teddy bear physique.

"Old cemetery?" I asked, and when he nodded, the triangulated peak of his rain hat advanced across his forehead.

"You're Kate," and he readjusted the cap. "Up there," and again as he pointed, his hat slid forward making it difficult for him to both move the hat and point, "is a pioneer cemetery that recently earned state historic status. Tombstones go back to the mid-1800s. It truly is a stone city. Some elaborate headstones still stand. Vandals have destroyed others. Some sad epitaphs; some not too sad." He grinned and I noticed the crease between his eyes that angled like the creek outside my Iowa town, and I noticed the large brown eyes. In a novel I'd read the description, "drowning pool eyes."

"My favorite: 'Little June. Went too soon'."

My peal of laughter might have astonished him, but because he repositioned his errant hat, I wasn't sure. "I'd take you there today except I'm off to open the museum. Drop by at anytime. I've a bit more about Franklin and Amy."

Laughter died. Yes, Franklin. Amy. After Neal left I regarded the western hill. Why couldn't I go? Despite wet jeans and the wisdom of awaiting a decent day, I moved rapidly along the sidewalks. Water gurgled down storm drains. Sticks, leaves, a condom, mashed paper cups congregated on the grating. I drank in the special smell of wet concrete and rubber tires, of car exhaust. Rain trickled along a parking meter post, smeared display windows of boutiques, beauty shops, and a stationery store. Rain fused its sound with that of the hissing fountain in a mini-plaza.

I slowed to review my cemetery decision. If I couldn't locate Franklin's grave, what would that prove? What help would a grave be anyway? Neal had assured me that Franklin and Amy had lived. Regardless, I kept on.

Parallel to tin warehouses the sidewalk narrowed. Cracks upended the concrete. I walked more carefully as the broken sidewalk inclined, and free of houses, and finally of sidewalks, I mashed leaves and twigs scattered across the roadway. Here dampness embraced another fragrance, like menthol, and I sniffed a fallen leaf. Eucalyptus?

A chain and padlock barred entrance through ornate grillwork, but a side pedestrian gate squeaked open when I shoved against it. I smiled wryly. Could it have been only last week that I'd traveled cross country leaving a sheltered existence for. . .a graveyard? Could I actually be hunting the marker of a man who died long before I was born?

Near the first plot my boots bruised cut grass and near another I plowed through matted weeds. Neal was right. Marble slabs and ornamental crosses made this a stone city. Markers reflected trends and economics as clearly as housing styles depict periods and wealth. I counted classic lines and Gothics. An infant tomb inscribed, "Our Babies," resembled a bed and doubled as a flower planter. On a slight rise, an Egyptian obelisk topped a granite base with a large "Millhouse" sculpted across each side. Often epitaphs ended with "Native of Wales," "Native of New York," "Native of Pennsylvania," as if to prove to mourners and to future generations that in an untamed West, the deceased had been mere transients. Their roots lay elsewhere—like mine.

Close to a family crypt I paused, for the name Nefeld was close to my maiden name, Nefeldson. Before I'd left Iowa, I'd not gone to the Harding cemetery with its snow blanket. I could imagine my parents' graves, their matching somber headstones, lined in martial fashion beside my maternal grandparents. Never had I dreamed that Dan and I would not be buried beside them. Would I die in California? Alone?

I turned toward a section with tiny plots where grief still seemed to hover. I wandered by toppled stones (the vandalism Neal had mentioned) and read next of plagues and fevers, of God calling people home, of shepherds and angels. Then I read, "Elliott."

"Jacob Penrod Elliott, born 1852—died 1902." Franklin's father? Chiseled on the adjoining white stone: "Beloved wife, Sarah Larson Elliott, born 1857—died 1896." I re-checked the name, the dates, feeling strangely moved by her age. Sarah must be Franklin's mother, and she'd never reached her fortieth birthday. Now I was older than she had ever been.

The next stone said simply: "Daughter, Anne Elliott. Born June 8, 1875—died July 19, 1876." Franklin's sister? Then I saw his name with the dates, 1877—1906.

The stone, slippery with rain was icy, solid, definite, just as was the adjacent stone for "Amy Bennett Elliott, 1879—1907."

Rain pounded the umbrella and the graves as I remained immobile, until I shivered in the damp chill. I retreated out the gate, down the hill and through the business section. A shortcut down a side street led by the museum where Neal said he had more data.

From the museum's entry way I heard him speaking about sailing ships that once docked at Madison's harbor. I peered into the living room. A group of children, apparently a class, half-circled him. In his one hand he suspended a ship's lantern and over the wire he smiled at me and nodded toward the rear of the museum.

"Can you imagine sailing in the Strait through thick fog with only lights such as these?" I heard as I slipped through the former dining room to his crowded office. File cabinets abutted more file cabinets leaving but a slender trail to his desk. A computer was stage center with file folders, books, envelopes stacked in the wings.

I sank into his desk chair, appreciating the thin stream of heat that escaped a floor register. Through a high window I watched rain drops hit electric wires.

"Sorry," he eased along the office path. "Have a class from the parochial school, so must get back, but I did locate a picture for you." He bent over my chair to nudge aside papers before he unearthed a photo. "From what's jotted on the back this was shot in Mr. Elliott's bank, the lobby."

In the background teller's cages resembled dreary caves. Shining square floor tiles dominated the foreground and between the two extremes posed a line of men, likely employees. At the left end, most presidential in attire and attitude, Mr. Elliott rested a proprietary hand on a younger man's shoulder. With a smile—the smile I'd enjoyed but hours earlier—beginning to break at the corners of his mouth, stood Franklin. Incredible. The Franklin I'd conjured duplicated the Franklin who had lived.

"I'll search for more in our archives," Neal said. "Plus, I have additional material about Amy at my house." Once more he grinned. "Must get back, but please stop by soon."

I rested in the desk chair and trained my attention on one figure in the photo. Impossible. Improbable. Unreasonable. Whatever word I gave to my situation it didn't matter, because explainable or not, Franklin did still exist.

CHAPTER FOUR

"*D*ear Molly,

No rain today, just drab skies, so I'm hoping rain won't fall this evening when I drive to the airport to meet your father."

I dropped my pen upon the lined paper. Not only did I dread the awesome trip to San Francisco, but I wasn't ready for Dan's return. Too much had happened.

But two days ago, drenched from the cemetery and walk from the museum, I'd unlocked the front door, aware that Something did share my house. And while standing in the hallway listening to the quiet, it seemed the rooms whispered confirmation.

I'd wadded newspapers and piled kindling in the living room fireplace. As a smoky blaze struggled to exist , I considered my "ghost." Fascinated and bewitched by him, I could do worse than copy his dictated poetry. As I stretched out before a more robust blaze, I wondered for the first time about life. Did it have varied levels or dimensions?

Such line of questioning continued throughout the remainder of that uninterrupted day. Often I regarded the rosebud. Did it tell me to install book shelves along the southern wall, to arrange my chair and desk in the western corner near the front windows and to re-read Amy's few diary entries? Whatever—in short order I'd memorized them.

Next day I experimented with positioning pictures against the walls on the lower level, and through another downpour drove to the grocery store at the mall, ate lunch at a drive-in, and all the while drafted mental questions for Franklin. When night abruptly canceled day I took pen and notebook to the north room, where I put on the necklace.

Notebook. Writing. At the moment I was writing to Molly. What to add to that first paragraph? Not since Molly's junior high days at summer camp had I written her and then my letters contained congratulations on each earned badge. More recent communications? Notes tacked to the bulletin board. . . "Take out garbage." "Pick up your room." "Dentist appointment tomorrow, 10:30," and finally, "Steve called."

I tapped the pen top against my teeth as I considered energy spent worrying about Steve and her. Pregnancy? Bad reputation? Sexual diseases? Confusing lust with love? Would Molly pressure Dan and me to let her marry and move to that squalid farm south of Harding? And when I tried in euphemistic terms to broach any of these concerns, she'd set her jaw and in a defensive posture, folded her arms across her chest. At this distance, after encounters with Franklin and Lorraine, it seemed ridiculous. Why couldn't I have spoken directly about fears and worries? Why allow Molly's involvement with Steve to warp our relationship?

Without bothering with a transitional sentence, I scribbled, "Molly, I apologize for hassling you about Steve. Apologize, as well, for not explaining my feelings. I trust you."

Just in time, I caught myself from adding a cliched, "I want the best for you." Just in time I pulled back from probing about grades.

"Despite the weather," I wrote, "and not having met anyone except Neal, the museum director, and Lorraine, a part-time library clerk who lives on a sailboat, I'm beginning to like Madison and this house, even in its sad condition."

I longed to write the name, Franklin, in this letter, longed to describe him, but instead I told of the view from the north room's windows and of the back yard's mystique. Closing with love, I sealed the envelope and rewarded myself by sitting back and reliving last night's events.

"You look like a secretary," Franklin had said as he settled on the floor opposite me, before he smiled and nodded. "We definitely need to get a chair and desk in here for you."

"I have a desk downstairs."

"Let's do it then."

"What?"

"Move the desk to the north room. Can we?"

"Probably if we take out the drawers."

With the ease of youth, he bounded out the door.

Since high school days I'd owned this cheap plywood desk. It symbolized miniature lifetimes when I'd written poems long on passion, short on substance; emotional stories minus plot. On the scarred top I'd confessed crushes to my notebook, flooding pages, as well, with frustrations and disappointments about not being creative enough, attractive enough, popular enough, intelligent enough. Through such admissions I'd grown to accept an average state, an image fortified by my future. Gradually, over the years, words had dwindled. Rarely did I turn to the desk and the dog-eared notebook.

We piled desk drawers on the living room floor and experimented with hand holds.

"You want to back up?"

"You back," I said and lifted the opposite end, which half way up the stairs banged against the wall.

He asked, "Want to rest?"

"Keep going," and we did, centering the desk in the corner where I'd felt it belonged."

"Take it easy," he said. "I'll get the drawers."

"I'm not decrepit, just winded."

"I don't find you the least bit decrepit." He flashed his amazing smile.

He is not flirting, I thought, *I mustn't interpret an innocent compliment (one for which I'd really fished) and magnify it.*

So swiftly that I figured this time he must have floated, Franklin brought two drawers, two more, and then the long middle one, where pencils bounced against postage stamps and a box of smashed crayons topped erasers. Before I could apologize for the mess, he rushed out for my straight-backed desk chair.

"Do you want me to sit and you begin dictating?"

He laughed. "Not just yet. Sure, ideas are packed in my head, but they'll wait." With hands at his waist, he regarded the desk, "Now you'll have a spot in which to write." Excitedly he paced for moment; then lifted his right eyebrow. "Game to help me carry up the rug that once lay here? It's stored under the house."

Rolled and stuffed behind the furnace, the rug—dusty and smelling of age—was easier to bring up stairs. As it unrolled across bare boards he laughed with delight. "This is a special rug that I had woven. As I paced I studied the pattern, gained inspiration as I recalled how laurel crowns once graced the brows of poets."

I ran fingers over the nubby texture with its border of entwined laurel leaves. You could pick one leaf and be drawn into it, could follow each vein, each curve.

As if designing snow angels he lay down to press out creases imprinted by storage. I applied pressure on the rug's edge and said, "Yesterday I visited the cemetery."

"Is it as overpopulated as the rest of the Bay Area?" He grinned. "Find my grave?"

"Uh huh, and that of your parents, and Amy's, and an Anne's."

"My sister. Died before my birth. I think my father," and glorying in the rug he moved his arms and legs, "when he couldn't comprehend my obsession with writing, consoled himself by thinking of me as a second daughter."

"This bothered you?"

"When I was young. By the time I was thirteen or fourteen, when I knew I could never be a banker, never more than a lover of words, I began to devote even more effort to being true to myself."

"Your mother?" I mashed all my weight on a resistant wrinkle.

"Beautiful, talented, frail. She encouraged me," his arms quit moving, "and because Father loved her deeply and wanted to please her, he allowed me free rein."

"And Amy? You loved her deeply?"

An internal voice scolded, "Kate, why should it matter?"

"I loved her."

"Pretty?"

He nodded and sat up. "Petite. Never weighed over a hundred pounds."

Cross legged beside him, I felt big and ungainly, so tuned out the rest of his description.

"Don't you?"

"What?"

His deep laugh startled me. "I said it's an improvement that women can wear slacks. In those jeans, for instance, you look great."

"At the museum I saw a picture of you, taken at the bank."

"Ah, yes," he half-reclined, propped on his elbows, and pushed against a bubble. "Father's one attempt to give me a crash course in banking. Museum, hmm. Hard to realize that my picture's there."

"In it you look very much as you do now."

"Maybe there's something to be said for the supernatural state, watching others age as I've stayed the same." His shook his head. "I've speculated about how it would be to grow old, lose my hair, develop a paunch.

"But in regard to society's aging," and he motioned toward the front windows, "I've seen streets built for cars to provide people with speed, comfort and power so they can move more easily to deal with problems. Yet in doing so they've created more problems. Buildings rise, houses collapse, and does that change human nature? Electric lights, telephones—You see, that's one idea I'd like to capture," and he jumped up. "Changes and changelessness, particularly the latter. Since my spirit elected not to go on until I'd written my poetry book, I've verified that despite advances, death still cripples the survivors, that jealousy persists in damaging, that—"

He threw up his hands. "Sorry, but that gives you some concept of what's penned up, of how much I need you," and he crouched beside me, a muscular leg too close to mine.

"You may be expecting too much from me. I've not written in years."

"Why not?"

It wasn't fair to blame Dan, that was too easy, or days which by their very ease defeated creativity. "Other demands," I said.

"Such as? Talk to me, Kate. Tell me about where you lived."

I smiled, seeing Home, seeing this seasonal chapter when winter, now an anti-climax, deadened fields. I felt again the forerunner of spring, the gentling wind. So I told of that freshening and of lilies and irises, peonies, snapdragons, summer's hollyhocks. And that part of my soul trapped in Iowa inhaled the dusty scent of autumn and responded to maple leaves somersaulting through lazy air.

"Oh, Kate, never doubt that you're a poet. You juxtapose words, even bend your body to their rhythm." In his exuberance, Franklin squeezed my elbow, chasing away memories and a parade of scenes.

"It's late," I said.

"Tomorrow?"

Standing and free from his touch I was more controlled. "Tomorrow evening I pick up Dan at the airport."

"Will he cause any problem for us?"

"I hope not." I sighed. "Dan wouldn't understand this."

"He'll never see me. No one will but you. You're in charge. You have the necklace."

Now, some twelve hours later I could still see his riveting gaze, feel his arm on my shoulder, hear the melody in his voice.

Enough of that. I'd mail Molly's letter. A brisk walk would lessen this intensity I'd created.

On concrete steps leading to the post office, I paused to examine depressions carved by foot traffic. How many feet must tread on stones before erosion—

"Hey, lady, you have some kind of foot fetish?"

With a laugh I walked with Lorraine into the lobby, where she pointed toward a wall mural. "That's by Maynard Dixon, California artist, painted during the WPA period."

The scene depicted a wharf clogged with ferries, schooners, fishing vessels while in the foreground a man in top hat and a woman in a bustled dress peered at the fledgling Madison community. Were those the fashions Franklin's parents wore? I must get a book on late nineteenth century clothing, furniture, customs.

"Yes," Lorraine chattered on. "I know scads of trivia. I've listened to reference librarians.

"May the U.S flag be flown after sundown?" she squeaked.

Her voice deepened. "If properly illuminated."

"What's the name of Santa's fifth reindeer?" she lisped.

"Comet, little one."

I deposited my letter in the Out-of-Town slot. "You should compile a book of miscellaneous information."

"Brighter minds beat me to it. Besides the temptation to invent facts would be too tempting. I'd make up animals or a rare species—the Catabungas—who do nothing but dig tunnels."

"You'd have believers."

"Absolutely. Some people believe anything. Hey, want to go sailing this afternoon? Wind's picking up, and I'm eager to sail. Don't want to wait weeks for perfect conditions."

"Remember I'm the one who stumbled even getting onto your boat."

"Next you'll tell me you have flat feet and adenoids, but I'll ignore those limitations and take you anyway."

"Okay, these clothes all right?"

"Sure. If it gets cold I have jackets on board."

Since the passenger side door of Lorraine's green VW was permanently stuck, I scooted across a frayed, taped seat and collided with a stick shift.

"A little limited on aesthetics but the thing runs," she said as we lurched from the curb. "Actually it's Adam's. Along with the boat it's on loan and the state it's in today is exactly as he left it. One of Adam's virtues is that nonessentials like car appearances don't bother him."

When Lorraine parked at the harbor, I assumed a nonchalance I didn't feel, for wind whipped the dull water. As if starched, boat mast flags stood at attention. Oh, God, there was more breeze than I'd anticipated.

Once more Lorraine outdistanced me, and when I reached *The Eden*, Lorraine said, "Sit in the cockpit." She flung her shoes below and moved forward along the deck on bare feet. How did she gain her confidence, I wondered, watching her untie strands of rope bound around the masts and toss them in my direction.

Far out on the front part ("bowsprit" she called it), Lorraine stuffed canvas covers into large duffel bags. She primed the engine, threw "bumpers" onto the dock, cast lines behind us and with deft motions guided the ketch toward the harbor entrance.

As we merged with the open channel, a gust struck and the boat plowed ahead. I noticed no other sailboats, just a distant tugboat and an anchored fishing boat, a far cry from the post office mural. When Franklin and I next relaxed on the gray rug, if I could think clearly and not be so aware of him, I'd inquire about shipping.

The boat bowed and staggered. Spray coated my lips while Lorraine hurried about yanking up sails, tugging ropes. *The Eden* lurched erratically.

"Not to worry," Lorraine yelled from a deck suddenly wet.

With hands like talons on the cockpit's edge, I heard her reassuring words, "She's a heavy old boat. We won't turn over."

In but a couple minutes, she jumped into the cockpit beside me, "We're trimmed. Now, I'll play tour guide. On the left: Port Costanza, an early grain port. Across the Strait is Barriton, a town known for 'firsts'—first report of the Sierra gold strike, first Protestant seminary in the state, first—uh, go below. See how much depth we have. Charts are on the table."

Lines on the curling pages resembled pancake batter shapes. Where was this Indian Rock? Had we passed Sister's Lighthouse? Did these numbers mean feet? Fathoms?

"Don't sweat it, Kate. We're aground. Come on up. Enjoy the scenery."

In the far distance a skeletal bridge gleamed and Lorraine said, "Villicot Bridge." She listed communities at its feet; gave capsule appraisals. The one on the left, she said, contained vacant company houses from a closed sugar plant. Currently the former factory stored imported cars.

Peacefulness underscored water lapping against the hull, the wind's chant in the rigging. Moods from romantic novels once read filled my mind. At that company town, a plant owner who resembled Franklin searched the horizon for the frigate upon which his fiancé would be arriving. He ached for her and—

"This is the only way to travel even if you don't move," Lorraine said.

Half-shackled to misty dreams, I smiled.

"I don't want Adam to return, reclaim the boat."

I lost my dreams. "If he does," I asked, "what then?"

"I'll move on." Lorraine dropped the topic to explain about buoys, channel markers, and the sail boat's supremacy over power boats. From there we branched into books and philosophy until the sky darkened.

"A storm?"

"Nah, night."

"But I meet Dan at 10:39."

"Perhaps. We're stuck here until the tide changes, about 9:15."

"He'll be worried."

"Should have told you, on sailboats you can't keep schedules."

Usually pork and beans gave me heartburn, and after eating hot dogs I chewed antacids, but on *The Eden* I ate unheated beans from a can, two cold hot dogs dipped into a mustard jar and half a dozen packaged cookies, the cheap pink marshmallow variety I'd never buy.

"I eat thousands of calories when sailing. Theory goes that you burn it off. Good theory except I keep gaining weight." She grabbed another cookie.

Lorraine would never been mistaken for thin, but such confidence, such personality, radiated attractiveness. *Could I ever be attractive? Did Franklin find me so? Oh, stop it. Realize you're an older woman good for writing his poetry.*

Lights dotted the shore line, the wind cooled, waves thumped, and a bubble of laughter formed, the youthful kind which signals abandon. I felt young, delighted with the beauty on the water, knife streaks of light from the landed buildings, wide shadowed expanses, a contradiction to the narrowed shadowed horizons in Harding. The laughter bubble expanded, when I glanced at Lorraine, her soft blonde hair tangled by the water's breeze. I had a friend, and I had Franklin. Whoever/Whatever he was, he made me feel alive, and then laughter surged in my throat and pushed against my lips.

Such an unrestrained sensation recalled an evening when a friend (was her name Sharon?) and I chased beneath a ripening moon. With sixteen overwhelming us, we were entranced by night. We responded to its passion and galloped across a newly-plowed field. With senses preternaturally keen, we almost decoded earth's secrets that rose from the exposed soil. I laughed.

"What?" Lorraine asked.

"Was remembering an adolescent time which gave me the same sense of exuberance that I'm experiencing tonight."

"Definitely a call for a celebration." Lorraine dropped through the open hatch for her cheap red. Night donned a darker coat and regardless of the setting and the wine, I was conscious of the hours and of Dan.

Shortly after ten o'clock, Lorraine guided *The Eden* into its berth and without putting away the sails, hustled me along the slippery dock. "I'll drive you to the City. This time of night and with a couple glasses of my brew, you'd end up in San Jose or Eureka."

Although I wanted Lorraine to drive, I protested, "You're not exactly sober yourself."

"But I am. You build up an immunity to cheap red. Plus, I've had a friendly relationship with a couple officers."

I scooted across the VW's front seat, and as Lorraine shifted into reverse, the bug shuddered and died. I laughed. Even funnier was the idea of meeting Dan in dirty jeans with hair on end and make-up gone.

True, much sooner than I could have driven it, we pulled up before the baggage claim area. "Try and find Danny boy before I have to pay to park or before I get a ticket for stopping by a red curb."

Near a wall in the baggage section, Dan was defined not only by matched luggage, one carefully stationed by each leg, but by irritation. In aura fashion, it outlined him. Then I slowed. When had his hair thinned? His waistline expanded? He would be indistinguishable from other middle-aged businessmen, except at this point near a deserted carousel, he couldn't be confused with anyone.

As I shifted vision to recognize him, Dan blinked at me, plainly bewildered by my appearance. "Kate? What in the world?"

"I've been sailing."

"Good Lord, it's eleven-fifteen. I called the house." As if in proof, he waved his cell phone. "No answer. I didn't know if you were dead, in a wreck, but next figured you'd gotten lost."

And before me rose the image of a frosted glass window on Christmas Day. Where was he? Where had he been these last few days? I couldn't bring up the far past or the present one, particularly since we were regarding each other as near strangers. "Come on," I said. "Lorraine's waiting."

He frowned.

"My friend has a sailboat. Took me out today. We went aground."

His footsteps spelled out unease as he trailed me to the curb, and with a peculiar weariness he sank into the back seat. As Dan arranged his bags, Lorraine hit the gas pedal and bellowed at an approaching officer, "Up yours, fellow."

As she blended with the string of freeway-bound cars, she cranked up her window. "I wasn't blocking anyone, kept the motor idling, but he's been eyeing me, itching to write out a ticket."

She glanced into the rear view mirror. "Hi, I'm Lorraine, Kate's friend."

"Yes, well." Dan upended a suitcase that had fallen onto the floor. "I appreciate your picking me up."

"No problem. Least I could do after sailing us onto a sandbar. You know," she said to me, "that's the third time I've misjudged that spot," and never again during the ride did she directly address Dan. "Obviously charts are accurate, but I play it too close." Her sentences evolved into anecdotes about ocean-going ships that had borne down upon *The Eden*, about seasickness near the Farallone Islands and man overboard drills on someone's sloop. Like a divided person part of me was swept along with such incidents while my other half, with antenna honed, registered Dan's puzzlement.

After Lorraine dropped us off, we stood uneasily at the bottom of the front steps, and I realized he didn't know what to say.

"Where'd you meet your hippie friend?"

"Library."

Silently we mounted the steps, stumbling in the dark. Ah, yes, I'd not been here to turn the porch light on. Dan banged luggage against a step, the railing. In the living room, unease didn't lessen. He jingled some coins in his pants' pocket and clucked his tongue—always a sign that he was analyzing the situation—as he surveyed a disarrayed living room. "Our stuff looks funny, doesn't it?"

"I'd like to redecorate with period furniture." As I spoke I imagined seeking Franklin's advice, and I smiled.

Catching my smile, Dan stepped toward me. "You startled me at the airport in those clothes, but, well, you're looking good. Pretty. There's something younger, more alive about you. Guess if that's what sailing does, we better get a boat." He chuckled.

But when I said nothing he said, "Do you think I invented this trip? I had no choice. You think I went off to see Sheila?"

"It doesn't matter, Dan."

"Doesn't it?" He turned away and swallowed. "I gave up a lot for you— for us." And he sounded as weary as he looked.

"It's late," I answered. "Like something to eat?"

"No, thanks."

While he unpacked his luggage I lay on my side of the bed to recount incidental concerns: no communication from Molly since her phone call, the bad rains, and some of the upcoming repair projects. "Replace window panes in the dining room, paint the house exterior, as well as the interior. There's the bathroom. The dining room ceiling is cracked, and we have low water pressure."

"Quite a list," he said, and those were the last words I remember him saying for so deeply did I sleep that I didn't hear the alarm. His hand on my shoulder woke me.

"I'm leaving for the City," he said, and I answered, "Breakfast?"

"Had some cereal."

I sat upright. Never, except when I'd been sick, had Dan prepared anything.

"Sorry about last night," he said. "Like to go out for dinner this evening?"

Then the front door closed, and in the fragile dawn the car engine coughed. Lulled by the atmosphere of the house, I snuggled under the blankets. Odd how Dan's entrance, his statements, his movements, had altered the restorative threads within these rooms where, upon his exit, the fabric began mending itself.

Mid-morning sun woke me. All right, I'd tackle more cartons, clean the spare bedroom, add projects to the repair list, after I visited Franklin.

Partly to disguise trembling legs, partly to disguise eagerness, and partly to appear businesslike and ready for dictation, I settled at the desk before putting on the necklace.

From behind me he spoke, "I've missed you."

So he wouldn't see the effect of his words I examined the waiting notebook.

"And I you."

"Your husband got home safely."

I swung toward him as I resisted an impulse to confess that my marriage couldn't compare with his and Amy's, as I resisted the temptation to blurt out the dismal/familiar account of a husband's infidelity—and their resultant shared love. But the story wouldn't improve in the retelling, in the admission of how I'd pleaded with Dan not to leave me. Perhaps in a poem I would eventually employ that emotional panoply, but at this instant with Franklin disturbingly near, I'd pose one of my questions. "So you can see us?"

"I choose where to look and essentially it's within this room. Your life with Dan is none of my business, is it? But do tell me about an airport. How it smells? Sounds? And bridges? Do they actually hum when you drive across them?"

Since he sat on the rug and seemed in no hurry to record his verse, I joined him and tried to depict the airport's jangled emotions, how welcomes intersected farewells, and I told how the Bay Bridge and the Golden Gate affected me. I told him about sailing, and he countered with reminiscences of Italian fishermen who dumped salmon from hand-tied nets, of feluccas that populated the waterfront a century ago.

"Barges and schooners would dock at Madison or at Port Costanza for grain and fruit produced from farms and ranches that filled this valley, these hillsides. As a boy I'd wander for hours, finding no one. I'd ride Pharaoh in places where land has been re-contoured. We'd ford Palmyra Creek—seals swam there—but that creek's gone, I'm sure.

"Ferries carried passengers until the Vallecito and Barriton Bridges were built. I remember giant train ferries and some paddle wheelers running between San Francisco, Sacramento, and Stockton. Often they put in at a Chinese community in the delta where there were inexpensive girls and a chance to win big at the fan-tan tables."

Sunlight caressing Franklin's left cheekbone cast his eyes into shadow and brightened his full lips. He was beautiful, as was his voice chanting about the sailing ships' demise, the death of commercial fishing. If his speech translated into written language, the results would be profound.

He spoke of earthquakes. "The worst, aside from the famous one in 1906, occurred during the Richardson's stay. It tumbled Mrs. Richardson out of bed, smashed cups, saucers, vases."

In turn I told of Midwestern tornados, how the Winslow house, just south of town, whirled on its foundation, how caps were lifted from bottles in one side of a soda pop carton.

The light, like an unstructured sun dial, crawled along the laurel leaves and showed that too many hours had elapsed, but I found it hard to move, to leave.

"We'll write another time," he said. "Let me help you today," and he jumped up to extend a hand. I bumped against a decidedly un-ghostly form.

For the remainder of the afternoon I relaxed, finding it easier to stack dishes in the dining room built-ins and wipe cobwebs from corners as we talked. When had I ever spoken to anyone about whatever flitted across my mind? Strangely, in brief days I'd discovered two people—well, one person and one "entity"—with whom I'd establish an almost instantaneous rapport.

When I mentioned house plans, he asked, "Would you consider having it as it once was? For example in the living room, those bookshelves on each side of the fireplace had glass doors. Over the mantle hung a mirror in gilded frame. Twin horsehair chairs were by these front windows and between them was a circular table with ostrich feathers in a vase. The sofa was a heavy mission-style piece, up against that southern wall."

"What happened to your furniture? Any way I could track it down?"

"Doubt it. After Amy's death, her family cleaned out everything. Anyway, in one dining room corner we set a grandfather clock, had a rectangular table, as you do, and we centered it under the chandelier. The bathroom? Well, stay with progress. Originally the toilet tank hung on the wall, but wouldn't it be wonderful if you could find a claw-foot bathtub?

"In the little front room," and he dashed ahead of me, "off the entryway, we kept plants and wicker furniture. The master bedroom had print wallpaper, a highboy and a canopy bed. Amy pieced a quilt. You guessed it, lumpy and uneven."

He sprinted upstairs and motioned toward the vacant room to the right. "A company bedroom although we never entertained over night guests. Amy put comforters (ones she bought) on the single beds. A chest of drawers, Gold Oak, stood against a wall, and a Queen Anne chair, a gift from her family—which Amy didn't like—truly hid in a corner. We papered walls with a blue hydrangea pattern and she chose lace curtains for the windows."

Together we entered the north room where from its windows we could see the gradual progression of downtown lights as they blinked on.

Undoubtedly Franklin guessed that Dan would soon arrive, for he touched the necklace and asked, "Tomorrow then?"

As I reached for the clasp, his breath feathered my cheek. "Until then, Kate. . .No, to me, you are Katherine."

CHAPTER FIVE

*H*ints of gray shredded the night, signaling an end to this artificial weekend. I lifted my head from the pillow. The illumined clock radio dial showed almost five o'clock and cast muted light across Dan's profile. *In his way, he's trying*, I thought, *for he'd hurried home Friday night to take me to dinner.*

And I had tried. Could hours with Franklin have gentled me? With this altered perspective, wasn't I seeing Dan more charitably? More compassionately? For during the meal at Madison's Little Italy Restaurant, I expressed sincere delight that Old Jer had liked Dan's conference report, as Dan valiantly ate lasagna and garlic bread. Neither does he like, but to please me he'd ordered the special and Chianti, although previously he'd complained that an invisible residue coated his teeth after he drank red wine.

"Have some good news," he said. "Clark and his wife—Peg, I think—invited us to their home tomorrow evening, along with a few other couples. Clark's from the office, lives in Rivera. You know, that plush community near Berkeley where we first looked?"

Images of contemporary houses, flagstones or curved sidewalks, cul-de-sacs, tidy landscaping sprang to mind, but they didn't entice me to go to Rivera and meet Dan's co-workers. And, yet, just weeks ago I longed for potential new friends, unaware of our past. I longed for acceptance not only of Dan and me as a couple, but I longed for proof that he wanted us to be known as a solid couple.

The desire not to go to Rivera had lasted the entire Saturday when rain bound us to the house. Dan willingly pounded nails and rearranged furniture, agreed to furnish rooms in a late Victorian style, "As long as it doesn't cost an arm and a leg."

Impressed at what I'd accomplished, he wondered aloud how I'd managed several heavy objects. Without argument he unpacked and stored his items: shotguns and waders, a tattered plaid shirt and crushed baseball cap, high school athletic medals, and a lopsided spice rack, a legacy from seventh grade shop class.

On Saturday night while I waited for water to trickle into the bath tub, I faced the mirror. Of course, the evening would be fine. Of course, I must regard this as the proverbial new beginning. But at the actual cocktail party I was the brown mouse among women who visited gyms, exercise classes, and plastic surgeons. Taut faces, flawless make-up, and designer apparel signaled interests far removed from scrawling poetry in a run-down house.

Lips in one bronzed face parted, "You and Dan have bought an old home in Madison?"

"One that needs work." Around me in an irregular triangle, wispy sounds, like a desert breeze, rustled until the breeze spoke, "Oh, my." "Repair." "Goodness."

Bronze face said, "Madison is a stable blue collar community, but it's a bit distant. Didn't you check in Rivera or Costa?"

"Nothing was in our price range."

Smooth Neck said, "Occasionally properties become available where owners will arrange flexible financing."

Dan rearranged the tenor of the women's group when he stepped closer and agreed that life in Rivera would be superior. Perhaps he'd fantasized such a life in an upscale community with Sheila, for these were the kind of people with whom Sheila would belong.

"This is our camping out phase," he laughed, causing the breeze to expand. "As soon as something we can afford, change that to *anything* we can afford, hits the market we'll grab it."

I kept my smile in place. Surely he was joking or being an appreciative guest, for only that afternoon he'd contacted a roofing firm who'd send appraisers out on Monday to evaluate the roof's condition.

However, as we drove home I discovered he was serious.

"The way I see it, Kate, we fix up the place as inexpensively as possible. Sell it, make a profit, and move to Rivera. That's the 'in' address. We bought too fast, that's all. If we'd had more sense, we'd have rented, checked around before buying. I saw that very clearly tonight."

"But you approved of my redecorating plans. . . . Dan, I love that house."

"We've not been here long enough for you to love anything. At the moment, it's base." He swallowed and stared at the road, an off-white beneath freeway lights. "You've left Molly and have given up your home, have been through hell with me. What I intend is to find a house for you, as close to but better than the one in Harding. A single story. And our best bet, for many reasons, is Rivera. I did well in San Diego, pleased Jer, and you saw how they liked me tonight. I'll be getting a raise soon, advancing."

Advancing. A new life. But I thought of the north room, of Franklin, and of how he'd said, "Katherine." He'd call me Katherine. No one had ever spoken those syllables with his inflection. Immediately I was comforted.

Early Sunday morning the phone rang. While Dan answered, I curled under the covers, listening to the degrees by which his voice lost its groggy tint.

"All right, Irma, put her on."

I tied the sash on my robe and hurried into the kitchen.

"So, if Steve had car trouble, why didn't you simply call Irma?" Dan demanded. "What?" He rolled his eyes. "Molly, that was stupid. Naturally, she'd worry. Where did you sleep?"

Dan mouthed, "Molly was out all night."

I started to say, "Is that all?" All? A month ago I, too, would have been frantic.

"If Irma grounds you, that's fine. I'd do the same. Oh, no, don't give me that about being an adult." And as if Molly were before him he moved his hand from its position at the elastic band of his pajama pants and shook his finger. "Oh, sure, you're eighteen. Sure, you can do what you like, but, by God, not when I'm paying the bills, and Irma and Dexter are responsible for you. Is that clear? Okay, here's your mother."

As he thrust the receiver toward me, he stalked from the room. I paused in an attempt to manufacture an emotion stronger than annoyance. "Honey?"

"Mother," she sobbed. "The car broke down."

"Don't lie, Molly. If you sleep with Steve then you take the consequences. Dealing with the Hawkins is one."

"You don't sound like yourself."

"I'm not sure I am myself anymore."

When Dan re-entered the kitchen I sought a clipped tone. "Now, I suggest you apologize to Dexter and Irma, follow their rules, or they might ship you to us." As the threat left my mouth I thought, *I do not want another person in this house.*

"Moth-er, I have to graduate here. Have to. I can't leave Steve."

"Then, shape up," and I handed the phone back to Dan.

In the bathroom as I turned the hot water faucet, I imagined Molly in a few minutes also turning a lavatory spigot to wash away tears. Sympathetic to her distress, my eyes watered. I should be in Harding to hug her, to repeat assurances. Slowly Molly's tear-stained features faded to be replaced by her other facial expressions: wrinkling her nose at the home perm's odor; batting eyelashes sticky with mascara; frowning over a history text; zippering her lips with a forefinger to keep from eating dessert; smiling at a puppy, laughing at Dan's jokes. In Molly's life smiles had dominated, so I selected a recent one wreathed with love and maturity when Dan and I capitulated to her pleas to stay with the Hawkins.

And I clung to that picture while Dan ranted about Molly's conduct. "You'd think she'd show some consideration. . .worrying Irma and Dexter. . .this is how she thanks them?. . .Steve. . .no respect. What in God's name were they doing all night? Don't answer. That's a rhetorical question."

When his anger down shifted to irritation, I broke into the sound track. "Why don't we work today on the bathroom drain and the one in the laundry room?"

Reluctantly he dressed and drove to the hardware store to buy a snake. With him gone, I hesitated at the stairwell. No, with Franklin I required leisure. To summon him for odd moments was unsatisfactory. We required time to talk and share.

"Think about plumbing," I lectured myself and left the stairwell to remove drain screens. For most of Sunday Dan and I struggled, plunging and twisting the snake until water gurgled free. We replaced washers and faucet handles, mixed and applied tile grout around the bathtub.

When evening fell, Dan laid a fire and we sat quietly. He didn't switch on the television but admitted he'd been apprehensive about the new job. As he talked about the office, the different politics, I told him that I would have been petrified to drive the bridge, to find parking, to walk across the building's marble lobby and press the elevator button. As the elevator swept upward, my stomach would have knotted, and fear would have exited with me on the twelfth floor, where Dan said cubicles joined cubicles.

"It's far different from Harding," he said, an understatement.

"Do you miss it?"

He poked at the log to avoid eye contact. "Yes. Harding will always be Home. There's something darned marvelous, you know, about walking down the street and hearing someone call your name. It's reassuring to have your doctor, dentist. . ." He broke off and dropped the poker onto the hearth. "In Harding, I knew who I was."

Unable to think of an answer, I sat with him united by a history that no one could erase. Only the spit of flames broke the silence.

"I miss Molly," he said at last, and I nodded.

"Do you miss—Her?" And, as I spoke, discovered only pain's outline.

"It's getting better." He studied his hands.

"You still love Her?"

I felt him debating his response. Finally he said, "I never before realized that it's possible to love two people at the same time." Then he added, "But I never wanted to hurt you."

"I believe that. But, why, Dan?"

He snorted, "Why? I don't know if there's an answer. It simply grew. I mean, Sheila and I, over the years have always teased each other, flirted, you know that. At the Hansen's barbecue a year or so ago something just sort of ignited between us. We talked some on the phone, met for lunch." He stopped.

"Go on. It's okay," for it was. I felt removed, almost dispassionate.

"Eventually there was more, but what I hadn't counted on, what she hadn't counted on either, was feeling like we did. Hey, at the outset she and I told each other that this was wrong, that we were just attracted and we'd have a—an—interlude. We hadn't figured we'd care so much for each other."

"You talked about divorce? Marrying each other?"

"We did. Explored some impractical plans." He stared into the fire before suddenly he moved, surprising me, to bury his face in my lap. I patted his graying hairs, rubbed his temples, feeling a near-grief for him, and for what we'd had so long ago. His breath warmed my thighs when he said, "But I told Sheila we had no future. I would stay with you."

Short days ago I would have experienced triumph, but instead I thought about a handsome young man with magnetic eyes and sensual lips.

Now, on this Monday morning, dawn teased the east and the alarm buzzed. I boosted the thermostat and in the kitchen fried bacon and eggs.

After dishes and after Dan's car cleared the hill, I dressed and laughed aloud when infant spring, in the guise of sunshine, broke through the panes. An omen? But I needed none. Joy pulsed in this house.

I slipped the jewelry in place and he stood before me with that dazzling smile. "Did the weekend grow an extra day?"

"It was a very long weekend," I answered.

He advanced toward me, "Katherine," and rested his right hand on my shoulder. "I hope in some way I can help you, that you won't see me as self-centered." He placed his left hand on my other shoulder. "You are sensitive, kind, and lovely."

My mouth dried, my heart raced, and in the distance something foreign jingled.

"Doorbell," he said.

"Bet it's the men to check the roof."

By the time I reached the front door the two roofers had already left the porch, but they climbed the stairs again to hand over a business card and say they'd be examining the roof.

Unable to be comfortably alone with Franklin while they were present I decided to hunt for the north room's wallpaper, which Franklin had described as a gray-blue with ivory-colored roses centered in each panel.

Yet as I walked from the house, I moved slowly. Could I be suffering from some kind of breakdown? Had Dan's affair, leaving Home and Molly pushed me over an edge? If so, now that Dan was trying, why couldn't I do the same? Subconsciously did I want to punish him? And what about Franklin? I could have manufactured him as I'd manufactured worlds as a child. But how to account for the museum picture? He had lived. The library book vowed that ghosts and apparitions were possible. If people had encounters of the third kind, weren't additional encounters possible?

Maybe when individuals, like Amy, entered those unexplained situations, humanity had no options but to consider them mentally ill or possessed. Therefore, the moral was to keep quiet about extraordinary visitations. And, what harm could there be for me in such involvement? Franklin and I were going to write. He was kind, gentle, handsome, and he enhanced my days.

"You're in outer space. Must be a man. I've called your name twice." Before the library Lorraine rearranged her backpack. "Yep, you have a lover."

"What?"

"You have that distracted air. Notice I don't."

"Did you break up with Peter?"

She puffed out her cheeks, preparatory to a massive sigh. "Would be easier if I could. Then I'd locate a new man, but, let's face it, I'm nuts about Peter. Unfortunately, he knows this. He spent the weekend with me because his wife was out of town, but last night, like a male version of Cinderella, he leaves at the stroke of midnight so he can get home and have adequate rest before he meets wifie's plane this morning. Shit. So, where are you going?"

Without giving me time to reply, she fell in beside me. "Why do I love him? He won't separate from wifie. Sometimes I fantasize he will, but fantasy is all it is. And, yet, without fantasy, what's left?"

In Belleci's Paint and Paper Store, we wandered along aisles scanning displays and leafing through bulky sample books before I spotted a gray-blue pattern with misty roses. It couldn't be. When the clerk approached, and speechless, I pointed to the design, he said, "You're in luck, lady. We have that in stock."

"Hey, what's wrong with your talker?" Lorraine laughed. "Need some liquid? Come on. I'll buy you a cup of coffee. It costs seventy-two cents at Mona's Café because seventy-two is her favorite number."

Mona also favored mismatched cups and chairs that teetered on a sagging floor. In my euphoria I praised the restaurant as charming, with personality.

"Okay, who's the guy?" Lorraine clinked a yellow porcelain cup on a green plastic saucer.

I shook my head.

"I tell you, Kate, when you decide to move, you move fast. I predicted you'd find someone. Dan will be livid."

Her words, like a needle, pricked my balloon. "I'm not hunting for a man, and I don't want to make Dan jealous." But could Lorraine be right? Could this be about self-worth, about vengeance?

"Whatever the reason, whoever he is, I say, 'go, girl.' You look fantastic. Keep this fellow on the side whatever you do."

We strolled down Vermosa Street, the brush of Lorraine's backpack against her pea coat the only sound for a moment. As if of one accord we moved toward the waterfront, each of us, I believe, in unspoken agreement that I'd go but part way with her before turning back.

A block from the railroad tracks she said, "See you soon," and I watched as she continued north. Even in her stride, I could read distress. Strange how body language speaks more clearly than words. Strange how revealing it can be. It was Franklin's body language that I read, and as I moved away from the sight of Lorraine's retreating figure, I laughed at my word choice— a body in relation to a ghost.

As I again neared downtown, I noticed to my left a residential street of small one-level houses, Brandis. I'd see if it was a short cut to my hill, now rising to my far left. These houses, bungalows, were older, maybe built from 1900 to 1920. They had porches and flower gardens, earmarks of long-established residences. As I passed one, where ivy shielded the porch, I heard my name, and Neal stepped from behind the wall of green.

"You live here?"

With a majestic sweep of his arm that encompassed the side rose garden, denuded by winter, and the picket fence marking the opposite side of the lawn, he announced, "On this entire estate. Come in for a tour of my mansion."

I hesitated. By now the roofers would be gone, and I could be with Franklin.

"Well, if you can't see all rooms—I've an impressive total of five—at least step into the living room, where I have an oil portrait of Amy Elliott."

From the porch we entered directly into the living room, one that didn't compute with this large, bear-like man. If I'd been asked to describe where he lived, and I've not given it any thought, I'd have pictured a stark environment with leather furniture. But in a space surely not more than nine feet by twelve, overstuffed couches and chairs interspersed with occasional tables competed for attention. Figurines and reading lamps cluttered the tables.

"An old ladies' room," he said, and I didn't correct him. "I've lived here my entire life with my mother and an aunt. This is the way they liked the room, and when they died—just months apart—both asked me to keep the room as they'd left it."

I felt a slight chill. Another example of the past dictating to the present, and right beside me was another example of a man who listened to yesterday and honored it. I smiled at him, feeling warmed by his returned smile. Not handsome, he instead emitted a goodness, a stability, a non-judgmental aura that could prompt one—a wife surely—to confide her ideas and fears.

"You live alone?"

"Since Mother and Auntie's deaths, yes." Had he then at some point been married? Was he gay?

When once more I surveyed the claustrophobic room, I paid attention to the darkly-papered walls that contained a pattern of funereal looking flowers. Scattered in random fashion across the wallpaper were framed paintings, equally drab: bleak waterfalls and lakes, a wolf in snow country baying at the moon, but in the back corner—a woman's portrait.

Neal tugged the chain on a lamp closest to the woman's picture, and its dim yellow rays caught in the painted blonde ringlets.

"The artist began on Amy's picture several months before her wedding, a gift her parents commissioned. The artist became ill so the portrait wasn't completed until after she married. I think that the picture lost some significance for them, because Amy insisted on wearing a present from her husband, a man they didn't entirely approve of."

"They didn't approve?" I repeated as I skirted the nearest table where a delicate figurine of a shepherdess and twin lambs teetered precariously near the edge.

"Guess Franklin not only couldn't hold a bank position, but he had a reputation as a dreamer, a charmer."

"Charmer?"

Neal reached up and with his one hand fumbled with the painting. "My great aunts vowed that he could entice someone—we'll interpret that to mean females—to do whatever he desired."

As Neal struggled with the frame, I debated if I should help him. Had he gone through life, through all his probably fifty-some years, with one arm? How many activities had been denied him? Could he drive? Open a jar? Tie a shoe?

There, he held the picture in his hand and shrugged, as if wondering how to proceed with his definition. "My great aunts maintained that he enticed Amy to—to well, not wait for marriage to—to well, let's say, 'make love.'"

I veered around a chair with fat arms and beside Neal confronted Amy Bennett Elliott's oval face—high cheekbones, a broad forehead, eyes widely spaced like Jacqueline Kennedy's, a pert nose—

"Lovely, isn't she?" he said.

Of course she was, but I couldn't answer for my gaze traveled across her features to the rosebud necklace gracing her slender neck.

When he noticed my focus, Neal nodded. "Yes, that's Franklin's present. My great aunties called it, 'cheap, a rosebud made of bisque. Didn't even buy her a diamond or a pearl,' they grumbled, 'but a lump of ceramics not even glazed.'" Neal continued speaking, but his voice came indistinctly, as I concentrated on the rosebud. He said something about her youth. "Barely eighteen when she married Franklin." Something about early widowhood. "Devastated. Her family begged her to come home." Something about the family's hope that she could remarry someone "more responsible." Something about the great aunts saying, "It's a blessing there were no children." Something about "Became more and more of a recluse. Wouldn't let Auntie Stella or Auntie Beatrice into the house." Something about Stella and Beatrice as spinsters. "Amy was much younger—the family beauty— the one her parents and Stella and Beatrice knew was special."

"Amy's death?" I finally asked.

"From pneumonia, I believe. Apparently Auntie Stella and Auntie Beatrice had left her alone for a few weeks because their father died and they were involved in details, a funeral—to which Amy didn't go."

"They broke down the door to get her?"

His brown eyes widened. "How did you know that? But, yes, that's exactly what happened. She was hallucinating, claimed that Franklin visited her."

I stared at her wide doe-like eyes. Indeed she was as Franklin had described her. Franklin.

"Thank you," I said, "but I better get on home. See what the roofers found. May I hang the picture before I go?"

He nodded. "Two hands are better at that."

As I replaced the portrait's wire on its nail, the rosebud necklace at my eye level, he said, "There must be more about Amy and Franklin in my mother's bedroom. She kept records and diaries. Come back some time—usually I'm home on Mondays when the museum is closed—and dig with both your hands," he smiled, "through the trunk and see what's there."

With both hands. An opening to talk about his missing limb. But Neal's story at this point was far less important than was Franklin, who waited for me to put on the actual necklace, so I snaked around the room's obstacle course, said "Goodbye," and hiked up the hill.

As expected, the roofers had gone, leaving their triplicate form tucked beneath the front door mat. I paid no attention to comments, price, or itemized repairs, but dropped the form on the kitchen table.

Before Franklin or I spoke, I handed him the wall paper sample, which he positioned against the north wall. "Very close, Katherine."

"Then I'll buy it, and we'll wallpaper." With pure joy, I clapped my hands and spun around. For some reason I didn't want to tell of Amy's portrait, of remarks about a charmer reputation. All that mattered was that we restore this room. With it capturing what he'd loved, surely it would help him write more effortlessly. But, was I being presumptuous? Maybe he could write under any condition, so I apologized. "Wall papering can wait. You've postponed writing for ages."

"Ah, Katherine," and he sprawled on the rug. "You don't turn on a writing valve and it automatically gushes out. There's a rhythm, a preparation. Also," he kneaded his hands, "while I've had large blocks of time in which to think about verse, I've been unable to write any down. As a result some great ideas, excellent images, have evaporated. In essence, I need to begin again."

I sank down beside him, lulled by his voice, an actor's voice, I decided. "Particularly when we must work in synchronization, we must totally trust each other, practically think as one. We must become more," and he cupped his hands, as if to extract the proper expression from the air, "intimate." And I gulped. "We must establish utter closeness, so my words will flow and so that as you write them, you can suggest improvements. I think that wall-papering is an adventure in togetherness."

I rejected the niggling worry that Franklin was stalling writing his poetry—a worry furthered by Neal's comments—and consoled myself with the authenticity of Franklin's sentiments. With him, I measured the number of square feet, wrote the figure on a notebook page, and walked back down the hill.

I returned with rolls of "Forgotten Rose," with brushes and a tray, and as I slowly mounted the front steps I recalled an innocent time, before Sheila, in which Dan and I had wallpapered Molly's room. In a pre-adolescent horse phase she'd selected an equestrian print. After we aligned a palomino's head with a mustang's flank, our patience dwindled. By evening Dan shouted, and as strips of paper, either over or under-pasted, slithered toward the baseboard, I cried. Dan retreated to the garage. We pacified Molly with horse posters and never again mentioned wallpapering. Later, Irma Hawkins said, "If a couple survives wallpapering and curtain hanging, they have a good marriage."

Good is a relative term.

But on that late Monday afternoon, Franklin and I fell into a measured movement. Easily, smoothly, a choreographed dance of sorts, we wet the panels and brushed them on walls, where the roses stayed.

"Where do you go when I remove the necklace?" I asked at one point, when we slid a panel through the plastic tub of water.

"For one who treasures words, I haven't a vocabulary to explain. 'Disembodied' may come close. Have you ever had the sensation of floating, of gazing down on your body or on a room?"

We snugged the panel against the textured wall. "No," I answered, " but does this floating happen for days, for months?"

His smile was sad. "Time's a human measurement. Only when humans are involved do I react to it."

As I immersed another panel in the water tray, my fingers nudged his. Through translucent liquid I regarded my skin, wrinkled at the knuckles; veins that formed a bas relief on mine were flat on his

"The manifestations that some humans calls ghosts," he said, "are souls on one level. There are various ways to manifest, depending on your, well, status, where you are, to whom you're appearing, your vibrational frequency, your needs." He grinned and propelled the panel through the liquid. "I'm not very far up the scale, Katherine. There's so much beyond that I don't understand, some that I do, and that I can't yet explain to you. Just like there's so much in this dimension I didn't see when I lived here, areas that I tuned out. On this plane, your plane, no one sees, hears, understands even a fraction of what is possible. It's similar on the other side, but don't worry about it. Let's be glad that we have this opportunity."

"Just one more question?"

"Sure."

"If there's a desire—like poetry—or a place—like your house—or a person you can't bear to leave, you then have an option to stay?"

"Simply put, yes." He ran the wallpaper brush across a bubble disfiguring a leaf. "Most don't stay attached to humans because it can be painful and unfair. And, of course, attachments vary. For instance, some humans claim that they have a guardian angel, an invisible spirit. Some spirits cling to objects; others to places, like I do, and they choose forms or don't choose forms, it depends."

"Do you associate?" I sneaked in another question, curious if he had any contact with Amy of the wide eyes and long hair.

"No, it's a lonely choice if one elects not to go on, but for me it's similar to writing, which is one of the loneliest choices a human can make. With this passion to produce a poetry book, I longed, no, yearned to hang around."

As evening fell, we finished the wallpapering. Exhausted, I lay on the rug and inched myself around admiring our work. "Gorgeous."

"It is. Oh, Katherine, thank you. Thank you." His hands cupped my face and he drew near.

"Kate, I'm home." Dan's call rasped through the air. Vaguely aware of Franklin's final words, I tore off the necklace and dashed from the room. When I got downstairs, Dan was in the bathroom giving me minutes to compose myself. As I reheated a left-over casserole, he wandered in and I announced, "Today I wallpapered an upstairs room."

He arched an eyebrow and I said, "I've decided to write and I need a studio."

As he mixed a Scotch and water he said, "Kate, you couldn't paper anything."

"I did. My mess is still there," and I led him to the north room alive with the odors of paste and drying paper.

When I snapped on the light, he whistled, "It's perfect, professional." He examined a seam while giving a wide berth to the plastic tub. "I can't believe you did it."

Meticulously he checked each wall. "You did this alone? How'd you move that desk?"

I swallowed. "One of the estimators helped. You know the roofers came this morning."

"This rug?" Stooping, he skimmed the palm of his hand across the nap.

"Under the house. See, this room's quickly shaping up."

"And you're going to write—"

I sucked in my stomach and stood tall. "Poetry."

He's going to ridicule me, I thought, but he bit back any remark and reassessed the room. "I don't know. Maybe it's the shock of our whole new life, but it's—" and as if searching for stability, he shoved his fingers across the desk top surface, the lone item from Iowa, and we listened to the subsequent squeak on wood, "well, strange. You seem strange, this room is strange. I don't know," and he laughed apologetically, "but I feel something in this room, like something's going on. Does that make any sense?"

I nodded. "It's a creative strangeness."

"For you, but I feel, uneasy."

"Let's have dinner, and take a look at the roofing estimate. That should offer another kind of uneasy."

As I set the table, he checked the form. "Jesus, thirteen thousand dollars? For the roof? What'll they ask for painting, for shoring up walls, for replacing this?" And he pointed to the dented linoleum floor.

I turned the hot water faucet. "At least the plumbing's improved."

"Temporarily. Soon that line'll need replacing. There's corrosion. Means new pipes. We'll start actively hunting in Rivera. Sure those houses are expensive, but they don't eat you alive in repairs."

I refused to listen, to quarrel. Dan was tired. He'd felt something of the north room's power, and with the estimate he was angry, lashing out. Fair enough.

After dinner, he retreated to his computer, which he'd set up in the entryway room, where Amy once had her plants.

I retired to the bedroom and thought about the unreal, unnatural day: Lorraine, Neal, Amy's portrait, and Franklin. Always, always, Franklin.

CHAPTER SIX | MAY

"*D*ear Molly,
This will likely be my final letter since your dad and I will be coming back for your graduation in ten days."

The phrase, "ten days," as if embossed, rose from the page. I had but that much time before I'd leave remodeling and poetry writing, leave my house and Franklin. One of life's ironies, I thought again, for just three months ago I would have done nearly anything to have maintained my life in Harding, and now I would do almost anything to stay in Madison.

I re-read the written sentence and the words "your dad," caught my attention.

How altered was my relationship with Dan. I'd sacrificed town, house, friends, daughter, and pride to stay with him and had struggled with moments of blackness—ones unleavened by color—when I realized how deeply he loved Sheila. Love was much harder to deal with than an affair. In January and in February there had come periods when I'd sympathized with his division, but that seemed part of another life, because emotions felt with Dan, whether good or bad, had vaporized, and I watched him as an objective viewer. He would cock his head, aware of my remoteness, and puzzled ask, "Where are you, Kate? You're in another universe."

But I must get on with the letter. "I've been a poor correspondent, but I never dreamed remodeling would claim so many hours."

Again I lifted my pen as I reviewed the efforts. The living room, basically finished, boasted newly-plastered walls. Broad oak planks, smoothed by the sander I'd learned to operate, glowed with varnish Franklin had applied. The fireplace gleamed, a pristine white, while sheer curtains draped the enameled window frames.

A carpenter Dan had hired to replace the window's splintered ledges, worked with his partner today in the living room.

Seated at my north room desk I could vaguely distinguish the drill's faint whine, a hammer's tap. Closer, the sound of a turning page caused me to glance across the room where Franklin read in the Morris chair.

After having seen an illustration of his comfortable chair, I'd crisscrossed the county searching flea markets and garage sales, antique and used furniture stores. At last in a Port Costanza warehouse—the interior converted to stalls—I discovered the Morris chair supporting a "collectibles" sign. Without arguing over the excessive price, I bought it and insisted the proprietor tie it in my trunk. On that drive home guilt accompanied me. Blithely, I'd spent Dan's money on a chair destined for my room, and this after he'd surprised me with a car, a used Plymouth.

To bring the chair up the steep flights of stairs, I waited until evening and Dan's arrival, for Franklin never ventured out front.

With the chair arranged in the western corner, Dan had peered about at the hurricane lamp, at book shelves partially filled with poetry editions, and taking a step toward them said, "Every one of those books is old."

"When hunting for period furniture, I've bought books from the turn-of-the century."

He pulled an anthology from its niche and rifled the pages which released an evocative scent of past time. "Not exactly sex and action," he kidded as he scanned a Wordsworth poem.

Treading a narrow path, as if worried I'd bristle at his comments, he added, "but good—good." And as he carefully replaced the volume asked, "How'd you get these shelves up here?"

"Had them delivered."

He surveyed paint glistening from baseboards and closet door, from molding and window frames before he touched my desk where notebooks, pens, paper scraps and an opened dictionary covered the top. "Writing?"

"Un Huh."

He affected a helpless, half-defeated shrug. "It makes you happy?"

"Fulfilled."

Once more he examined the room and clucked his tongue against the roof of his mouth. "And you don't feel uncomfortable in here?"

"Just the opposite." But I sensed the room's agitation, so eager to remove him from a place uniquely mine, I took his arm and we walked downstairs. An apt analogy for our life, I felt, walking beside him, not with him.

Yet while I didn't care to walk with him, I didn't like my duplicity and invariably made mistakes. For example, one night while I read, Dan concentrated on a television movie. Suddenly the passage reminded me of a poem with which Franklin and I had been struggling. "Franklin, listen," I cried.

"What?"

"Oh, sorry," I laughed, "was so involved with this novel that I spoke the character's name."

Another evening I suggested that we paint the stairwell the next day.

"Kate," Dan answered, "I go to work tomorrow, remember?"

So each time I replaced the necklace on its shelf, laying it just so with the rose bud directly in the middle and each side of the chain arched upward as if eager to meet, I drilled myself. "Dan is coming home," and I prepared a mental agenda.

Yet this pretense was a cheap price for days consumed by happiness, work, writing, and yes, with love of Franklin.

Once more I forced my attention back to Molly's letter.

"Thus far we've not done anything to the kitchen, our bedroom, or the spare bedroom," I explained. "The backyard's a mess, and your dad's been dragging junk from the tool shed. There's a dilapidated gazebo which I'm eager to repair and paint."

Last Tuesday, May cast a spell luring Franklin and me outside. While California winter differed markedly from the Midwestern variety, spring sang the same prelude I'd always heard. Maybe spring is identical everywhere with its innocent promises. He and I pulled weeds, pruned tree branches, transplanted ivy and propped up a tilting gazebo wall.

"When building this place I dreamed of sleeping in the gazebo on summer nights or reading poetry on hot afternoons."

"It will be our next project," I said. But on Wednesday the carpenters returned. By myself in the jungled backyard I lost enthusiasm, feeling defeated at the task.

To Molly I wrote, "In that gazebo and in my north room I *will* write poetry. And you can stifle any gagging noises."

In a cautious manner Franklin and I had discussed poetic topics. Even more cautiously we'd spun trial verses. We labored over exact synonyms, sometimes concentrating on a word and on meter to the exclusion of content. Countless lines that I'd committed to a notebook page disappeared beneath a heavy black mark.

"No, Katherine. We need a tri-syllable word there. No, X out that phrase. We can do better," and as I "Xed" I wondered why, if Franklin could pick up items, could function in this house in an amazingly human way, he wouldn't hold a pencil? Write his own verse? Why pace around the room?

"I'm compelled to move," he said. "I have to hear a physical melody in order to create. On horseback I composed some quality material, but at home when immobile, I saw ink dry on the nib, as everything died. When I walked, the melody sang again."

Writing for and with him proved to be more exhilarating than anything I'd ever known, except, and I grinned, for the love I felt for him. This was part of the whole enchantment. His gaze could stroke my body. With his hand, like the kiss of milk down, he'd brush my forehead. When he leaned over my shoulder to read a stanza, his breath warmed my earlobe and skimmed the back of my neck.

One evening, after we'd agreed that his first poem, "Beautiful Destruction," was a completed draft, he kissed me.

Long before Sheila entered our lives, Dan's kisses had become perfunctory. Since Sheila they were, at best, civil, but Franklin's lips conveyed passion and a latent surge of desire surprised us both.

But to no one except Lorraine could I even hint at my happiness. When she commented on my appearance, I'd laugh and thank her. She'd answer, "Hold on to your secrets, Kate. Sometimes by sharing them you dilute their mystique. As for me, talking about Peter merely enhances what we have, probably because we have to hide, and you're the only one I tell."

About Lorraine, Dan limited his comments but on the rare occasions when she dropped by, his stance and forced dry laugh left no doubt that her dress, personality, philosophy—everything she represented—alienated him. Although Dan told me to mingle, he meant, of course, with "the right people." He hoped I'd shop, lunch, and form friendships with the Rivera wives.

With them I went to San Francisco, and he was pleased. True, I enjoyed strolling along the sidewalks, inhaling the fogged breeze, seeing cable cars.

. .But to the others buying and gossiping were important so when Peg, one of the wives, invited me again, I declined, and didn't tell Dan. Instead I emphasized my joining the Madison Historical Society.

"Well, you'll be the youngest fossil."

"Figured I'd learn about the past in order to refurbish the house correctly." And he left that alone because an accurately refurbished house would bring a better price. However, my motivation stemmed from Franklin's curiosity as to how Madison judged his parents, Amy, and especially himself.

Originally I'd had no intention of joining the historical society, didn't even realize there was such an animal, but on a Monday, when the museum was closed, I went to Neal's house, since he'd invited me to drop by and with two hands dig through his mother's trunk. So at ten on an infant spring morning, I walked across his porch.

When he answered my knock with a startled expression, I apologized, "Should have called."

"No, no, it's fine. I'm just rather a mess," and he swiped his hand across dark whiskers. "Taking it easy today, didn't shave. But come in, please."

Even on this sun-splashed day, the living room was dark, as if it were saying "history can only be remembered as painful or depressed." As if reading my thoughts, he nodded. "A repressed room, isn't it? I spend very little time in it, but I imagine you've come to find out more about Amy and Franklin."

"If it's convenient," and I followed him, as if through a lair, which reinforced my initial impression of a bear. Although a large man, who seemed even larger in a sweatshirt and thick corduroy pants, he easily sidestepped tables and chairs en route to a short hallway which contained three closed doors and one open door at the far end. He tipped his head in that direction, "My room." With his hand he palmed a closed door, "The bathroom, and those others are Aunt Josie's and my mother's room, as they left them."

"You said your aunties were Stella and Beatrice."

"No," and he ushered me into Mama's room, which smelled of bottled age. "My great aunties were Stella and Beatrice. They were Amy's older sisters. Some ten years after Amy's death, Beatrice surprised everyone and married. She must have been thirty-eight by then. She promptly had a daughter, Josie, and the next year gave birth to Sarah, my mother. Our family appears to have had rather an aversion to marriage. Great Auntie Stella never married and my mother's sister, Josie, never married. My mother married late and had only yours truly."

"You've never married?"

He smiled. "Nope. Must keep the tradition alive."

"Well, that hardly keeps the family alive."

At that he laughed, a booming laugh that cleaved its way through history's mausoleum, which contained a tidy single bed draped with a gray, hand-tied comforter, black and white photos of somber individuals rigidly positioned upon a dresser, a charcoal-colored rocker and dark velvet drapes drawn across a window.

On this glorious day, Neal switched on a floor lamp that towered over the rocker. To its right lay a trunk—painted black, naturally. When he unlatched it we peered in at stacks: black photo albums and lidded boxes. If I reached for the top one, I imagined I would find a crushed bouquet, commencement programs, play ticket stubs, an autograph album—

"Extract that second box, that purple one, and you'll discover some Amy-related mementos. I'll go shave and fix tea? coffee?"

After he left I settled into the rocker with the purple box. I extracted Amy's baptismal certificate, an award for elegant penmanship presented to an outstanding eighth grade student, and an embroidered sampler, "Now I lay me down to sleep," to which an affixed piece of paper identified it as, "Amy's first cross stitch." Below that was an envelope addressed to Beatrice, but on the flap a different handwriting demanded, "Keep! Regarding Amy."

Long lodged within the envelope, the letter fought for its accustomed cocoon. By inching one corner upward and applying tension to the other, I removed the single sheet, dated May 13, 1904.

Dear Beatrice,

After much debate I've decided to write this letter, one which I'm unsure I'll actually mail. But since we've been friends for years and since I care deeply for you and your family, I feel duty bound to relate certain facts. If the situation were reversed, I would want to be informed.

I understand that Amy and Franklin Elliott are serious. While the Elliotts are an upstanding family, I regret that the description "upstanding" does not apply to Franklin. As neighbor to the Elliotts for more than 20 years, I'm aware of disappointments he's caused them. It's no secret that Franklin shirks work, that he's a loafer. That in and of itself may not be sufficient reason for your family's alarm, because Mr. Elliott will always support his son and son's family. However, of deeper concern is Franklin's untrustworthiness. Charming and handsome, he uses people. Examples? In high school Franklin did poorly in algebra. He then dated Celia Appenstock, the top math student, but not a particularly pretty young lady. He bewitched Celia and after he received an A in the course, which earned him a spot on the honor roll, he abandoned her. Second case: Franklin fancies himself a poet. Two years ago he entered a poem—one I've read and can report that it is poor—in the county contest. He didn't win, nor place, but he learned that the judge, Miss Corvay, from Port Costanza, would also judge the following year. A recent graduate of Stanford University, Miss Corvay is 25 and lonely. Franklin—in the interest of space, let's simply say that when he entered the identical poem the next year, he won. Third case: Franklin submitted a poem to a national contest. On the day that he received notification that he'd been disqualified, I was at the Elliott home. I saw the letter, which he tossed into the fireplace, a letter in which judges accused him of plagiarism. I've forgotten which poem he copied, but does it really matter? Deceit is what is important. In the years since high school, he's exhibited more of the same behavior, but I will stop for now.

As I have penned these lines, I have known anguish. This is not easy to do. Amy, a sweet, innocent child, deserves better.

Your loyal friend,

Emma

The handwriting was bold, assertive, and I immediately thought, *What was her grudge against Franklin? Did she love him and he spurned her? Was she jealous of Amy?* A vicious, untrue letter, it shook me and—

Neal stood at the doorway. "Clean shaven," he announced and brushed his hand along his chin, "and I'm ready for coffee or tea in my room."

With the letter I tagged him into his light-drenched back bedroom. Along the rear wall a series of windows faced north. If I'd not been upset about this letter, I would have neared them and checked to see how much of the Strait was visible; see if I could pick out Lorraine's boat. A stark room painted white, it had a large desk, floor to ceiling shelves packed with books, a single bed in the corner and twin easy chairs separated by a circular table. On such rested a tray with coffee carafe, tea cozy, and condiments. Although angered by Emma's letter, I wondered as I chose a chair, how he had managed the tray with one arm.

"Coffee," I said.

"Tea for me," he answered, and we exchanged friendly smiles. *Neal*, I thought, *is old-shoe comfortable, bathrobe comfortable*, and so I could launch right in. "What about this letter? What was Emma's problem?"

"Obviously, I never knew the woman. My mother never knew Emma. Mother's aunt knew Emma, and Mother served as the repository for family lore." He stirred sugar into his tea and as the teaspoon circled the cup's interior, he appraised me. "Am a tad surprised at your reaction to the letter. Thought you were interested in Amy and if Franklin were a cad, wouldn't that make you more sympathetic to Amy?"

I bought time by sipping from my china cup. Ah, great coffee. I took another sip while I cautioned myself to be on guard. Because of my love for Franklin, I mustn't blunder. A negative reaction to Emma's accusations was a mistake.

I replaced my cup on its saucer. "I think I'd bought into this perfect love scenario, about Amy and Franklin, and so anyone who dispels the myth, I don't like."

"A romantic?" he smiled. "Guess I am, too, or at least a sentimentalist. Otherwise, why would I keep the other rooms—all but this, my sanctuary, as Mother and Aunt Josie wanted?"

We chatted about the past, about what it might or might not teach us, and we questioned when we would have preferred to live. Neal picked 1849, the Gold Rush year, and I said, " Very early in the 1900s."

When we'd emptied the carafe and cozy, he rose. "Want to search further in the trunk?"

"Not today, thanks. But another time?"

He escorted me to the living room door and urged me to return any Monday. Then, as if a postscript, he added, "We're having a membership drive for the historical society. Meeting's monthly on a Tuesday night at the museum."

So I extended my palm for the membership envelope.

There was no reason for Franklin to be bothered by Emma's false charges, so I didn't mention her letter, but dwelt on the trunk in Sarah's room. "Sarah was Beatrice's daughter," I explained.

Franklin gave a disbelieving laugh. "Old Beatrice actually got married, actually had sex, and produced two daughters?"

"Right, Josie and Sarah. Josie never married and Sarah was Neal's mother."

With Dan detained in the city on that particular night, Franklin and I rested before the fireplace. With talk about Beatrice, he switched onto his side to regard the flames. "Can't imagine prissy old Beatrice in bed with a man."

"I take it you didn't like her."

"You take it right. It was mutual. She and Stella could only enjoy the straight and hidebound. Not for them flights of fancy or other lifestyles. I threatened their beliefs, I stole what they most valued, sweet, beautiful Amy." He was quiet, and propped his arm to support his head before he asked an unexpected question, "Why did you marry Dan?"

"I suppose because we were college students, ready, or thought we were, to be in love. However, I quickly learned that I couldn't share with him certain thoughts or feelings. He indicated they were dumb or foolish, and just as quickly I learned that I didn't care to hear about football or duck hunting. But, I would be lying if I didn't say I was content."

"How long, though, could you deny your creative spirit?"

"Probably forever. I never felt my writing was any good."

His face showed pure puzzlement. "I've never doubted my ability. When I lived and wrote, the editors weren't ready for me. Now, with your assistance, they can't fail to recognize my talent."

And before I could ask about former rejections, he lowered his mouth onto mine.

So what else could I add in a letter to a daughter I'd so easily relinquished? Unmotherly, abnormal, such a confession would sound to my Harding acquaintances and to Dan. If he knew how erratically I thought of Molly, he'd be appalled. That I could love her, wish the best for her, miss her, and yet dismiss her problems and successes, he'd never understand. Granted, without Franklin I wouldn't have understood either. I would have clung, called constantly, mailed daily letters and have begged for an Easter visit.

Okay, the letter. What about devoting some paragraphs to Lorraine, who amused Molly? During our routine Sunday evening phone conversations, my daughter would ask, "Does your friend have you smoking pot yet, Mom? Going without a bra?"

So I wrote, "Lorraine took me sailing last Tuesday. We left before dawn when the tide was with us. It was exciting, and yes, awfully cold, to be on the water and watch the sun rise. We had a strong breeze so she raised all sails: the mizzen, the staysail, the main. Aren't you impressed? We met a cargo container ship loaded with Toyotas coming upstream and passed the moored ship used by maritime academy cadets.

"There's such a feeling on the water. In the dampness, there's newness. Even sounds resonant on a different frequency—the gull's cry, our magnified speech."

Hold it, Kate, I thought. *Molly's going to pinch her nose and say, "Puke, Mom."* So I skipped ahead and detailed our stop at the Berkeley marina where we picked up Betsy and The Colonel.

"With his beret and cigar, The Colonel reminded me of retired military until I spotted the gold ring in his right ear and until I smelled him. 'Kerosene's permeated his clothing,' Lorraine said later, because he lives with Betsy and another woman, Ish, aboard a derelict schooner. Ish didn't go. She's expecting a baby soon. I didn't bother to find out if Ish and The Colonel are married, if Betsy and The Colonel (from their embraces they share more than a platonic relationship) are married or if all of them are married, or. . .

"But The Colonel's a superb helmsman. As we set sail, the wind rose, causing white caps. On my side, the port side, water washed across the cockpit, and when we tacked, spray drenched me. Lorraine brought out foul weather gear, so the cold and wet were tolerable. I enjoyed it, the entire drama.

"Betsy, Lorraine, and I manned (womaned?) the lines until we dropped the main, reefed, and put in at a cove on Angel Island, a green island with a mountain in the middle and a lush picnic area near the piers."

With such scenery I wished that Franklin could hike the island trails and climb Mount Livermore, but that would never be. On that April night before the fireplace I'd told him that life extracts compromises. With Franklin, compromises meant confinement to the hill house. He'd never walk with me, attend a movie, join me at a symphony.

I focused on the letter. "Deer, raccoons, and birds live on Angel Island. We didn't go ashore, but Lorraine told about its history, as a military and immigration installation. Mostly Betsy ate and smiled at The Colonel who— and this is the extent of what I learned about his personal life—has grandchildren in Jamaica.

"We sailed back to Berkeley, let them off; then bucked outgoing tide. By the time night fell, we were miles from Madison. Fortunately, I'd told your dad we might be late, because Lorraine anchored, and we slept until the tide changed.

"It's splendid to sleep on a boat. It rocks you, lulls you. About two a.m., Lorraine hauled up the anchor and we raised the sails. To be the only moving things on the water was quite eerie, beautiful."

As I recapped the trip, I ignored the fact that Lorraine moaned about her fixation with Peter, while I dwelt on Franklin, impossible, though it was, to admit he was a ghost. Ghost. How implausible that would sound. Outside these walls I, too, often lost faith, doubting that what I had inside my house was real. With Lorraine I kept purposely evasive. "Slightly younger," I admitted, "a poet."

I scanned my letter. Need I add more? Probably I should make it "meaty," compensation for my former scanty notes and sometimes unsatisfactory phone conversations. Maybe write something about Neal? By so doing it might disguise how rarely I spoke of her dad, who was spending longer hours in San Francisco. Almost monthly he attended out-of-town meetings and when home, worked from the computer. We'd turned the little room off the entryway into his office. Not partial to computers, I left his alone. And, yes, I'd wondered when he was away if he were meeting Sheila, and, yes, I'd wondered if they were exchanging e-mails, but I didn't care to go there. Dan had his world. I had mine.

When Molly and I talked on the phone, she expressed interest in Neal, the only one-armed person even marginally introduced in her life. I'd explained about the historical society and the museum with Neal as director. That was tame for her in comparison to his appearance. Based on my description, she, too, called him "Teddy Bear."

Could I glean anything to tell her from the last visit to Neal's house, which happened on another Monday? I had returned to the bungalow on Brandis Street with a list of Franklin's questions. This time, since I'd had the courtesy to call him, Neal was not only clean shaven, but had tea and coffee brewed.

He invited me into the dismal kitchen, but from the window I could view wisteria blooming. The gnarled trunk and purple blossoms obscured the glass, but a lovely fragrance drifted around aging frames.

From the wooden straight chair at the table, I watched Neal lift the coffee pot and move toward me. In this shadowy setting, it seemed he was moving under water. He must have misinterpreted my staring, for as he poured coffee into my mug, said, "You're curious about my missing arm."

"No, no, was peering through the dim light, but, well, sure, I'm curious."

He replaced the coffee pot and then poured tea into a companion mug. "An accident, when I was five."

I sipped my coffee, careful now not to watch him lift his mug, but what could I focus on but the overgrown wisteria? As I directed attention to the window's upper section, where a fingernail of sunlight edged the purple flowers, he told about his parents' unhappy marriage, exacerbated by Josie's living with them.

"Mother and her sister Josie always banded together against Dad. Even as a little boy, I felt the tension. For instance, Mother and Josie wouldn't cut my hair, saying they adored my ringlets. They were horrified when Dad took me to the barber shop. Since he worked as a salesman for the Nabisco Company, he was gone a great deal. Mother and Josie refused to let me play with other boys. Too rough. If I fell, they smothered me with worry. If I didn't feel well, they kept me in bed, brought treats and homemade soups.

"I remember Dad saying, 'You're turning him into a sissy,' and Mother in a melodramatic gesture, clutched me to her bosom. 'He's my child.'"

Neal stirred sugar into his tea, but the clink of his spoon against the mug was muffled. What would it have been like to grow up in such a stifling atmosphere? No wonder the father fought to do normal activities, such as get his son's hair cut.

Neal laid the spoon on the table top. "Maybe this is more than you want to know."

I leaned toward him and covered his hand with my fingers. "But I do."

"You're easy to talk to," he said. "I've not gone into detail about my past with others. Have merely said that by getting tangled up with a harvester, I lost my arm."

"Harvester?" My fingers tightened on the back of his hand. "As in farming?"

He nodded and moved his hand so that our fingers interlocked. "Dad had relatives on a farm near Stockton. Probably in an effort to give me a taste of another life, he took me to visit them one weekend."

"Your mother didn't go?"

"She was enraged at his insistence that just he and I go. Oh, she never let him forget it." Now his fingers tightened on mine. "He and I went out in the field. I remember riding on his shoulders, and I remember sitting on his lap on the seat of the harvester, and that's it. I don't remember tumbling into the blades, can't even resurrect the pain."

"Undoubtedly that's a blessing."

Neal captured me with his large brown eyes. "All I clearly recall is the hospital bed with the sides up, like a big crib, and that bothered me, because I was no longer a baby."

In order to sip his tea, he released my hand; then asked, "Your coffee cold?"

"Sit still," I said. "I'll get a refill."

How strangely right it was to reheat water for tea, to dump my cool coffee in the sink and pour a fresh cup. With Franklin, of course, I knew a rightness, but it was hedged with sexual attraction, was backed by awareness that poetry must be written. Rightness, thus, had limits. With Neal it came with a capital "r."

Neal walked to his mother's room leaving me to consider brown-painted cupboards. Who would paint a kitchen brown? I noticed the clean floor. It must be hard to operate a sponge mop with only one hand.

When he returned, he laid a photograph on the table. "My parents." His mother, Sarah, wore her hair in a bun. Her suit of some dark color was too big. "I think she had a nice figure, but she dressed in loose clothing so no one would see her shape."

"Your dad wore his clothes well." A big man—ah, that's where Neal got his size—stood beside his wife and faced the camera with an uplifted chin. "He looks positive, like you."

Neal sat beside me. "A façade, perhaps, because he killed himself."

"Ohh."

"About a year after I lost my arm. Think Mother's constant blame—" He need not finish the sentence.

We speculated about why his parents had ever gotten together, about sister Josie's role in the household, about how fear and guilt can emerge as driving forces and convince someone to take his life and leave a child fatherless. "But," I said, "you are so attached to your mother, keeping her house as she ordered."

"It's taken years to try for objectivity, to attempt to understand my father. As a kid, all I knew was that he had been responsible for loss of my arm. And all I knew was that Mother and Aunt Josie would do anything for me. That's mighty powerful. Not until high school did I start to realize what a 'safe' web they'd woven around me. I never learned to ride a bike, never participated in physical education classes (Mother invariably obtained a doctor's excuse), never drove a car. Never dated. Sorry. I'm whining." Abruptly he rose, bumping the table and the coffee I'd not yet touched splashed onto my jeans.

"Oh, damn." He ripped off a section of paper towel and daubed at the damp splotch on my thigh.

"It's okay, Neal. Let me," and then—perhaps aware of how like his mother that statement sounded—we laughed. I let him press the towel against my leg, and sop up the liquid puddled on the table, before I said, "This is a good moment to exit."

"You had questions, and I've selfishly talked about me."

"Not selfish. I'm honored you told me."

"My parents were selfish. Mother thought primarily of what she wanted for 'Her son.' Father's suicide was selfish. I vowed not to—Directing the museum I intend to help others, to—"

"You've helped me, Neal. Thank you." And because the situation verged on awkwardness, I pulled from my pocket Franklin's list of questions.

(1) What happened to the Elliott and Bennett homes?
(2) Does any of Franklin's poetry exist? (school literary magazine? English assignments? contest entries?)
(3) Were any memorials created for Franklin? (scholarships? statues? trees planted in his name? etc.)

"Still interested in Franklin, huh? Whatever, I'll find the answers for you."

Now, as I replayed my time with Neal, I debated what, out of all that, could I extract and summarize in the letter to Molly. Could I—

"Mrs. Andrews." A knock pounded on the north room door. One of the workmen.

Startled, I dropped my pen. "Coming," I called and ran to the door before he might possibly open it. With a hammering heart beat, I followed the fellow down stairs unable to absorb his disjointed analysis of encountered difficulties. "But," he repeated, "we protected all your stuff."

He motioned toward the living room, but I ignored the furniture they'd covered, for through the tall front window front I noticed that day had fled. As usual, I'd lost track of time and these men, who'd stayed after five-thirty, were apologizing for not getting done.

"No problem. Thank you," I said as the front door opened, and Dan's smile faded before the disorder.

Again the workmen defended unforeseen sanding and the amount of patching required. As they proceeded to additional labor costs, Dan tensed and when we were alone and after he'd bumped against a swaddled chair which sent dust flurries into a maddened dance, he announced, "We need to contact a realtor about a place in Rivera."

Still shocked by the abrupt jolt into a contemporary state, bothered by my inability to maintain a hold on time, and upset by the chaos in these rooms, I neither argued nor agreed.

He went with me to the kitchen. "Sure, we must improve this property. Otherwise, we'll not make a cent of profit, but let's put a deadline on spending. After the dining room's done, let's quit."

I opened the refrigerator door and extracted last night's roast. Even though Dan stood behind me I could picture the shifting expressions across his face, ones fueled by fatigue from the long commute, worry about money, hope that a move to Rivera would involve us with a crowd of friends. "Kate," and his voice was tired, "I'll go check the e-mail."

True, he might hear from Molly—the internet was their special communication venue—but in the very marrow of my bones, I knew that he craved Sheila's message.

When he returned to the kitchen, he had shed weariness, for his tone was soft. *How broadening love is,* I thought. *Thanks to my love for Franklin, I can treat Dan—can treat everyone—more kindly. I can forgive, be emphatic, generous, and so it is with Dan. Whatever message he's received from Sheila, it's improved his attitude.*

Although he continued with his sales pitch about leaving Madison, the anger was diluted. He perched casually on the high stool, one with slender legs embellished by clustered grapes and carved ferns that Franklin and I had retrieved from a tool shed corner.

"The Richardsons, who bought the house after Amy's death, used the stool in Mr. R's office, the room where Amy put plants and wicker furniture," Franklin had said. "The room Dan's appropriated for his computer.

"Henry Richardson was an architect. He sat on a needlepoint pillow stitched by 'The Mrs.' as he called his wife because he had, again his words, 'lean buttocks.'"

Franklin and I had sanded away an olive green shade applied by Lowell Samson, a teenager in the 1940s. Lowell had dragged the stool upstairs to the south bedroom, his army command post center. Along the wall he tacked maps, facsimiles of war zones upon which he pinned flags indicating troop movements. Seated on this stool, he planned strategies for the Allies.

To peel potatoes, to day dream, I claimed it. But Dan, hunched there in his business suit, black shoes tucked on the middle rung, was the antithesis of Lowell Samson or of Franklin. Franklin. *I still wore the necklace.*

I inched toward the sink, keeping my back to Dan to unsnap the clasp and jam the jewelry into my jean's pocket.

"So?" he asked.

"Let's wait with a decision until we get back from Harding."

He nodded, but then, as if I'd dialed the Molly station on his internal radio station, he launched his one-man Molly talk show, which lasted through the meal. "I don't know what she's thinking of, staying with that part-time job this summer."

"She said her boss promised her fulltime after school ended."

"Even so she can't make ends meet. And what's she doing about her future? Kate, we must insist she come to California. She can enroll at the community college, live at home, start preparing herself for a career. You're going to say she's not academic, and I agree that a four-year college may not be the answer.. But there are vocations—dental hygienist, medical techs, and what about computers? In our office—"

Because I believed the station had been switched to the "Events at the Office" program, I cleared the table, but Dan, undeterred by my actions, reverted to Molly. "There's no future in Harding, and Steve's no future. He'll never be successful. Kate, we don't want her on that stupid farm. It's poor land."

"That's her dream, though, to marry him."

"Well, dreams can change."

We were quiet, bound, I think, by a mutual consciousness of how our dreams had varied and diverged. For Dan, his current dream had been compromised, while my dream—

He clucked his tongue, and as I squirted Ivory into the dish pan, he sought the television set. As a background, an evening news reporter in her perky disastrous voice ubiquitous among newscasters, before I mounted the stairs and addressed the envelope to Molly. Although the room welcomed me, without Franklin seated in his chair I felt a lack.

I stamped the envelope and neared the closet to replace the necklace. I slipped a hand in my pocket—empty. Carefully, as I fingered each lining crease, I came to the hole at the bottom. With tiny steps I proceeded toward the threshold studying the floor. The necklace was not in the north room.

I crept down the stairs, but each step was empty. Bent over, I moved along the lower hallway into the dining room. Nothing. Surely it lay on the kitchen floor, but on the dismal 1940s linoleum, I found a piece of carrot, a sticky stain, and dried mud resembling pencil led.

My heart rate increased as I swallowed back a wave of alarm. The necklace must be in these rooms, and resting against the sink ledge I replayed each motion, how I'd turned away from Dan and dropped the jewelry in my pocket. Could it have fallen in my tennis shoe? I untied the laces and shook each shoe. A geranium leaf fragment floated to the floor.

On hands and knees I crawled across the linoleum, patting, patting. Dust from the dining room gritted against my fingertips. As I continued through the adjoining room, I employed the same tactics. With careful fingers, I next explored each corner of the stairwell.

The phone rang and Dan called me.

"Sorry to call so late," Neal said, "but wanted to remind you of the monthly historical society meeting." As if the depth of his voice provided a sturdy wing chair, I sank back against it and the details he gave. "Also, I've partial answers to your questions. The Elliott house was razed in 1963, and the Bennett place was demolished in 1925."

He paused and I knew he awaited a response or a question, but my mind refused to function.

"In Mother's trunk there's nothing about Franklin's poetry, but that's hardly surprising, since my ancestors weren't exactly fans. The same applies to question number three. At least in the trunk, there's nothing about any memorial. I'll check the museum archives, but I am curious about your interest in Franklin when Amy lived longer in your house."

"Guess because I would like to be a writer that history of another fledgling writer appeals."

When I replaced the receiver, Dan asked, "Could you give a listen? Old Jer asked me to redo the independent insurance agent job description for a speech he's giving at a high school career day."

I fought to pay attention. After all if I cleared my mind of the necklace problem perhaps its location would pop into my head. However, the nagging question of "where could it be?" kept sounding and while Dan's lips moved I heard little, saying, "It's great," when he finished.

After he fell asleep, I left the bedroom, closed the swinging dining room door and under harsh artificial light at an artificial hour searched the kitchen. I inspected dishes, moved pans, unfolded dish towels, rearranged can goods. I swept the floor and with microscopic intent peered at mounded dust and dirt.

Cold, weary, distraught, I curled up in bed and woke with Dan. Mechanically I stirred oatmeal, poured juice, bid him goodbye and as soon as the door shut behind him began hunting. As morning advanced, my ideas grew more frantic, sending me to impossible locations—the laundry hamper, the linen closet, even to unsealing Molly's envelope in case the necklace had slipped inside.

To ensure I'd not lost all reason, that I hadn't automatically replaced the necklace, I patted the closet shelf beside the diary. I searched through desk drawers and laid aside each piece of paper upon which I'd jotted down our stray strands of poetry.

Franklin had initially suggested we compile a collection centered around three objects: a chair, a bed, a table. We'd trace each item through a century and from each object's perspective view the human story as successive people interacted with the item. But it had proved limiting. I proposed we widen the selection of objects and to include seasons, for I'd long responded to nature as it related to humans and to objects. It seemed to be working, particularly the mirror poems with "Wintered Mirror" my favorite. Franklin had conceived of a mirror recording time's passage more accurately than a clock and had dictated as one line: "Each night if he wound it/ the clock proved true/ but the mirror it was without his hand/that told the proper time."

At noon I decided on systemization. From the front hall I sidled along the floor, and as if schooled in detection, searched for clues. Mid-afternoon I cried, an act that relieved some tension and made me think, *Why not appeal to Franklin for advice?*

Seated in my desk chair, I even held "Wintered Mirror" against my neck. "You know I've lost the necklace. Where is it? Or do I still need it? By thinking of you with total concentration, can you appear?"

Statue-like, I listened to the room's unsung music and closed my eyes, willing myself to see him, feel him. Even before I opened my eyes, however, I knew I was alone. Maybe sitting in his Morris chair would help. Nothing. Was I too tense? Blocking positive vibrations? I breathed deeply, slowly. Nothing. All right, I'd imagine him, and as clearly as if he were with me, I visualized his black hair, snapping eyes and devilish smile. I felt his lips move erotically across my cheek before they met my lips. I heard him pronounce, "Katherine," felt his hand on my forearm, saw the perennially crisp white shirt unbuttoned at the collar to expose smooth white skin, saw his black pants that, while not form-fitting, emphasized his hips and thighs. . . I was alone. For whatever reason, he or I required the necklace as a connection, for if he were sending instructions I wasn't receiving them.

When Dan came home his irritation flared. "Those guys didn't come back today?"

"Oh, the workmen, no."

"Why didn't you call them when they didn't show up?"

I said nothing in my defense for how could I have ignored absent workmen, dust, covered furniture?

As I plodded through the ritual of dinner preparation, Dan shouted his unhappiness into the telephone; then slightly pacified pulled out his chair at the table. "One of the fellows was sick today. Promised they'd be here early tomorrow."

After dinner he checked his e-mail and considerably cheered, said, "What about a movie tonight? We haven't gone in ages."

Yes, to leave the house, to blank out for a few hours the threat of hopelessness.

Dan selected a romantic comedy, but as the screen couple embraced I thought of Franklin, and as we drove home, making small talk about the fluffy film, I wondered for the thousandth time where the rosebud necklace was tonight.

Next morning I closed the north room door and analyzed an unfinished poem. Could words we'd agreed on, ones etched on paper, serve as a bond if I read them aloud? But they sounded trite and juvenile. In an imitation of Franklin I paced the gray rug, before seated at last in his Morris chair, I clutched the book he'd dropped. For a second, worrying ceased when I thought of the poetry collection we intended to publish. On the last rainy afternoon we'd shared, Franklin had tossed out possible titles: "In the House of Years, "Seasons Beyond Spring," "Embedded Voices."

"What happens when the book's done," I'd asked. "I mean if the reason you've stayed around is to see your work in print, then what's next? Are you then free to—to move up the ladder or whatever?"

He nodded and avoided my gaze.

Frowning now at the rug, I attempted to impose his form upon it, but instead I was aware of pounding and sawing. Our carpenters had returned. Well, I couldn't work. I'd go visit Lorraine, but she wasn't at the library nor was her battered VW in the marina parking lot. I tried Mona's Café. Today the ambience weighed heavily. High spirits and laughter belonged to others.

I hiked to the cemetery and Franklin's grave, where I felt suddenly embarrassed at this melodramatic gesture. "Okay, Kate, face it. The necklace may be lost, may be gone forever." And hurt, as deep seated as what I'd felt at my parents' deaths, at Dan's infidelity, at leaving Home, at losing two possible babies, consumed me.

Self-help books advise one to keep busy. Okay, I'd throw myself into physical labor, would apply paint remover to kitchen cupboards, observe blisters bubble destroy the brown color and scrape off layers to expose the wood. I'd paint on white, the original shade according to Franklin.

With a determined pace I shook away his name. I'd volunteer at the museum, spend more hours with Lorraine, and trust that after our Iowa trip, my sense of loss would diminish.

But I had no chance to call Neal, for my phone was ringing when I entered the house.

"Hello, stranger." It took a moment to place the crisp sophisticated voice.

Peg, wife of Dan's co-worker. "I've tried several times but couldn't reach you."

"Probably I was cutting pathways through the back yard maze or wallpapering."

"Someday I must see your property. Actually I was calling to see when we could get together. Lunch? Dinner? Brunch?"

Prompted by the decision to keep busy, I said, "Why not come for dinner on Saturday? I'll invite Beth and Jay, Connie and Martin. It will be informal. Workmen are here today, so I don't know what state the dining room will be by the end of the week."

I rattled off time, directions, and broke the connection. While the madness of keeping occupied possessed me, I invited the other guests; then leaned against the wall. Entertaining had never come easily and having asked affluent people to this mess, I'd stick with a simple menu. As the idiocy of what I'd done continued to sweep over me, I took little solace in the knowledge of Dan's delight.

"The worst is over," one of the carpenters promised. "Sanding's completed and we'll clean up. Tomorrow we'll paint the dado and next week can paper the upper wall if your order's in."

"Splendid." After Franklin had detailed the fern design needed in the dining room I'd lugged home sample books from Belleci's Wallpapers, but we found nothing similar. Then Lorraine suggested a specialty shop across the Strait in Barriton. One lunch hour she coaxed her Bug over the bridge to a waterfront store where I located green paper that was close.

As with the north room wallpaper, as with the refurbished kitchen stool, I experienced a surge of happiness. Eventually the house would reflect Franklin. Without asking the price I placed an order. When the clerk said, "It's shipped from Boston, so will take a while," I told myself that delay was but a minor setback.

In sharp contrast to the day I'd bought the wallpaper, a day when I felt young and vibrant, I knew in this aging afternoon the press of years. With Franklin I had reversed the clock. Now the expectancy of day stalking day as Dan and I faced retirement, if not in this house then in another, reinstated the sag to my body. With the carpenters gone, I climbed the stairs slowly. As always, the room refreshed me, banishing a portion of that weariness. But without Franklin would I ever write?

I must. Purposefully I approached the desk, opened my notebook to yellow-lined paper and an unfinished poem. What had Franklin and I intended? "Love haunts an autumn wind," I read, but no second line came. Instead I thought of Dan, of his pleasure about Saturday's dinner party. I gripped the pen. Under any guise, Dan mustn't steal into this room. Again I studied the words but impressions of Dan invaded—his tongue clicking against the roof of his mouth as he pondered an answer, his rolling a pair of socks into a ball, his neat tying of a plastic bag filled with dead branches from the backyard. How dismaying that my "other life" had infiltrated the heart of my room. I closed my notebook.

As predicted, Dan laughed with delight about the upcoming dinner. "But, Kate, we've got lots to do. It's already Wednesday."

Throughout Thursday and Friday I tried to padlock thinking and emotions. I had inhabited a frozen territory before; I could do it again.

At noon on Friday the workmen left. The bottom half of the wall gleamed and the border of each dado inset panel radiated a glossy white balanced by the subdued flat paint on the recessed portions. It was, I believed, as Franklin must have known it, and I ran up stairs calling out, "I wish you could stand in the dining room with me."

I sank into the Morris chair, but my tears quickly dried, as the room did not encourage sorrow. For minutes I lingered there until Dan's smile flashed before me. Damn it! Unfair. Why should he bother me in my sanctuary? Disturbed by the room's apparent betrayal, I completed a grocery list and backed the car from its tight garage .

The one note of brightness, I decided, as I shoved my cart along the Safeway aisle, was a familiar figure ahead. "Hey, lady," I said, "read any good books lately?"

Lorraine turned a pale face toward me.

"What's wrong?" I asked

"Life. It's a pile of crap."

"Peter?"

"Who else?"

"What's happened?"

"Can you stop by *The Eden* after shopping?"

At the harbor while Lorraine unlocked the gate, I watched baby ducks paddle behind their mothers, gulls arch in short flight, and sun freckle the water. I couldn't force my legs to move rapidly along the dock, couldn't push a lethargic body easily onto the sailboat. But there was no opportunity to explore my depression, to say, "my lover's gone," because after she poured cheap red into jelly glasses, she said, "Think I'm pregnant."

I swished a mouthful of wine from one inner cheek to the other as I grew accustomed to the taste.

"But you're not positive," I said.

She exhaled a mighty sigh. "I've a doctor's appointment next week, but I did one of those home pregnancy tests."

"And Peter?"

"Is sorry, feels bad, says, 'Now maybe you'll go on the pill rather than have faith in condoms' and will be glad when it's over."

"Your affair?"

"The abortion."

"Oh," and I gazed at the familiar line of nautical books, at the port hole with its constant varied circle of water, at the gimbaled stove.

"Naturally he can't go to the clinic with me, so if it's required that I have a driver, will you—"

"Why not wait until you're certain? Could be a false reading."

"But if I am, can I count on you?"

I gulped wine. I'd never known anyone to have an abortion, wasn't even sure what was involved. "I'm off to Iowa for Molly's graduation."

"I know. It will probably take a week or so for an appointment if I go ahead with it. Yeah, I've thought," and she fiddled with the zipper pull on her sweat jacket, "half-thought rather, of having the kid. Nutty. The only way I'm keeping alive temporarily is by living on this boat. It's not fit for a baby, and I don't want to work full time, and don't want to hassle with child care, don't want to raise a child alone." She met my eyes. "I can list twenty reasons why I shouldn't have a child except, Peter's the only man I've ever truly loved." A passing boat—moving too fast—left its wake to rock us back and forth. "By now I know what love is. Peter, even though he can be an s.o.b., completes me. With him I come alive in a way I've never done with anyone."

So well I understood.

"Corny as it sounds, I'd like to have his child. And yet—"

I stared at the ladder leading to the deck. "Whatever you decide, I'll help."

She ran the back of her hand across her eyes, then reached out to squeeze my hand. More than callused skin, I felt warmth. How different from the manicured hands of the women who'd sit at my table tomorrow evening.

"Your groceries are melting, Kate, and Danny Boy's going to be mad at refrozen ice cream. Go home. Really I'm fine now."

As I slid behind the steering wheel, I congratulated myself. I'd traveled more than linear miles from my former life, and such knowledge steadied me as I drove, and as I unloaded paper sacks. Such knowledge whispered, "Why not write about growth? By yourself, without Franklin, write."

In my desk chair, I searched my notebook for a clean page and felt words in hard blocks hit the paper:

> Like parchment
> the box collapses
> Floats suspended
> limbo style
> Touching earth
> it forms new ground.

Poor, but it was a start, and I'd done it alone. Pride helped, but not for long. Should a miracle occur, and I emerge as a poet, could desire for Franklin, for that completion which Lorraine named, ever be satisfied through writing?

That night nor on Saturday did I re-enter the north room. Peacefulness and poetry were nonexistent as Dan and I, stoked by adrenalin, sped through the day at high gear.

Forty-five minutes before the guests' expected arrival, I hurried from the bathroom, zipped up my peach-colored dress and opened the top dresser drawer where I'd stashed my jewel box. A plain pine rectangle with an Arkansas decal, it was a gift from Molly when she, at age thirteen, spent a week with a friend's family in Mena.

"For your quality gems," she'd teased, but the few pieces within the box fit the label better than they matched Molly's definition.

I raised the lid and gasped. The rosebud necklace. It couldn't be, but it rested there, between clip-on silver earrings and a copper charm bracelet, a miniscule crack marring the center of the rosebud. I couldn't move.

"Big decision?" Dan passed me en route to the bathroom.

"This necklace." I wiggled my index finger.

"Oh, found that on the floor the other evening."

"The. Floor."

"Kitchen. Think you'd gone upstairs, so I just dropped it in with the family jewels. Didn't remember seeing it before, but figured you and your friend had bought a K-Mart special or something."

My laugh bordered on hysteria, and with a baffled shrug Dan closed the bathroom door. When I heard the shower spray hit its normal pitch, I dashed for the stairwell. Not bothering with the light and with shaking fingers unable to master the catch, I pressed the rosebud against my throat. And he was there. I pressed my face into the white shirt front, and as I wept he murmured, "Katherine, I've missed you, missed you. Kept trying to help."

"I didn't know what to—trying?"

"Every time you came into our room I poured out the message that Dan had picked up the necklace, put it in the box."

"That's why I thought of him in here."

"Kate," Dan yelled from the bottom level, "stove timer's going off."

With promises to be back later tonight, I restored the necklace to its shelf.

"Not the most opportune time to work on poetry," Dan said as with oven mitts I removed loaves of browning bread from the rack.

As the door bell chimed and the six from Rivera entered with exaggerated panting over the steep stairs and with quips about heart attacks ("That hill." "Those stairs." "However do you manage?"), I slipped on high heels.

Dan, exuding conviviality, fixed drinks. I brought appetizers and listened to the three women experiment with polite remarks about the dining room.

"What a job you've tackled," Peg said.

Dan waxed on about making an old property marketable.

"There are those who prefer older homes. As for me, I like nothing more old-fashioned than my microwave," Connie said.

On a house tour, despite their civility, they saw no charm and were appalled at a single bathroom.

"Surely you'll install a second?" Clark said. "It would improve the selling potential."

As Dan agreed, I read his mixed expression—satisfaction in our party, renewed dedication to finding an acceptable address.

Forget it, Dan, I thought, and confident in that strength, secure in Franklin's love, I could pretend graciousness.

After the good nights, Dan hugged me, a caring hug, which was unnerving. "A fantastic meal, a fantastic evening. Thank you. But, you know, they're right on about this house."

"Could be. I'll go do the dishes."

"Let them wait till morning. I'll help you then. Come on to bed."

"You go on," I said, "get some sleep. I'm too keyed up."

He shrugged but didn't protest. After washing dishes, stacking them in the drainer, I tiptoed into the bedroom. Dan was snoring. I kicked off my shoes, shut the bedroom door, and hurried to Franklin.

CHAPTER SEVEN

*T*he airport terminal doors whished open upon a lobby, where noises bounced from a distant ceiling and exploded against signs and counters.

"It's so loud," I said.

"Doesn't sound bad to me. 'Course I've not been holed up in a house for a week. I've been battling traffic in the midst of the City. No, this isn't bad at all." Dan marched toward the United counter and set our luggage on the scales. He was right. I had holed up, but I'd not been immune to his resentment when dinner wasn't ready, when I neglected to pick up his suit at the cleaners, when I forgot to pay the phone bill.

At one point I tried to explain. "Ideas are tumbling in my mind. During the days we'll be in Harding, I'll be unable to write, and I'm worried that the poetry will shrivel if I don't get some of it down now."

"Don't you think you're going a bit overboard with all this? Don't—" He hesitated. "Of what earthly value is poetry? If you're determined to write, write something that might help someone, that might sell. Do articles. They have substance. Poetry's like ballet, like modern art—nothing to it. It's like eating cotton candy. Now when we're confronted with remodeling, bills, the expense of flying to Iowa, you hide out upstairs writing verse that no one's going to read."

I said nothing more, assuring myself that most of what I'd told Dan was true. I did need to record impressions, but also I needed Franklin in this lone week sandwiched between our reunion after the lost necklace and my trip. I must store memories to extract in the Midwest.

And because workmen were installing an imitation cut glass chandelier (Dan's selection, which he insisted added "pure elegance") over the dining room table and wallpapering above the dado, Franklin and I spent each day in our room.

In a pool of sunlight on the gray rug we loved, read books, examined texts, exchanged samples of style, clarity, rhyme schemes, and refined stanzas leaving me alternately tired and stimulated.

We experimented with sonnets and quatrains, with hexameters and free verse, and having moved into seasons combined with the objects topic, we began equating seasons with various forms of love and then with the colors of seasons and the colors of love. We roughed out, "A Yellowed Love," "And Love Chose Blue," and finally, "Love in Red."

> Clad in autumn flames
> she wore desire
> like leaves

matted in her chestnut hair," Franklin suggested.

> "Hungry for the man
> who stalks dry woods,
> for fall to touch her skin.
> Tired of teasing summer love
> she spreads her thighs
> for harvest," I added.

"Katherine, your writing is becoming positively sensual."

Idyllic hours. Never had I believed I could be with someone indefinitely, but in Franklin's presence I no longer valued privacy.

"Kate!"

I blinked at Dan's tense face in the San Francisco terminal. "What?"

He took my arm. "You were standing there with some kind of dazed smile, blocking others from the counter."

Dutifully I passed through security inspection, waited to board and snapped my seatbelt before beginning a poetry anthology I'd checked from the library. Momentarily, conscience pricked, for library reminded me of Lorraine, whom I hadn't seen since our conversation on the ketch. Locked away as I was, if she'd called or dropped by the house, I wouldn't have known. Purposefully I had resisted present day intrusions. Too soon, I must deal with Molly, for Dan was insistent that she return with us. Too soon, I must handle his demands that we house hunt. For just those few days I ignored Lorraine's pregnancy dilemma and the latest exorbitant repair bills.

Did love, of the all-consuming variety, make one egocentric, cause one to erect barriers? I unzipped my purse and felt for pen and paper. On my note pad I'd scribble this question about an inclusive love. I sensed more than saw Dan's reaction, and his disapproval blocked succeeding questions. I replaced the note pad and opened my book at random to "The Fisherman's Honor" by Li Qingzhao (1084-1151?). When I read, "Hard to find words in poems to carry amazement," I thought, *Oh, Franklin, even in the eleventh century, poets struggled for adequate words, for insights as to how to clarify abstractions.*

An hour out from Des Moines, Dan spoke about Molly, furnishing nothing new. Was it inevitable that we lose the ability to see with fresh vision? Must everyone fall into that trap? When did one begin to repeat ideas, to entrench himself/herself into a more restrictive philosophy? This time, though, I didn't jot down questions, for I hoped we'd exit the plane in a semblance of unity.

A second before she saw us, I spotted Molly standing within the crowd near the luggage section. So young she was, so pretty. When we threw arms around each other, I sobbed into that long hair she refused to cut or curl and in response her thin body shook.

She seemed delicate, a child, not the adamant teenager demanding to stay in Harding, nor the assertive young woman who set the mood for most phone conversations. In my mind's eye I'd escalated her growth, had put her on a level with me, with Lorraine.

Molly stepped back to appraise me. "Mom, you've lost years. I hardly recognize you."

Dan's massive hug, his "Oh, baby, you're a sight for sore eyes," saved me from replying. As a center post, Molly looped elbows with us and we bumped out the door.

"You here by yourself?" Dan asked.

"Un huh. Borrowed Steve's Ford. The Hawkins wanted to drive me, but I needed to see you alone. When we get back to their house, there'll be confusion."

My radar picked up Dan's reaction to "needing to see you alone." Right there on the sidewalk before the terminal, I figured he'd immediately unveil his plans for her, but he kept walking and listened patiently as she recounted final school days, tests, parties.

En route to the parking lot I inhaled the sweet scent of Midwestern spring, wishing I could box intangibles, those secret untranslatable parts of a locale and attendant emotions. I'd present the package to Franklin. When he removed the lid, we could share everything.

Dan settled into the back seat and with the trite, "Home James" remark, waited for Molly to turn the ignition key. A blanket was stretched across the lumpy front seat and a dream catcher dangled from the rear view mirror.

As Molly eased into traffic, Dan complimented her driving skill, likely his final compliment because instead of thanking him, she said, "Steve's bought an engagement ring. He'll give it to me after graduation."

Quiet. Dan would gather more ammunition before launching an attack.

"We're planning a July wedding."

"Then you're not pregnant," Dan said.

"Daddy! No. We don't want a baby until we get on our feet. Steve and I've talked it over with his parents. Tim, Steve's brother, doesn't want anything to do with the farm. He'll graduate from high school next year and his parents hope to help send him to college. Money they might have used for Steve, they'll pay as wages for his farming. At first, it will be a little rough 'cause we'll live with Steve's parents, but as soon as we have enough saved—and I'm keeping on at the drugstore—we'll rent a place in town, which I know will be tough on Steve to drive back and forth 'cause he has to get up so awfully early, or the Myerson's who rent a house down the road from the farm might be leaving and we might get their house."

As round one, Dan deployed the inexperience missile. "You haven't seen the world, haven't dated anyone but Steve. How can you know Mr. Right isn't out there?"

"If Steve's enough for me, why do I need to go searching?"

For another mile or two, they volleyed back and forth the idea of inexperience and sampling the world before Dan raised objection number two, age.

"Most teen marriages end in divorce."

"Lots of later marriages do, too. Boy, you should count the number of oldies getting divorced—even your former partner Hank."

Did Dan stiffen? Unconcerned, I drank in the scenery, the green corn stalks. Green in this country came from a more generous palette than on the West Coast. Without paper and pen I trusted I could store away perceptions about nuanced shades of love in nuanced shades of color.

"Well, you need to prepare yourself for some occupation. If you and Steve divorced, or if, say, he was killed in a farming accident, how would you support yourself?"

Her fingers clenched the steering wheel and in a movement so like Dan's, she clucked her tongue. "I can always go to school."

"Can you?" And then Dan, his body bent forward as far as the seat belt allowed, pressed. "School requires money, you know, so why not get some education now when we can help? I'm not saying don't ever marry the guy. I'm not saying don't accept the ring. Wear the damned thing, but live with your mother and me one measly year. Enroll at a business college or take one of those year-deals at community college where you can become a paraprofessional something or other."

"Daddy, I can't leave him. A year's forever."

While Dan dwelt on time's swiftness, I was sure he didn't notice heifers, like mottled statues beside their mothers, nor appreciate glossy weeds gentling barbed wire.

Next he introduced finances. "I'm not speaking against Steve's family. Certainly the Idersons are decent people, but they live barely above subsistence level. They own poor land. There's no future there. You and Steve can work your fingers to the bone, and you'll still have zilch."

"We'll have each other."

"Consider your children. What can you give them? Think beyond yourself."

She can't, Dan, I thought

His voice held desperation. "You're bucking a trend, you realize. This generation's opting to marry later."

Molly rolled her eyes. "Dad, hard as it is for you to understand we LOVE each other." And in another Dan imitation she raised her head so her chin atop her gorgeous long neck pointed in bird dog fashion toward a bug-spattered windshield. Then the chin swiveled in my direction. "Mother, you've not said a thing."

"I don't know what to add. Basically, I agree with your dad. He or I could produce countless arguments. Would they make any difference?"

"Nope," and she grinned.

"So?" I shrugged.

Dan muttered. To him my shrug indicated I was letting him down, was bailing out. He cleared his throat to effect a masterful tone. "I intend to talk to Steve and to his parents."

"Fine." She fluttered her right hand in some vague motion. "In fact, the Idersons have invited us to their house after graduation, a little engagement party."

In the lengthening silence, aware my question would displease Dan, I asked, "What kind of wedding?"

Molly beamed. "Small. I figured you guys wouldn't be in favor of my marriage and asking you to fork out for a big ceremony would be too much. Steve and I will have a family affair, plus a couple friends, in the church parsonage."

"No long white dress?"

"White's for virgins," Dan said.

Ridiculously, I felt disappointed. How I'd treasured months of planning, had relished selecting a white satin gown with covered buttons. I would be denied the emotional hills and valleys of helping with a daughter's ceremony.

"You're being sensible, of course, but I can visualize a Victorian wedding, a high-necked lace dress—"

"Your mother's gone bananas on Victoriana."

"Mom," she shook her head, "just a nice, short service."

Yes, that was appropriate for Molly who did not float on dreamy clouds. She'd be content, truly content, with a quick service and probably a life with Steve. My daughter was Dan's daughter.

With a divided nature, I neared Harding. How reassuring to feel Irma's hug and hear her say, "I've missed you". . . yet how I missed my house on the hill. How delicious the freshly-sliced tomatoes and the snapped beans seasoned with bacon tasted. . . yet how I yearned for my notebook lying on my desk. How disorienting to look beyond the Hawkins' property line at a house no longer mine . . .yet how my soul kept winging west to Franklin. Such divisiveness shadowed hours as I talked with townspeople, wandered into stores once landmarks in my former microcosm, or regarded my original house from the Hawkins' porch.

Then on the evening of Molly's graduation, the two factions merged. In her cap and gown she smiled broadly while Dan snapped pictures, and her exuberance and the recognition that this marked the end of high school fastened me to a spot on Irma's porch.

In the flurry of a fast-paced meal and in locating a parking place at the high school gym, I had no opportunity to dwell on anything else. At the back of the crowded gymnasium, Dan and I scanned rows of occupied folding chairs until I saw a waving hand. Mrs. Iderson had saved us seats.

We headed toward a contemporary American Gothic, a gaunt woman with hair secured in a bun. Drops of water still beaded Mr. Iderson's slicked-back hair except around his ears where strands had dried, allowing errant spikes to spring up. His suit rested uneasily on his large frame. The print dress bagged on hers. I felt ashamed. Why should I who disdained the Rivera set, who admired Lorraine's unconventionality, react so to this couple? Had I so quickly fallen back onto traditional paths? Suddenly my questions, even my passage to the reserved seats, were stalled at the sight of a tall blonde woman at an end seat of the left section.

In the space of a micro-second, myriad thoughts bombarded me. Why? How out of the hundreds in attendance had I picked out Sheila? Not in the main section, she was at the far side as if a distant relative or casual acquaintance, not where a parent of a graduate would sit, for her oldest son Caleb would receive his diploma tonight. She was alone. Neither younger son was with her. However, in that flash of time not only was I able to wonder but was able to envy her outfit—a classy white pants suit with a fashionable white duster. Tanned, slim, lovely. In that instant observation I also saw the naked hunger when she saw Dan.

In that same instant I saw his same longing. His face tightened with such need, such love that I ached, thinking simultaneously of how he'd never regarded me that way and wishing that he had and thinking how painful each day must be for each of them living life at a reduced level, and thinking, incongruously, of what color must be their love.

We bumped purses, feet, and crossed legs as we excused ourselves to reach the Idersons in the middle of a row. Dan and I didn't look at each other. Instead we spoke with Steve's parents until the band struck up "Pomp and Circumstance." The audience stood and Dan, as if afraid of being tempted to turn toward that far section, stared intently at the line of graduates.

When abreast of our row Molly smiled and waved, showing off the tiny sparkle on her finger. Steve hadn't waited until later. By some locker room door had he jammed the ring on her finger? No flowers, music, not even candlelight?

Six students behind Molly marched Steve, as ill-at-ease under his mortar board as were his parents in their outfits. He was just a kid, wouldn't be nineteen until September. And suddenly all attempt at spanning social stratums collapsed along with my infatuation with their brand of love. Dan was right. Molly mustn't marry Steve.

This certainty gathered momentum throughout the ceremony, throughout speaking with others after graduates threw caps in the air, throughout an exchange of waves with Hank (seated in the middle section with his two sons), and throughout the trip to the Iderson farm. Carefully Dan and I discussed the evening and Molly's ring. Just as carefully we avoided any reference to Sheila, who had managed to exit before we left the gymnasium.

When we parked the Hawkins' car in the farm lane, the smell of near-poverty greeted us. Steve's car swung in behind us, its headlights piercing the blackness to play across a peeling barn and flowers scrawny beside a clothesline.

Molly hurried toward us, her happiness defeating starkness. As she embraced me, I questioned how I could demand she forfeit what she wanted, wanted at least at age eighteen. Should I pray for miracles, that she'd change her mind, decide on college, find another man, break the engagement? Or maybe I could hope the marriage wouldn't last.

As for tonight, I felt compelled to make it as lovely for her as possible—play a part, at which I was becoming proficient. Accordingly I congratulated Steve, complimented Mrs. Iderson's cake inscribed with "Congradulations, Steve and Molly," and sat in a kitchen dulled by years and despair, by failure and stillborn hope. I laughed at jokes and nodded at the kids' anecdotes about what had happened before and during the ceremony.

"Wasn't it something the way Miss Herrick stuttered over Truman's name? She was sloshed."

"Mark wasn't wearing any underwear."

"What about that lei Susan's uncle sent from Hawaii?"

With their laughter and creation of a shared history, their eyes spoke of a strong young love, of a purity that left me speechless. Just minutes before I'd been convinced that they must separate. Yet could I be wrong? What right had Dan and I to inflict such pain? They'd undoubtedly face enough pain of their own making.

I envied Molly's steadfastness, her lack of doubt. In a reversal, she seemed the adult and I the confused teenager. I'd never gone through the depths of all-encompassing love. Names of high school dates I couldn't recall. I'd been the obedient, compliant daughter. Was rebellion, uncertainty, a rite of passage all must go through at some point?

The Idersons contributed little. Their younger son Tim wandered off. Markedly depressed, Dan didn't talk with our hosts or with Steve, so at the round table, pitted by years of wear, we endured, listening to the clock tick dire warnings, as my desire for Molly's memorable evening leaked away.

Within an hour we left. At the door she kissed me and promised to be along soon.

"Stay out," I forced one last display of gaiety, "as long as you like. Celebrate."

In the car, Dan contemplated the bleak setting. "I wanted so much more for her. God damn, God damn."

Irma and Dexter had left the end table light on its lowest setting. At least we'd be spared further pretense tonight. In the guest room, Dan sank heavily onto the bed. His sadness infected me, and when he extracted a handkerchief from his back pocket, I, too, cried. He pulled me down beside him and we sat clumsily on the edge of the bed.

"It will be okay," I finally said, unsure for whom he had shed tears.

He nodded and stuffed the handkerchief into his pocket. Sitting side by side and facing the house that once belonged to us, I said, "Do you plan to see Her?"

To his credit he didn't say, "Who?" but shook his head.

The room closed in upon us, and I wanted to raise a window but to move—to do anything would, I felt, destroy any chance of communication.

"She," and time that had leaked away at the Iderson's stopped, "left tonight. Ever since. She's lived with her mother in Minneapolis."

"The boys are with Hank?"

He nodded.

"So," and cautiously I spoke, "you've been in contact?"

"Would this upset you?" And defeat dragged behind each word.

"When I begged you to stay with me, I never begged you not to see her again."

We were at an impasse. He clucked and said, "Can we talk about Molly?"

That we did and in so doing remembered stages in her life: riding a bicycle, bringing home a stray dog, falling from a park swing set, drawing a picture for us after my second miscarriage on which she'd printed, "You aways haf me," which we interpreted to mean, "You'll always have me." As we shared our reminiscences, I leaned against his shoulder. Dan rested his cheek upon the top of my head and recalled a father-daughter banquet at a church hall, while I remembered her diving from the highest board at the swimming pool.

It was natural to raise my head and meet his lips, natural to undress and let my body rise and fall in unison with his. Madison was far far away and Sheila and Franklin didn't exist. That night Dan and I were entangled not in lust, not in love, but in what we'd had, the child we'd made, and our sorrow about her.

Next morning, relaxed in that pampered bliss that comes when someone else cooks and serves food, I ate pancakes and sipped coffee from an aqua mug that Irma had fired in a ceramics class.

Dexter entered through the back door. "Truck's here to pick up the rummage. That stuff piled in the corner of the garage goes?"

Irma shot me that I-don't-trust-his-judgment look. "In the right hand corner, not the left. I better show you." With a groan of imposition, she hoisted herself from the chair.

From my position near the window I watched them nod over boxes and sacks. When they carried the collection to the truck my disinterest evaporated, for Dexter had ostrich feathers.

"Wait!" The screen door banged behind me. "May I buy the feathers?"

Dexter passed me the carton. "Honey, you can have those old things."

And while I told about the house, about hunting authentic pieces for it, I thought, *Oh, Franklin, I'm bringing us a gift, one from my former life. We'll set the feathers on the circular oak table in the living room.*

As if the feathers released some precious elixir, I again was able to gain detachment. Removed from Dan's distress, from the Hawkins's dim predictions about Molly's future, and from assorted individuals who strolled in and out of our limited hours, I listened to Molly's ideas and vowed we'd attend her wedding.

Despite detachment I was prompted, by I know not what, to borrow Irma's car and drive to my parents' graves. The cemetery, three miles south of town, had been a white rectangle in February. The narrow roadways in that section of the graveyard drift full in winter, adding one more barrier to a visit with the dead. I smiled at that thought. In Harding, would I ever have imagined that a visit with the dead could prove interactive?

But what of Mom? Dad? Had they also had the option to wait around Harding? I braked, swung right through the cemetery gates, and bumped along the gravel road. Potholes, courtesy of winter, plagued the road. On each side, though, grass had been mowed and occasional floral decorations, like paint daubs, colored the grounds. Ah, yes, this weekend was Memorial Day—Mom had called it Decoration Day—and relatives would leave vases and fruit jars filled with flowers on various plots. On the back seat floor of Irma's car rode one of her ceramic vases ("A bit of a problem on one side," she'd said when I protested her giving it to me to leave at the cemetery), alive with peonies. My parents would like that, would like to be remembered.

As I coasted down a knoll, I returned to my question about hanging around Harding. Nope, I couldn't believe that either parent had desired anything badly enough to resist the other side. How little I had known them. How little they probably knew themselves or each other.

Dad, employed by the highway maintenance department, took pride in driving snow plows each winter and graders each summer. But pride in keeping highways open would hardly qualify as a reason to remain in this dimension. As for Mom—a stay-at-home Mom, as I had been—she took pride in her neat house, in pickled beets she canned from our garden, and in her healthy zinnias and peonies. Not enough, I'd wager, to haunt the simple house, where I grew up.

I pulled off the road, at least felt the right wheels depress the earth, so perhaps another car could get around, and stared at the tombstone city. My parents had loved me. This I never doubted, but it was an unemotional bedrock of love, which I reciprocated. I never gave them any trouble, aside from my dreamy tendencies which concerned them. I'd done well in high school and college, had married Dan, a local product, of whom they profoundly approved. "Good man, Kate," Dad had said. "Practical fellow."

They'd adored Molly and after I suffered the second miscarriage, Mom had said, "I lost two before you were born." I was shocked. "You never told me that. How far along were you?"

Mom flushed. "Far along," sounded sexy, intimate. "Unimportant," she finally said. "Of importance is that we had you, and you are fortunate to have Molly."

"Were you depressed? Sad?"

She shrugged. "You deal with life, Kate. You don't walk around being depressed and sad. You snap out of it."

And that's the extent of what I gleaned about the dual pregnancies, but it showed me—if I hadn't already known—that one did not let others see one's suffering.

I reached for the vase of peonies. If I positioned it just right, the dip in the rim would nestle against their headstone.

As I strolled down the row toward their plain stone—"Don't spend money on a tombstone," Dad had lectured before his death, so Mom and I complied, even had her name etched on as well to save a few dollars—I thought, *What one image comes to mind about each of them?* I see Dad in his roomy arm chair tugging on his galoshes. Behind him the window is dark, thick with a storm. The floor lamp is on, and it shines on his right cheek, leaving his eyes and forehead dark. I hear the definitive click of each buckle; then he raises his head and smiles. "County Road One's nearly impassable." He seems heroic to me, a child, and that's what I choose to think.

I brushed cut grass from the bottom of the stone and centered my peony arrangement on the concrete ledge before her name. Helen. Had she liked her name? If ever I'd asked, she would have frowned, puzzled by such a nonsensical question. "Like?" she might have said. "Like doesn't count. It's the name I was given."

My picture of her? I remember stepping into the living room on a spring evening. Uncharacteristically Mom sits by the window. Its open lip emits a stirring fragrance, and she breathes in unaccustomed nature. She doesn't realize I'm there, so I observe her profile. With eyes shut she radiates peace, contentment, is as close to "being dreamy" as I've ever seen her. Her lips curve into a smile. Wherever she is, she's happy. and I experience a pang, for never has she directed such an expression on me. And, yet, now on the grave, I claim that memory. While Mom never appeared introspective (introspection was a luxury), she did harbor some secrets, had something that was beyond consulting the Wednesday newspaper advertisement for grocery store bargains, something that meant more than meat loaf and Monday laundry.

Until I heard the approach of another vehicle entering the cemetery, I remained at the grave, letting questions explode in my mind—questions I would never have faced if Dan and I were still living a life in Harding that replicated my parents. I flattened my palms against the gravestone and whispered, "Goodbye. Tomorrow we're off for California."

The next morning en route to the Des Moines airport, Dan, Molly, and I spoke rarely, and when I held my daughter close it was the memory of her as a young child and of the past that evoked tears.

Dan blew his nose loudly, then grumbled only half-jokingly about "those ugly feathers" I carried on board.

Early evening, when a delicate tinge shaded the hills, we came back to Madison. I nearly commented on how welcome were the rooms despite needed repair, but Dan hit the play button on our message machine in his computer room.

Therefore, I roamed through the downstairs, cherishing the mounting tension about meeting Franklin in the north room. As I returned to the entryway room, where Dan was still playing messages, I heard Neal's voice, "Kate, found some old newspaper articles in which Franklin's mentioned. Stop by the museum when you can." How warm his voice. How much voice quality conveyed. I could imagine him reading texts for audio books, could picture a sightless person smiling as his voice like a golden bath filtered through the speaker to spread around her.

"Franklin?" Dan frowned.

"I'm finding out more info about the man who built our house."

Apparently satisfied Dan smiled, "One message was from Jay. He's asked us to dinner at their place tomorrow, and they've found us a house."

"What?"

"Kate," and his irritated sigh said more than any words. "Rivera. Remember. Jay and Beth. At the end of August their neighbors are being transferred, but the neighbors' house hasn't yet been listed. We can check it out tomorrow evening."

I didn't know where to start with an answer, but the ringing phone postponed my inarticulate attempt.

"Glad you're back," Lorraine said.

"Me, too."

"Okay, I'm coming on with this heavy favor. Can you take me to the abortion clinic tomorrow? "I longed to say, "No, I've just arrived. Tomorrow

I want to dedicate to Franklin."

She must have sensed my hesitancy. "Sorry to do this but clinic rules demand I have a driver."

"What time?"

"It's awful, six-thirty a.m."

"Who was that?" Dan asked as I replaced the receiver.

"I'm driving Lorraine to the abortion clinic tomorrow."

"That kind of friend definitely makes Rivera look more and more appealing." He switched on his computer. "I'll e-mail Molly that we made it."

And probably he would e-mail Sheila, but I left the room to unpack.

Dan's soiled white shirt, the graduation night shirt, smelled of sweat. It had been an eventful evening. When I withdrew my yellow dress it, too, would carry a composite accumulation. As I moved to drop his shirt into the laundry hamper, I noticed a loose button. When I reattached it tomorrow, it would be an automatic action. All my adult life I had mended clothing, an act of love. But what kind of love? Did I still love Dan? I clutched the shirt against my chest as if a concrete object might contain the answer. Maybe that was what Franklin was searching for in his original notion of utilizing objects to tell narratives, for what is a life story but a study in love or lack of it? If caring was love, if compassion was love, then my answer was yes to my question concerning Dan. If wanting the best for him was love, then the answer was yes, even if the best was being with Sheila. I felt no anger, no jealousy. Could love be that passive?

I wished for my notebook. No, I wished I had the ability to express these questions in a more literary, more profound manner. With Franklin, could poetry adequately address such things? Or did such thoughts cross my mind because of my age? When young, as was Franklin, as was Molly, love between a man and a woman wouldn't be seen as compassion. "Mom," Molly would say, "compassion sounds pretty non-sexual."

I laid the shirt on the dresser, ready to mend in the morning. Non-sexual. Well, with the exception of two chance sexual encounters in the last four months, Dan and I had lived like siblings. What if that defined our marriage until one of us died? After my humiliating pleading, he'd agreed to stay, but I couldn't force him to love me, and I knew I'd never love him as I had prior to Sheila and prior to Franklin. The color of our love was brown, pale brown.

He strode into the bedroom with a smile. Ah, he must have connected with Sheila, but he said, "Left a short message for Molly, told her we'd made it back just fine. I was good, Kate, didn't bring up her engagement at all."

"Neat," I said and in a companionable state—like brother and sister?—we finished unpacking. Dan stored the bags in the closet, stretched, yawned, put on his striped pajamas and relaxed in bed. Soon he slept.

At last I crept up stairs, whispering "Franklin," as I affixed the necklace. And as he extended his arms, he answered, "Katherine."

Fog muffled the piers, distorted bleating horns and drew a nimbus effect around Lorraine as she clanked the gate shut behind her.

Pea jacket, jeans, boots, and a bandana on her head prompted me to say, "I should have worn jeans instead of Middle America polyester." As we left the marina I spilled out Middle America details, climaxed by the wonder of coming back.

"Your guy, Franklin. Were you able to see him last night?"

"Briefly."

The fog, at ease upon the water, rapidly dissipated as we drove into the central section, and when we neared the clinic on the opposite side of town, found it backed by a clear sky.

A nurse called Lorraine's name but minutes after we tried to settle on plastic chairs in the waiting room. I tried not to stare at the two younger than Molly. One woman in her mid-thirties wore a tailored suit as if after this minor detour, she'd command an office or a class room. To my right a teenager in tight Calvin Kleins and a baggy sweat shirt brushed her hair, streaked with orange-red highlights. Heart-shaped ear rings bobbed on thin wires gouged through her ear lobes. An amateur job of piercing, it matched the amateur application of thick mascara and purple nail polish. Unlike the sense of judgment I'd experienced with Mrs. Iderson, I felt this child inhabited a life dealt from a dog-eared deck.

A groomed woman in a blazer and gray skirt sat to my left. Her hand with its weighty wedding band, lay in her lap, while her other hand gripped the arm of a man in a business suit. Husband? They would have discussed how a child at this stage would stall their careers. Beside each other on a tufted white sofa they would have categorized pros and cons until they opted for this solution to an unplanned pregnancy.

I rubbed my brow feeling momentarily light-headed at the emotions surrounding me, at the emotions that had brought this assortment to this room.

"Whitney Kessler," the nurse called. After making a face at her friend, one of the very young girls confidently moved toward the corridor. Her friend began reading and underlining a text book. Here were individuals trapped by complex issues, all stemming from moments of love, attempts to gain love, or a mistaken love.

I walked to the drinking fountain and as I depressed the lever heard the words, "What if you're involved in a pretend love? You've invented a romance that has no consequences. No unwanted children. No inconvenient wives. You came up with a perfect man."

As I drank, another woman followed the nurse along a hallway. "What if you've made up a handsome young man with your interests and sense of humor? He's your defense against conflict and tragedy. You can run to him, so you needn't cope by yourself."

Where were these questions coming from? Why was I thinking along these lines?

Exhaustion, I assured myself. I'd just returned from a tiring trip, a daughter's graduation and her engagement. I was facing an unpleasant dinner party that night. I was concerned about Dan's intention to move and put our house on the market. And there was Lorraine.

Yet, as I resettled onto the plastic chair I could not shake the feeling of bigger issues, the feeling that decisions—all centered around love—were pressing in. On a magazine's glossy page I saw a Victorian house featured in a paint advertisement. While it didn't resemble mine, it conveyed an aura of place. Yes, place. Love of place. I had loved Midwestern seasons and now loved my Madison home. How did one measure or define that kind of love?

I dropped the magazine on the floor when Lorraine finally sank down beside me.

"You okay?"

"Sure," she answered. "I'll rest and go to work tomorrow afternoon."

As we headed for the automatic door, I asked, "Like to come back to the house?"

"Naw, the boat's home, at least temporarily. I'm comfortable there. Plus, Peter will be over later to check on me."

"And?"

"Oh, Kate, I don't know." She slid into my Plymouth. "I just don't know. I love this man." In unison we clicked our seat belt buckles. "He wanted a little on the side and got more than he'd bargained for. He loves me, oh, not in that total-renouncing-everything manner that we all yearn for in books and movies, but he'll miss me, even mourn me when I take off. And, God knows, I'll suffer." Her hand shook as she passed it over her eyes.

We stopped at the red traffic signal. "But you're not leaving?"

"Someday Adam will want his boat, and I'm not sold enough on Madison to move on land. When Adam shows up it will be a sign to clear out."

At the ketch I shoved back the hatch cover, unfolded the scratchy wool blanket and tucked it over her on the port side bunk. I suggested food I could bring, recommended a book, and proposed jelly jar wine. She smiled and said, "Go home."

When she fell asleep I left and as I drove, thought of Franklin, allowing his form to blot out everything. I parked in the garage and ran to the second level where his arms drew me close. I rested my head against his chest until he said, "Shall we get to work?"

He commenced his pacing, but for the minutes that he toyed with a troublesome line, I wrote in my notebook:

> We fashion pools of love
> in which to dive
> Shattering for a moment
> our reflected gaze.
> The surface mends itself
> holds us immersed within
> the depths of our invention

CHAPTER EIGHT

hrough hazy dusk Dan and I rode toward the Rivera dinner party. Probably ugly strings of cars, dying weeds beside the freeway, and smog blotting the sky contributed to my sense of displacement.

Greeted by superficial affection—"Kate, darling! Marvelous to see you. How was the trip? Ohio, right?"—I hunted for a role to play and downed three glasses of wine. Even my former mousey personality would be preferable to my shifting moods. As if I'd passed through too many time zones too quickly leaving bits and pieces of myself scattered across the globe, I tried to draw everything together. I'd fix my mind on specifics, such as the rust-colored couch. Expensive, it smelled new—a sharp contrast to my twenty-year-old couch which I planned to exchange for a horsehair sofa with a triple-arch medallion back and hand-carved flowers on the middle section and arms.

A maroon floral-patterned rug for the living room. . .hardboard boards polished around its edges. . .a rocker. . .cerise banquet lamps. . . marble-topped occasional tables. . .realistic oils ranging across the walls. . .ostrich feathers. . . .

Wine from a decanter gurgled into my glass and brought me back to Jay's smirk. "At least," he said, tipping the carafe upright, "I didn't say, 'penny for your thoughts.'"

"They were hardly worth a penny."

"Probably thinking of your daughter," Beth said. "It must have been difficult to leave her back there originally; then return only to leave her again."

"Yes." I peered over the glass rim at Jay freshening drinks before he glided into the men's stronghold at the far end of the room.

"My youngest goes off this fall." Connie rose from the depths of a bronze velvet armchair to lean forward. "Stanford. She graduates with honors next month from Norwin High."

"Her major?" Beth asked.

"Oh, Jen's torn between law and medicine. Probably medicine, specializing in pediatrics."

"Specialization's the way to go." Peg's skirt swished as she carefully crossed one leg over the other, which called attention to new sandals and a flawless pedicure. "Tad, our older son, is in veterinarian medicine, will be an ophthalmologist."

"For animals?" I asked.

"Why, yes, dear. So many pet owners demand quality care. Similar, isn't it, to the medical field? Years back we relied on the traditional family doctor, and, now, no one does."

The three agreed and named their internists, gynecologists, therapists. . .

"Well," Beth sighed, "Scott's finishing his junior year at Berkeley and is obsessed with swimming."

"With that scholarship he received and those records he's set," Connie said, "no wonder he's obsessed."

"He's maintained a 3.9," Beth acknowledged, "and does well in architectural drawing, but will anyone hire a magnificent swimmer-architect?"

Expected polite laughter fanned us, and I drank more wine.

"What will be your daughter's major and what university has she chosen?" Peg's question linked me with them.

"Marriage."

"Family counseling is so important," Beth said.

"I meant that Molly's not going to college. She's getting married this summer."

Connie's, "Oh, my," expressed it all. My glass was empty, but as I searched for Jay, Beth stood to check, "One last thing in the kitchen and then we'll eat."

"Married." Peg pronounced the word as if she were a linguist rooting for its derivation.

I should have let the two pitch syllables back and forth but the wine and my emotional state goaded me into speaking. "Molly's known Steve since childhood."

"But the baby," Connie protested.

I tensed. "She's not pregnant. She's in love. She'll be a good wife and isn't that important? Everyone can't be brilliant. Everyone can't be college material."

Connie eyed her gold bracelet. Peg regarded the laughing men, and I wished for more wine. No, actually, I wished for Franklin.

We waited until Beth swept through the dining room where goblets cast starred light back toward the source, a candled chandelier.

"Do come on," she called.

Peg and Connie joined the men as I willed the room to stop its slow rotation. I'm drunk, I realized, and the statement shocked me, forced me to decline wine with dinner. With my lips in what I assumed resembled a friendly expression I sat, a rock among the conversational tide pools.

Before we ate the *piece de resistance*, Beth's chocolate mousse, Jay tapped his glass. "Listen up. Four houses down, a corner lot's coming up for sale. When the guy, Joe Keithly, told me I said, 'Don't list it, yet. I know a terrific couple,'"—here Jay included Dan and me in his benevolent smile—"'who want a home in Rivera.' I told Joe that Dan and his wife, plus the rest of you, would be here tonight and asked if we could take a look."

I held a bit of mousse on my tongue, letting it dissolve but it failed to delay the inevitable and, in a less-than-clear-headed condition, I trailed the group down the sidewalk to a contemporary home with solar panels, skylights, computer terminals, stuccoed walls and acrylic sculptures. As seven enthusiastic people trooped from room to room exclaiming over innovations, I stood before a Plexiglas abstract where a humanoid raised a claw.

As if I had been gifted with the ability to read another's thoughts, I knew not only that Dan liked the property, but that he could see Sheila in this setting. She'd straighten a tipped painting over the fireplace. Completely white with a red centered dot, it would be striking, avant-garde, above the granite hearth. On backless high heels she would saunter across the ivory carpet and line duplicate place settings on a starkly black dining table. With the look she'd worn at graduation, she would turn toward Dan. Ah, yes, this was a Sheila house.

"Oh, Kate." Connie joined me. "It's a wonderful property. You needn't do anything. No remodeling, nothing."

And while others shared a night cap back at Jay's, I listened to their excitement. The treble clef of female voices chorused about moving companies, shopping centers, and exclusive clubs. The males' bass boomed with "great deal", "interest rates", "twenty-five year loan", "getting rid of the old house."

The chorale faded, replaced by the accompaniment of our car tires striking asphalt and the cricket-like rattle from the dash as we exited Rivera.

"I really liked it," he said simply.

A van passed us in the fast lane as I debated how to respond. "It's not my house," I answered. "It's a house for Her, for Sheila."

I'd hit the mark. He blanched and clucked his tongue against the roof of his mouth, but no pronouncement followed. Once more I imagined his thoughts, could hear him wonder, Should I admit I dreamed of her living there? Should we talk about her? Isn't it better to let it alone? and to the third question he answered a silent, "yes."

But avoidance was merely a stop gap. I tossed in bed and after lapsing into light sleep, dreamed a beast stalked the tree to which I clung. Its roar was male but the foot falls padded in feline fashion. Although safe on a sturdy limb, I felt the trunk sway and shudder as the animal butted against it.

Breathing hard, I sat up in bed and tried to ignore the obvious symbolism. A full moon cut a jagged yellow through the curtain, an out-of-place curtain brought from Harding. I moved to the window, saw moonlight brightening shrubs and bushes that bordered brick pathways I was reclaiming in the back-yard. Perhaps it was the moonlight's power. Perhaps it was the nightmare or my unsettled life with Dan. I'm unsure about motive, but I slipped from the bedroom and in the north room gathered up the necklace in the dark.

Franklin spoke my name, and I felt him stiffen when he pulled me against him and touched my silky nightgown.

His hand that slowly moved across my back exerted pressure and I more tightly embraced him pressing my body harder against his form. His fingers traced my nightgown strap and eased it from my shoulder. The gown breathed as it fell to the floor.

I lifted my head to meet his lips with a fierceness as deep as that of the beast that growled in my dream. From the rug we rolled onto the bare floor. Then, Franklin abruptly froze and I, too, heard, "Kate?"

Footsteps thudded. I tore off the necklace an instant before Dan rushed through the doorway. He clicked on the light switch and together we blinked against the glare.

"My God, what's going on?"

Some instinct warned me to act cautiously, so I smoothed the bunched edge of the rug.

"Guess I had a nightmare," I said.

"You were moaning and thrashing around, beating on the floor."

"Apparently the day was just too much. Must have sleep walked or something."

He glanced at each corner and even inspected the empty closet. "It's ridiculous. You've never done this before," and as if I were in a police line-up, as he could discover some clue, he continued scrutinizing me. "You really are all right?"

With a nod, I flipped off the light and we descended the stairs. To his credit he dropped his questioning except to ask, "Like some warm milk?"

"I've never drunk warm milk in my life. Have you?"

He half-smiled. "No, it's popular in stories, though." Ill-at-ease we stood at our bedroom door, and he inclined his head upward. "What should I make of that?"

"I've nothing more to say, Dan, but, please, don't worry about it," and I crawled into my side of the bed and turned away from him.

Sleep held me prisoner until nearly nine the next morning when the telephone woke me. I stumbled toward the receiver to hear Lorraine ask, "Want to ride along to Barriton? An antique store's across the street from the library where I'm leaving some book donations."

"You feeling okay?"

"Sure."

On the drive across the bridge she never alluded to yesterday and that suited me, as did the lamp in the antique shop. Although swirls of metal lace were caked with dirt, the twin bulb sockets, pull chains and the carved reeded column were intact. "It's an omen," I told myself, "that everything is fine, that everything will be all right.

As I paid for it, Lorraine honked the VW's horn and yelled, "Get it in gear, Kate. I have to get back to work."

Through the shop window I motioned at my prize and when I dashed to the car with my purchase, she teased, "You done good, kid," a sentiment felt but expressed differently by Franklin when I showed off my "find."

"Grand," and he stroked the lines of the lamp. "Been thinking," he continued with no obvious connection to the lamp, "about Neal. Didn't you say that he had some information about me?"

"Yes, but you want it today? You don't want to work on 'Spring Love'?"

"Well," and he drawled the word as he applied his charming smile. "My curiosity has grown."

So I wandered down the hill and in my accompanying fantasy imagined entering the museum where Neal lectured a high school group. He nodded to me, so I continued alone into his office. On his desk lay papers, pages, letters, booklets that dealt with Franklin. I perused each item, aware that no one would see whatever facial expression revealed whatever emotion.

In reality, however, the museum rooms were vacant and Neal sat at his desk.

"Hey, there," I greeted his back.

In his swivel chair he spun around and when he smiled, I thought *somehow he always makes me feel that I've come home.* "Glad you're back," and he gestured for me to pull up a metal chair folded against a file cabinet.

As he inquired about my trip and as I settled onto the squeaky chair, I tried to ignore the desk corner closest to me with several books, for the top one was labeled, "The Laurel Wreath: Literary Selections from Madison High School, 1893."

"In our archives—translate that to boxes in the basement—I couldn't find anything about Amy, but did come across these high school literary publications with Franklin's poetry." He handed me the first "Laurel Wreath." The cover's illustration reminded me of the laurel design in my north room. In the Table of Contents I located Franklin's name in bold print opposite the title "Springtime." As I leafed through the booklet to page 24, I felt that no one in nearly a century had turned these pages:

> When springtime touches our favored shore,
> it breathes promises of much more—
> of blossoming beauty and star-kissed nights,
> of balmy days and lingering lights
> of sunset that streak our hills to
> turn our thoughts from winter chills.

If I looked up and found Neal watching me he'd see my reaction. Bad poetry. No, adolescent poetry. I'd just assumed that my Franklin would write something more erudite. So I read the other selection on page twenty-four and those on the opposing page. None twisted words for rhyme or settled for simplistic verse. Could Franklin have believed this was good? Perhaps for some reason he'd quickly composed this?

"Here's the literary issue from 1894."

This time Franklin's contribution appeared on page twelve. Closer to the front of the book, it, therefore, must be better. But it wasn't. Granted, he didn't adhere to a rhyme scheme, but his stanzas about a white horse galloping through mystical fields with a beautiful woman had no point.

Without comment, Neal passed over the final magazine, printed during Franklin's senior year. "Ode to High School" started, "We'll leave these halls with regret/salted by memories." While the line, at best, was ambiguous at least he'd progressed to a fresh use of "salted."

"Know nothing about poetry," Neal offered, "but—"

"You don't have to know anything to realize that this falls short of quality."

But that must be one of the reasons Franklin's stayed around, to prove himself, to prove that he can produce poetry that speaks to more than high school students.

"There are countless times that we long to do something for which we don't have the talent."

I longed to argue with Neal. Of course Franklin had talent. It simply needed time to develop (and the years he'd awaited a channel had supplied that).

"Sorry, Kate," he continued, "it would be quite nice to own a home where a famous poet had lived."

Unsure what to say, I sat there with the "Laurel Wreaths" on my lap. "I write poetry." Where had that come from?

"I'd like to read some of it. I mean it," and we laughed. He fiddled with a pen from his desk top. He depressed the pen's push button and then released it. "One of next year's tentative projects is compiling a short, reader-friendly history of Madison to sell here at the museum. Might this interest you? To help me with it? We have some money and we think we can get funding, so could pay you a wage."

A job. He was offering me a job. "Yes," I said. "Yes." With Franklin as an advisor, I might be able to bring in a fresh perspective or challenge facts that were incorrect. And probably because I was thinking of Franklin, I said, "Do you believe in ghosts?"

He raised his brown eyes from studying the pen and checked to see if I were serious. "Well, I've had no personal experience. Mother hasn't haunted me." He grinned. "The only hauntings I've had come from those still alive." Now he abandoned the pen and opened his desk drawer to extract a post card. The decorative side showed a photo of the Florida Keys and the reverse side read:

"My dearest Neal,
    Do wish you were with me. I'm alone now. Have a condo. Call me 305/231/1717. Consider that an order.

                            Eternal love,

                            Dolores"

A peculiar feeling akin to jealousy, pricked. "This Dolores haunts you?"

"Yes. I brought it on, I guess." He shrugged. "After Mother died. . .Let's say I'd had limited experience with women and Dolores moved next door, rented the house. Some years older than I, divorced, mother of five mostly grown children, she was assertive." He laughed. "Anytime she wanted something, she'd say, 'consider that an order.' And her tone was commanding. Anyway, she'd practically dragged me to the altar before I had sense enough to back off. After I insisted that I just wanted to be friends, she did rather haunt me. I'd come home from the museum and find her on my porch. I'd be at work and she'd call to breathe heavily. One evening I looked up from reading and saw her face mashed against my bedroom window. Fortunately, one of her children in Florida, convinced her to move there."

"Other loves?" I ventured. "A current woman friend?"

"No way. My lone adventure with Dolores has taught me that I'm destined to remain a bachelor."

We heard the front door open, so Neal rose. "Ah, here's one more reference about Franklin," and as he left the room, calling out to the visitor, "Good morning and welcome," I scanned the newspaper section he'd handed me. I couldn't find Franklin's name, but a column at the bottom of the page must be what Neal meant. It included a an item about Miss Corvay, resident of Port Costanza, a high school English instructor, who had resigned her job due to alleged improprieties as poetry judge and alleged improprieties with a high school student.

The yellowing newspaper crackled in my hands. This tied in with the letter in Neal's mother's trunk—that letter from Emma which I'd never mentioned to Franklin. Could the letter have some validity? Could Franklin have charmed—or more—Miss Corvay in order to win a poetry contest? I felt chilled. Had he also plagiarized a poem as Emma contended? Had he charmed—or more—that student, was it Celia? to pass a math class?

I restacked the newspaper and the literary journals on the corner of Neal's desk. The office wrapped me in a calming silence. And on the periphery of silence I heard Neal conversing with the visitor. *So*, I thought, *what does it matter if Franklin wrote poor poetry as an adolescent? What does it matter if he "charmed" younger and older women? That occurred decades ago. The Franklin of today is solely mine and is sincerely intense about writing poetry of substance.* I'd hold to that and not to thoughts that stirred and tried to ask, "Are you being charmed? Is Franklin using you?"

By the time I reached home, I'd squelched doubts about Franklin's past by repeating, "It doesn't matter. We change." So much depended on circumstances. If, for example, Dolores hadn't rented beside Neal, he'd not have had a woman's company (good or bad). If we'd not lived in Harding, Molly would not have met Steve, Dan would not have loved Sheila. If we'd not moved to Madison, I would never have encountered Franklin nor turned to writing poetry.

Clouds had moved in and the north room was dim when I attached the necklace. I lit the hurricane lamp. Bouquets of garden roses bloomed on each of the lamp's three successively larger bowls to cast rings across the desk and across a fraction of the rug. I liked to think of us forever drenched by the lamp's subtle power, secure within those boundaries.

"And the information?" he asked.

"Three "Laurel Wreath" journals with your poetry."

"That's it?" he put hands on his waist. "I won a contest and my poetry was featured in the local paper."

"It's all Neal found, at least for now."

Franklin chuckled. "When you have but one arm, it probably takes longer to unearth material." He paced along one side of the rug. "Shall we get to work?" He paced along the other side and now his black shoes shone within the illumined portion; now he moved away.

"Sight is more intimate," he said. "No, cross that out. And cross out 'eyes speak for bodies bound to others'."

As usual I proposed words. Many he accepted but even when I lined out our efforts I knew a completeness. If ever I were forced to leave or if Franklin went on to another destination, I wanted to remember this scene—joined together on work I valued with a man I loved in a room we'd designed.

Beyond the bathroom, the pendulum clock chimed twice. I settled back in the steamy water, enjoying the methodic striking of the hour, and I pictured the claw footed tub I'd like in the future.

The front door opened and I heard, "Kate?"

"In the tub."

"Okay if I come in?" Dan asked.

With tired steps he moved to the toilet, closed the lid, and as he sat down his shoes scuffed the tile and a bone popped in some joint. He looked at his fingers which he arranged in a teepee fashion. "Was detained in the City so didn't call Joe Keithly in time. Another interested party contacted them and second party will take it. It was a hot property. So, you needn't worry about moving right away."

Leisurely I descended the outside steps, my pace reflecting the contentment in which I'd basked since last week's reprieve as well as this pre-summer day languor. Halfway down the flight I paused beneath cypresses planted by Franklin and Amy. Branches interwove to form an arch, and I was grateful I'd declined Dan's offer to "prune that thicket."

From the front windows, Franklin had pointed out plants and bushes that survived from his day. Only a few had endured drought, flood, neglect, and pollution. But the cypresses persisted. "They prove the Chinese legend," Franklin said, "that cypresses have more vigor than other trees, and, therefore, are often planted on graves to strengthen the soul."

To the left on its post, the slanting black mail box contained advertisements, a bill, and a letter from Molly. I stuffed everything but her white envelope back into the box and ambled toward the library where I'd read the letter while waiting for Lorraine's lunch break.

The letter in my rear pocket seemed to issue its own directive, propelling me, regardless of the day's casualness, to hurry. How silly. If there were bad news, Molly would pick up the phone or e-mail Dan. But intuition told me that her letter wasn't filled with happy wedding chatter.

Spring floated through the library door which was propped wide by a desk chair. I waved to Lorraine behind the desk, but she barely nodded, intent on a complaining patron. "There's trash on these shelves. Filth. Nothing decent to read."

I chose a table near the magazine rack, close to the "S" periodicals: *Science Digest, Smithsonian, Sail, Saturday Evening Post, Scientific American, Sports Illustrated.* The covers, a montage of society's interests, blurred together. At the neighboring table a man folded a newspaper page. A fly buzzed. Would California's summer be as hot as Iowa's? The library had no air conditioning; neither did my house.

Quit stalling, Kate, and open the envelope.

"Dear Mother,

It's after midnight and Steve's gone home. Irma and Dexter are asleep. I should be, too, since tomorrow's another work day, but I'm too upset to sleep. Actually, I'm shocked and so if what I'm saying doesn't make much sense, it's because I don't have my feelings sorted out. Like I'm mad and bewildered and hurt and wondering if I can trust those I love, and then feeling sorry for you. Now let me say that it's not about the wedding. July six is still on. But I can't help but wonder if Steve will ever be like Dad. I mean when you married you must never have thought that what would happen would happen. And so besides being mad at Daddy, I wonder how I can keep Steve from messing around, or do all men mess around? And have you ever messed around or wanted to? I mean, I just never thought of my parents in that way. Sure, I know you and Dad have flaws, that you aren't always right, that you sometimes embarrass me and things like that, but to discover that your father has had an affair, might still be having one, well, that was part of the shock.

"Guess I should explain that today I was in the drugstore stocking a cosmetic shelf so had my back to the counter. The two women talking in one of the aisles never saw me, and I never saw them, which is unimportant. What's important is they were talking about Sheila and Hank splitting up. They said Dad and Sheila had an affair, that's why the insurance agency broke up and that's why you and Dad left town.

"Part of me kept saying that it was gossip, but part of me knew it was true. It explained the sudden move and everything. During the afternoon I considered lots of stuff, but I kept remembering when you'd called right after you moved to Madison and how lonely you were. I'm sorry I didn't know what had happened. Maybe I could have said something better.

"And then I felt mad at you for not telling me, that I had to hear it this way and then I thought how lovely you looked at graduation and when I was telling all this to Steve, he agreed that you looked good. He said, "like someone in love, all soft like,' and then I wondered if you were having an affair."

I exhaled and glanced around the library, at the rows of books, the reproduced Stuart portrait of Washington above the exit sign, the discreet restroom notice, and finally at the desk where Lorraine, freed from the complainer, grinned and mouthed, "Three more minutes."

Her grin helped, and I returned to the binder paper with its sprawling penmanship.

"I don't expect you to tell me if you are 'involved,' because, I guess, at this point it doesn't really matter as long as it's just that. Oh, Mother, I don't want you and Dad to divorce. I don't want him to marry Sheila.

"I can't imagine either of you married to other people. Maybe I'm being selfish and immature, but if I am, I do have a favor. Please stay with Daddy through the wedding. I want you, no need you both, to be here.

"I've bought my dress. You know I was going to get something plain, but I saw this one in Des Moines, and I thought, *Mom will like this. It's Victorian.*"

CHAPTER NINE

The day resumed its somnolence as Lorraine and I strolled toward Mona's Café. As we passed the museum, Neal called through an open window, "Don't forget the historical society meeting tonight. The surprise issue is 'Adopt-A-Grave.'"

"Sounds jolly," Lorraine yelled as I promised, "See you then."

"You really intend to go?" Lorraine asked.

"With something like 'Adopt-A-Grave' at stake, how can I miss? Plus I don't care to stay home this evening."

"Danny boy?" She detoured around a pile of poop. "Someday you'll leave him."

"That's wild."

"Ah, Kate. That notion's been knocking around in some part of your brain ever since you got that lover. It's obvious Mr. Mysterious Franklin's for you. I don't know if he's married or not, but you and he are simpatico."

"That we are, and, no, he's single. It's just I have never consciously stated it—the leaving Dan, I mean."

Inside Mona's, we twisted around occupied tables to claim the lone corner spot. A wadded napkin uncurled upon hash browns, a spoon handle protruded from a bowl. Yet we zeroed in on the quarter and the dime by the ketchup bottle.

"Cheap tip," I said.

When the waitress scooped the coins into her pocket, Lorraine ordered, "A hamburger loaded with onions."

"No heavy date, huh?" I asked, observing the waitress's free hand deftly stack dirty dishes.

"You got it." Lorraine tilted her chair to balance on the rear legs.

"Same for you?" the waitress asked me.

"Minus onions."

"Lordy, girl, you're not seeing Franklin this afternoon?" Lorraine asked when the waitress left.

"Might."

"Doesn't this guy ever work?"

To avoid her direct gaze I studied the table top, its scattered bread crumbs and empty pepper shaker.

"As a writer, he doesn't keep regular hours."

"Can't figure a writer in Madison." The clunk of her front chair legs hitting the floor worked to underscore the question, "Published?"

"Not yet."

The waitress's arm came back into view and as she swabbed the table, I noticed fine hairs glistening above her wrist. Franklin had dark hairs or hairs that appeared coal black against his white, white skin.

When the woman left again, Lorraine said, "Hope he writes porno."

I laughed. "No, just poetry."

"Oh," she moaned, "even if he publishes, there's no money in poetry, so after you divorce Danny Boy, how will you and Franklin live? Does he have other income?"

I shook my head."

"How does he manage?"

"It's rather a hand-to-mouth existence."

"Which means you'll have to work."

Mugs, in which coffee sloshed like miniature tidal waves, plopped before us, followed by heavy plates.

"There'll be a clerk position open at the library soon."

I didn't pick up my sandwich. "You're quitting?"

"In six or seven weeks." She pawed through her duffle bag purse, clinking keys and dislodging a worn wallet before she slid a post card across the table.

"Lorraine: Update. Back mid-July with crew of one. Take care, Adam."

"Crew of one?"

"He's bringing a lady friend and wants the boat back. Fair enough. He's given me ample warning."

"Give him the boat. That doesn't mean you must quit your job. There are apartments, you know, like over Lonzo's Furniture Store by the railroad station. I've seen a 'For Rent' sign on a window. That shouldn't be expensive and it qualifies as unusual."

Lorraine rested her elbows on the table and propped her chin on doubled fists. "I'm gonna leave. If I stay I'll be committing a form of suicide. The abortion—the thoughts I had before it, the self-analysis afterward— crystallized everything." She sipped her coffee and surveyed the other diners. "When Peter came to the boat after the abortion, he was kind, solicitous, sorry. He stretched out on the other bunk and drank wine. He mused out loud, pondering a vasectomy because he and his wife wanted no more kids. I knew they still had sex so that didn't bother as much as did the point that his life's established, that he never intends to have children with anyone else. The more he drank, and he was feeling mellow about a court case, the more expansive he grew. He even said he was fortunate to be loved by two women.

"Taking those examples—barring other hints which over the months I've conveniently dismissed—it shows that I'm perfectly free to hang around and drool over Peter. God, what a name. Peter. Isn't that the first word you ever used for penis? It would be masochistic to continue. Then, when Adam's card arrived, I knew it meant time to move on."

"But I'll really miss you."

She grinned and rubbed her rough, callused hands across mine. "Mutual. But we'll keep in touch, and, Good Lord, you've got major events ahead— daughter's wedding, a job search, moving in with or marrying Franklin."

I pushed back beginning sadness to ask about the evening meeting. "I'll meet you there," she said. "Might be a kick."

Our strides matched for a block before she turned toward the harbor. Once alone, I re-examined her decision. Maybe something would change her mind, but I doubted it. Already I felt bereft, felt the anticipatory grief that had prepared me for other farewells. When rumor circulated that Dan and I were leaving Harding and friends expressed regret, I could see them removing me before I left.

In flashback I sit in a parents' meeting at Molly's school. Parents chatter and exclude me from discussing the spring money-raiser. Of course, I will not be part of it, but over and above that I perceive a certain weaning away, the same process terminal patients observe in regard to their families. With this subtle preparation, a little death, I could more easily hand the realtor our house key and kiss Molly goodbye. It would be thus with the time that remained with Lorraine.

I trudged up the hill. Perspiration beaded my upper lip and stained the armpits of my blouse. Impatient to read Molly's letter to Franklin, to tell him about Lorraine's news, I reached for the rosebud, but his instant words delayed mine.

"Katherine, I have it, the conclusion for 'Love on a Windy Day.'"

In the file folder that contained our nearly-completed works, I riffled through papers from a yellow legal pad with their assorted stanzas and extracted the poem.

"But words snagged on whipping trees, await a freeing wind," he said.

"Franklin, yes, yes, that's it."

He looked over my shoulder and read the entire poem aloud. "That was your inspiration, Katherine, to reverse the first two lines and thanks to you the next four lines work beautifully. We've done it."

Perhaps spurred by Lorraine's comment about publishing, I said, "Think I'll submit this to a magazine. Maybe to *New Poetry*," for I'd checked back copies from the library. Although Franklin's name would be on the book, for we'd decided that I'd explain that I found the collection in the north room closet, I'd written ninety percent of "Love on a Windy Day," so below the title in a firm hand I printed, "by Katherine Franklin Elliott."

Dan, late for dinner, was pre-occupied by an office problem, one I couldn't untangle. Apparently while other agents and a secretary had disagreed about a claim, an irate customer with a loosely-related interest had wandered in. In Dan's efforts at diversion or diplomacy, the cases became snarled and misunderstood. Therefore, I didn't mention Molly's letter and wasn't even sure Dan heard me say, "I'm off to the historical society meeting."

Through a watercolor evening with the sun a pink orange behind the hills, I drove to the post office and mailed, "Love on a Windy Day," before going to the meeting.

Mostly elderly women stood in random clusters on the museum's walkway, while on the porch, propped against a pillar, an unlit cigarette dangling from her lips, waited Lorraine.

"Here I was ready to wow you with a rebellious smoking act and you one-up me with your sparkle. You've seen Franklin."

"Mainly I'm sparkling because I mailed off a poem, one I largely helped him write."

By far the most casually dressed and the youngest, we took seats toward the back. I waved to Neal who sat in the front row beside the society's president. He made some facial expression I couldn't interpret, but I sensed he was glad to see me. He looked nice in a blue shirt and it wasn't until later that I realized I'd not noticed the dangling empty sleeve.

The president introduced the guest speaker, a thin man with a high voice, intent on describing Madison a century ago. I copied key words, so I could ask Franklin questions. He then could detail the vineyards that once dotted hills and tell me about the four families who'd owned wine companies. Had Franklin talked with the Delios, the Viatris, the Lucidos, the Gallis? Had he ridden his horse across their land? Speaker dwelt on the beneficial climate, soil, terrain, and shook his head in sorrow over the last winery. The Lucidos pre-1900 plantings continued to bear fruit. Possibly those plantings, which Franklin had passed, produced today. The thought pleased me.

To generous applause he ended his speech, but before the audience could stir, the president said, "One important item of business. For years we've deplored the sorry condition of our pioneer cemetery. With minimal city/county funding we've been helpless while weeds have covered graves. We've sorrowed when vandals defaced, removed, or smashed markers."

Murmurs from the group supported her Pentecostal fervor.

"Therefore, why don't each of us adopt a grave? Be responsible for the upkeep—not cost, mind you, no need to purchase new stones, for instance. But we can pull weeds, repair fences around those plots that have them, periodically can decorate."

"Here, here," and one white-haired man partially rose from his chair.

Swiftly a proposed motion was passed and the president borne on enthusiasm clapped her hands. "We have pictures of some graves. You may recall when Eva Norchowski and Mary Dryer mapped the various plots. In the process they took slides. Some graves need little attention, but t.l.c. is never amiss. Then, if those present tonight would sign up for a particular grave, the adoptions will be finalized."

Laughter and a conversational buzz ensued before the lights went out and the first slide wavered across the screen. A woman to my left called out, "That's Hiram Jackson's, the first sheriff. I'd like that one."

"All yours, Mrs. Monelli," and the president scribbled in her book.

Perhaps it was the tenth slide that showed the Elliott plot. Due to the camera's angle, Franklin's tombstone was most prominent.

"I'll take that one," I said.

"You're?"

"Kate Andrews, a new member."

Another slide clicked into the projector, another volunteer agreed, and the president's pen kept scratching. After I spoke, I felt Lorraine's stare, but I concentrated on the screen. When the show ended I listened to plans about a work party. Then leaving the others to their drawn-out goodnights and mouthing, "See you," to Neal, trapped by several talkative women, Lorraine and I took off.

"Give me a ride, and I'll give you some wine," she said.

As we rode through Madison's deserted streets she said nothing more. Strangely reserved, she didn't remark when I bounced across the railroad tracks and appropriated two parking spaces at the marina. Had I hurt her feelings? Did she think me silly to join the old people on the graveyard campaign? She unlocked the pier gate and through a saltwater-air darkness we walked to *The Eden*.

On deck I chose my favorite seat because to my right I could see Madison and its lights. To my left lay the inky expanse of water. From below, Lorraine brought wine, jelly jars, and jackets with their musty odor. I tossed one around my shoulders aware that it no longer smelled peculiar, but right.

I passed through the usual stages of adjusting to this wine—bought, she'd said for just over a dollar a gallon at some Berkeley co-op which experimented with pressing, fermenting, and bottling.

"Okay," I asked, "what's wrong?"

"I have a weird feeling and am not sure how to express it. But when that slide flashed on the Elliott graves and you immediately spoke up—"

"Franklin Elliott built our house."

"Franklin. Elliott. That's exactly it. Your 'lover' is named Franklin, an uncommon name. Your Franklin writes poetry as did the 'original.' So tell me where your lover lives, not address, just approximately. This sounds dumb, but—"

In one gulp I emptied the jar's contents. Its bitterness burned as I answered, "He lives with me."

A long pause separated us.

"Kate, you mean you've been teasing. He's a made-up lover."

"No, he's real."

"What?"

"He comes to me as a physical being."

A round of silence briefly cushioned us, and I surveyed the town lights, so like fireflies. But when Lorraine spoke, she said sharply, "Tonight we're on different wave lengths or something. Have some more wine and then go on. When and where did you meet Franklin, 'lover' Franklin?"

I should have lied, should have said, "It's a coincidence each has an identical name, and it's uncanny that each is creative." Yet, tonight I wanted to be honest with my closest woman friend. "I realize how bizarre this will sound, but try and listen with an open mind. It began shortly after we moved in." With a voice surprisingly even, surprisingly decisive, I spilled out everything.

Except for pouring wine, Lorraine didn't move, and when I stopped she remained immobile. The lone sound came from a boat horn blasting a signal at the harbor entrance.

"I'll counter with a story." Lorraine spoke cautiously as if selecting vocabulary with care. "When I was growing up, Sam and Martha, an older couple, lived next door. Reliant on each other, they didn't mingle much with anyone. They had an intact life, no kids, a pleasant home. Martha liked me and on occasional summer afternoons invited me into their kitchen to sip lemonade. The room stayed cool and a little dim. Lined in knotty pine, it was more refined I thought than our papered walls at home.

"I must have been about twelve when Sam suddenly died, a heart attack in his back yard shop. Neighbors wondered how Martha would manage, but, as in the past, she kept to herself. Whenever anyone saw her she acted gracious, but distant.

"One evening, maybe six months after Sam's death, Mom sent me to borrow an egg. Through the back door I saw Martha at the table eating dinner. But the table was laid for another and she talked to the empty place, Sam's place. I wanted to back off but if I didn't get the egg, what would I tell Mom? And I didn't want Mom or anyone to learn about Martha and her pretend husband."

"Then after what I've said, you believe that Franklin's imaginary?"

Lorraine went on. "I made a lot of noise on the porch. When Martha unlatched the screen she was smiling, happy, and it came to me, what's wrong with what she's doing? Pretending Sam was there gave meaning to her days. When I got older I could appreciate additional advantages. Martha controlled that relationship. She could devise whatever she desired. Much more satisfying than the typical man-woman situation in which you cope or react. Invisible Sam was fine for her. And, Franklin, yes, I do think you've invented him, has been good for you."

I clanked the jelly jar against a stay as I leaned forward to protest, "But I haven't made him up. Look at the proof, his picture in the museum."

"Kate, simply because a photo shows a person with a resemblance to someone you've fantasized isn't proof. Hey, you read a book and think about the character. When the movie is released, you say, 'My gosh, that's him.'

"You asked me to have an open mind. I ask the same of you. I'm no psychology student but I think that traits you've projected onto Franklin are ones within yourself that you don't recognize. This handsome male encourages your writing talent, provides you with an unbiased appraisal of your marriage, your life, your child. Shortly, you'll be able to drop him."

"Like a toddler outgrowing his security blanket?"

"Damn, I'm doing this badly, but, in a way, yes. You throw away crutches when the foot's healed and it's time to walk."

The taff rail pressed against my back, and I squinted upward at the mast where tail-tells dangled limply. "You don't think there's the slightest chance Franklin lives, that he might truly be a ghost?"

"Nope."

"Am I crazy? Think I should see a shrink?"

"Again, no. You've developed a creative solution which temporarily works. Like taking sleeping pills. At some point, although you may have slept, you realize life's a little out of kilter if you're zonked on sedatives."

Her lucid ideas rained down making absolute sense. What if she was correct? My right hand with the empty jar shook as a dank breeze crested the water. Lorraine viewed life with clarity. She'd illustrated that ghosts, phantoms, are products of one's imagination. Needy, ignorant, superstitious people accept emanations and the supernatural. As she'd pointed out, I was needy.

"Face it, Kate," an inner voice (the one that spoke at the clinic) insisted, "you're a middle-aged woman. To attract a younger, virile man you'd have to fabricate him."

"You okay?" Lorraine asked.

"Sure, am grateful for your frankness."

"Do this for me," and in the dark her jacket rustled as she leaned toward me, "tell yourself repeatedly that the necklace has no power. Put it on. Convince yourself that it's merely jewelry and you'll see nothing. That will prove you're strong, that you can stand alone, that you can write, that you can do anything." She laughed. "By then, if you want a real guy, you'll find him."

As she accompanied me to the gate, she linked her arm with mine. "I've read some of those ghost chaser books. Actually find them amusing. But even if you took their 'facts' seriously, those 'experts' report that spirits don't assume human form, don't speak with our voices, much less have sex."

When I reached for the door handle, she hugged me. "You know, I think it would be good if you went ahead with this Adopt-a-Grave business. Working on Franklin's plot will reinforce that he's dead."

"Sure, thanks." If my smile was forced, in the blackness she wouldn't notice. I started the car engine and backed toward the road, but as I steered around the curve, my foot fell from the gas pedal and tears blurred my vision. Why couldn't she have accepted my story? Share my belief that Franklin inhabited my house? Why couldn't she rejoice with me?

From some sealed compartment, a childhood scene assumed shape. After frustrating hours at school I'd completed a painting. With fingers cramped and clumsy from holding the brush I'd applied color upon color. I'd even cried in frustration, but a week before Christmas the painting came together. I carried it home, a gift for my parents. I didn't wrap it until Christmas Eve so that each day I could admire my princess in an enchanted forest alive with beauty. I anticipated Mother and Dad's pleasure, visualized the picture hanging over the couch, the first thing guests would notice upon entering our living room. It would be the welcome note when I arrived home every afternoon.

That Christmas Eve I hardly slept. In gray dawn, in robe and gown, I pressed my package upon them. Tearing off the twine, Dad laughed, and I clenched my teeth against a hurt too big to handle.

"Honey, what is it?" Mom asked.

Aware he'd injured my feelings, Dad said quickly, "You've used lots of bright colors."

While we unwrapped other presents, ate dinner, and drove to my cousin's house, I fought to smile.

Mom taped the picture in a kitchen corner, one designated for school work. On December 26 with my parents' vision, I analyzed my drawing. The forest and the princess I'd seen so well had been replaced by brilliant crude shapes. Conscious of my parents' love, knowing they'd never intentionally hurt me, I knew they were right. In the same manner, my friend, prompted by the best of motives, had given me pain, but she must be right.

I wound past sleeping stores and headed up my hill. After parking, I peered at the house. Dan had left the porch light on. "How kind," I muttered, but the sentiment was shallow and I felt shallow, bombarded by doubts I thought I'd laid to rest.

Doubts, however, attached themselves in parasitic fashion and feeling drained, I stepped into the entry way. To my left, Dan worked at his computer in the small office.

"Left the coffee pot on for you," he called.

"Thanks." I got my mug and then faced the kitchen stool. Had I invented Franklin's involvement with that stool? Impossible. I couldn't have sanded, painted, and yet, wasn't I guilty of previous distortions, guilty of selling myself short? I steadied myself against the sink. Madison stretched beyond the uncurtained windows. On that dark night, months ago, I'd stood here, and what? In deep unhappiness conjured a man to free me from despair? Channeled a powerful hunger toward false nourishment?

I set the mug on the drain board and rehearsed Lorraine's disclaimer. "There is no Franklin. There is no power in the necklace."

"If Franklin's an invention, Kate, do you want a life without him?" questioned that inner voice.

"There is no Franklin. There is no power in the necklace."

"You've gone this route before," the voice said, "and then all over again you convinced yourself."

"There is no Franklin. There is no power in the necklace."

"Don't you have a duty to discover truth, though others may not see it, to learn from your passage on earth?"

"There is no Franklin. There is. . .."

When sunshine flickered across my face, I flopped onto my stomach. Better it were a clouded day, one to match my mood, for loveliness shouted to be shared. Slowly I crossed to the dresser where I'd put Molly's envelope. I'd not shared its contents with Dan last night, for he'd stayed at the computer long after I'd gone to bed. I glanced at the clock. In Harding it would be nearly nine."

"Mom, did you get my letter?"

"Yesterday. Are you free to talk?"

"Irma and Dexter are in the vegetable garden, but in a few seconds I have to leave for work."

"I'm glad you wrote."

"And Dad?"

"Haven't had a chance to show him your letter, but, yes, the gossip's true. Hank found out about the affair last Christmas. There went the partnership. That's why we moved. And, you're right, I was crushed."

"Now?"

"I'm fine."

"Oh, Mom." Relief pulsed through the connection. "Then there's no chance you guys will divorce?"

"We'll be there for your wedding."

"After I mailed the letter I did more thinking and can understand why you didn't tell me. I mean, you probably thought, 'why screw up her senior year, make Molly think less of her dad'. Right?"

"Right."

"But why? Why did Dad?"

"I can't answer that."

"It wasn't fair to ask you if you were having an affair, but I was upset."

"It's okay. I don't mind. There's no one." And my throat ached.

Molly, now freed of concern, spoke about her dress, the shoes she intended to buy, how the minister's wife had promised to belt out Lohengrin's march on the out-of-tune Baldwin.

After the conversation, I dressed before going upstairs. For a moment I hesitated on the north room's threshold. If there were such things as vibrations, the room hummed with them. I rubbed moist palms upon my blouse and marched to the closet. For hard minutes I regarded the necklace and then spoke distinctly. "There is no power in the necklace." And to demonstrate my strength I'd sit at my desk and complete a stanza. I, Kate Andrews, was capable of writing. I'd select a subject far removed from love.

I'd write of death, and by mid-morning I re-read my effort:

> Breathe laughter onto hollow bones
> Your breath returns
> Dress skeletons with warmth
> and coldness clothes your hands
> Whisper memories against a silent ear
> hear echoes of your own response
> So cradle fast your oneness
> against the graveyard's door.

I could rearrange, revise, and develop something potent. Lorraine was correct, but kneading my forehead, I wished for a surge of happiness in such knowledge.

As I tread back and forth across the gray rug, I resisted memories. I must reinforce the truth that this was my rug, my room, my writing, and that I could do it. With each step assurance increased. Easier it became to repeat, "There is no Franklin. There is no power in the necklace."

I neared the closet shelf. Why not toss out the jewelry? However in my palm the rose bud nestled, a special item. I'd keep it. Perhaps in some distant year, wear it. It would mark forever a turning point, an overcoming. Fired with resolve, I placed it around my neck. I needn't speak the declaration, for I felt my own capability in the marrow of my bones.

"Katherine." He didn't touch me, but his eyes and voice conveyed his love, his need. "Please, please don't desert me."

CHAPTER TEN | JULY

*I*talian cypress and eucalyptus trees deflected morning heat and their shade, like a canopy over a perpetual graveyard chill, gave an illusion of coolness. To arrange yellow rosebuds, ones Franklin had clipped from the gazebo's trellis, I had come early to the Elliott plot. At this hour, too, I hoped to avoid society members who had adopted nearby graves and who had competed with one another to tell family histories during the previous clean-up day.

At the last historical society meeting these same individuals had seemed to surround me when we "adopters" had voted to decorate graves for the upcoming Fourth of July holiday after the Madison Independence Day Committee had proclaimed "a simple Fourth", a day with picnics, softball games, sack races, community sings, and walking tours—including one of the cemetery.

Dan choked on his breakfast toast with that news. "Tour a graveyard? Now doesn't that sound fun."

I smiled. "It won't appeal to everyone, but one of our oldest members knows who's buried where. As the tour goes through the cemetery—and it is lovely there, Dan—different guides will relate capsule histories on the more important or interesting persons interred and will point out how tombstone carvings have evolved, how stones reveal status."

"I'll pass," he said as would both of us, for on the third we'd board a plane to fly to Iowa and Molly's wedding.

Today, July second, I'd avoid the official work party and go home to pack.

The graveyard appeared empty. One other car was parked in the graveled lot, but I saw no sign of its occupants as I stepped on twigs and acorns that littered the packed adobe soil.

Passing the column topped by a white angel I neared the plainer, more dignified Elliott markers. Little had changed in the month since I'd been here. No weeds grew. Removing browned flowers left from the first clean-up effort, I laid the touch of yellow on the grave of Franklin's mother.

"Oh, Kate." I whirled around Maybe 100 yards away and from the next line of tombstones, an arm waved. Neal stepped around a triangular shaped obelisk. As he walked in my direction I realized that the parked car was his. So he did drive. I must ask if he'd waited until Mother died before he learned.

"I've missed you," he said, and as I said, "Ditto," I was surprised to find that I really had. Teddy Bear man deserved his name in many respects.

"Kept hoping you'd drop by the museum or my house," and he motioned for us to move into shade bent by the mausoleum. We slid down onto the hard-packed warm soil and rested our backs against the solid, cool stone.

"Mother would approve," he said, and when I arched an eyebrow, he laughed. "One of her theories was about hot and cold, meaning that you must balance temperatures. For instance, if you ate ice cream at the same time you must drink a hot beverage—coffee, cocoa, or tea."

"Yep, she would approve," I agreed placing my palm against the heated earth and then pressing it against the wintered stone.

"She'd also approve of my efforts at cleaning up our family plot for the Fourth."

"You're avoiding the work party?" I took off my straw hat to fan my face.

"I've had enough contact with work party members throughout the year," and in a falsetto he said, "Oh, Neal, here's Papa's blue ribbon from the 1920 county fair. I just know its final home should be in the museum." He squeaked a few notes higher. "I've brought a rusting soda can. It must be historic."

As he continued, my laughter built. How cleansing is a belly laugh. *What a tie shared humor brings*, I thought, as he laughed so hard he couldn't formulate another example.

We relaxed against the mausoleum and stared at the Strait below and before us. Calm water today. Only an occasional sailboat with sails reefed. Probably he'd comment on Madison's nautical past, bring in how vessels once dotted the water, but he seemed content to sit quietly. "It must be hard," I said, "dealing with individuals who think that their family mementoes are worthy of inclusion in the museum."

From the corner of my eye I watched the mid-section of his gray T-shirt rise and fall over the roll around his waist. "Even historical society members are prone to believe that anything old is valuable merely because of its age.

About a year ago, at one of our programs, an appraiser did a spin off from 'Antique Road Show.' Fantastically popular program—we picked up about 50 new members—but the crap that people dragged in was—" As he searched for a descriptor, he brushed an ant from his slacks.

So I launched into possible adjectives, "Stunning, unbelievable, incalculable, unpredictable. . ."

"I'll pick incalculable," and he laughed.

Now coming into view a tug boat guided a freighter. In silent agreement, we watched it come abreast and watched the tugboat at the aft swing the ship to port. "If I had had both arms, I'd have gone to sea, or done something around water. I admire captains, tug boat captains."

And since his voice held no bitterness I didn't respond, just studied the tug as it maneuvered the vessel and was aware that never in Harding, Iowa, would I have even dreamt of ships or of a strait.

"I do want to include a healthy segment about shipping in the Madison history booklet."

"The booklet you mentioned?"

He nodded and with an apologetic smile inched away from me. "My bulk. Hot soil." Neal shrugged. "Yes, the booklet's what I want to talk about. The Madison Foundation Board distributes money bequeathed from former families, one of whom is the Elliotts. The board requests that local agencies apply for funds. For example, last year the Rotary obtained money for park benches in the downtown. The year before a conservation group proposed salvaging a wetland, and the board donated funds. So the historical society president—yes, Julia who wants Papa's blue ribbon displayed—pitched a dramatic plea and won them over."

At the same moment that I smiled I saw that the ant he'd brushed from his slacks had returned with a party to invade my jeans. I rose to brush my rump and as Neal positioned his arm against the ground to propel himself upward, I asked, "That means guaranteed financing for the booklet?"

On this slanted hillside I looked up to see him nod. "At subsequent meetings, the board will demand specifics, and because it's summer the board doesn't meet until September, which gives us time to prepare an outline."

At his feet a pebble rolled. "So I have the job?"

He extended his arm and we shook hands. "Come by later this month, and we'll talk."

"Thank you, Neal. Thank you."

He squeezed my hand. "We'll work well together, Kate."

Excitement didn't surface until I drove away. Without my seeking it, I had been offered a job. Someone trusted my abilities. Unless I counted high school baby sitting, I'd never held a job. As a young married I'd taken care of a neighbor's kids one summer, had fed pets and watered houseplants when friends vacationed, but a real job—

Near the library I pulled into a parallel parking slot; then laughed when I left the car and regarded the angle. I was at least two feet from the curb. "Oh, what the hell," I said to the world, "give me a ticket."

While Lorraine spoke into the phone, I waited beside the counter and my elbow nudged against a stack of returned books. When I read the top title, *Mysticism and You*, I glanced away. Must avoid any apparent interest in mysticism, a subject that Lorraine and I had painstakingly shunned since I'd foolishly confessed my "romantic fantasy."

Often I'd met her for lunch at Mona's, and one Friday we attempted to sail but when the wind died, she'd started the diesel and powered back to the marina. We discussed where Lorraine might go after Madison, talked about Peter, batted back and forth advantages/disadvantages of divorcing Dan, virtually dissected Molly, debated national issues, compared impressions of authors, mined nuggets from childhood, but we skirted clear of ghosts.

However, there were veiled references. "You're looking great, but are you *really* okay?" I assured her I was, that I'd come to terms with "my problem."

Yet coming to terms with Lorraine's departure was another matter. During June, because Franklin and I were writing well, I'd spent less time with her. In the deep of night, when thinking is clearer, I evaluated our friendship, attributing it to Lorraine's honesty, humor and courage, but one afternoon while Franklin paced debating between "blessed" or "happy" in one line, I thought that in some indefinable manner, Lorraine gave of herself.

With Irma Hawkins, for instance, I was conscious of others in her background: husband, relatives, friends. She never emerged distinctly from that network. The Rivera women—Connie, Peg, and Beth—had if not identical personalities, then ones that blended into each other, so they had but leftovers to hand me. Lorraine brought to our friendship a single-mindedness, a totality.

"What's going on?" Lorraine, off the phone, re-introduced me to the present.

Pushing the limits of library quiet, I spilled out the sequence in the cemetery, and she said, "Fantastic. Damn, wish we could go celebrate."

"I don't have time anyway, need to go home and pack."

"Right. Tomorrow's the big fly-out day. Hey, what did you decide? The lime green or the blue dress?"

"Chicken me, I'm taking both. Molly can pick."

Possibly the library's atmosphere calmed me, or maybe sharing my excitement helped dissipate it, but, more likely, the subject of the dresses was responsible for deflating enthusiasm. It reminded me of an incident with Dan.

On a Saturday when he was particularly edgy, checking his e-mail every few minutes until I wished that Sheila would please contact him, I said, "I'm off to shop for a mother-of-the-bride dress."

"I'll come along."

He never shopped with me. He disliked crowds and gift selections, but when I objected, he said, "It'd be good to get out of the house." Perhaps he was subscribing to the watched-pot-never-boils rationale, hoping that Sheila would send a message while he was gone.

En route to the mall, though, his monologue tracked, as it had since May, trouble at the office, that complicated situation I didn't comprehend. "Okay, so I did mess up, didn't handle it right, but that's not enough reason for Jerry to favor Clark, to direct contacts his way. I goofed, but damn it, Jay, Martin, and Clark needn't treat me like a leper. They no longer refer to golf, to lunch, to drinks."

Not one of the wives had phoned me, I recalled, since Beth's dinner in May.

"Course they think I also fouled up by not buying the Keithly house. Appears they've written you and me off."

"If we'd moved they wouldn't have 'written us off'?"

"Doubt it. They see me as incapable of getting my act together to snap up that property. I've muddied the office predicament. Two strikes." He braked at a stop light. "I'll get out before the third. I can't be fired or asked to resign. I'll leave before that happens."

Leave. The word dropped between us, and we let it lie like an invisible rider in the front seat. In previous exchanges we'd circled the issue of the future, neither of us quite willing to face it. Could we indefinitely continue in this half life? Was it better if he went to Sheila? Try a separation? How would I support myself? I was still a stranger in Madison and my one friend was moving. Then there was Molly and her plea that Dan and I stay married. We had shared history and that counted heavily. With such weighty thoughts, Macy's at the mall looked positively frivolous.

We wandered through a variety of stores, and I found nothing until Dan—I suspect weary of everything and eager to get home—said, "This is you." He took a blue dress from the rack. With pleated skirt that added inches to waist and hips and with a beaded bodice, it was, "A typical mother-of-the-bride dress," I moaned.

"Isn't that what we're after?"

"I want something attractive, not so matronly."

"Well, try it on at least."

When I emerged from the dressing room a clerk, scenting a sale, waited beside Dan to praise the dress as I revolved before a three-way mirror. The color flattered me, and for this small ceremony did it matter? Whatever I chose it wouldn't conflict with Mrs. Iderson's outfit and I wasn't trying to rival the bride. I took it.

Three days later, however, when I went with Lorraine to pick up a diesel part in Port Costanza, I spotted a lime green dress in a boutique window. We swung around to study it through the VW windshield. A princess style with high lace collar, it crossed several centuries.

"Buy it," Lorraine urged.

"Naw." Dan shook his head when I modeled it for him.

"Molly's dress is Victorian."

"Big deal. It looks wrong on you."

As the saleswoman's remarks had altered my perception of the blue dress, so Dan's response altered my concept of the green. Consequently I'd pack both.

I drove home from the library and gathered mail from the box. Once inside the house's shadowy coolness I noticed the return address, New Poet, so I made a jagged skyline of the envelope flap as I fumbled for the letter.

"Dear Katherine Franklin Elliott:

Thank you for submitting, 'Love on a Windy Day,' to *New Poet*. We have tentatively scheduled it for the October issue. Upon publication you'll receive complimentary copies. We appreciate your thinking of us and invite you to send future submissions.

Sincerely,

Theodore Barton
Editor

I read every syllable slowly, then read each out loud before I yelled, "Franklin."

"My word, Katherine," he said. "We've done it. It's the beginning."

He gathered me close and in the face of the day's miracles I forgot to pack, forgot to notify the newspaper to stop delivery, forgot to tell the post office to hold our mail. Instead, I spent the afternoon on the gray rug, drinking wine, memorizing the letter, talking poetry, and loving Franklin whose pleasure about breaking into print on a national level thrilled him. "And Elliott. It will be published under Franklin Elliott, an entree for my book."

Groggy, slightly hung over, I awoke to the alarm. Dan jammed feet into his shoes and brusquely knotted his tie. Sleep had refused to ease last night's hostility, spawned by a bad day at work, a jackknifed truck that stalled freeway traffic for hours, and a deliriously silly wife with empty suitcases and no dinner ready.

When I proudly produced my letter he said, "What's this all about?"

"About me. My poem's going to be published. Look out, big time, here I come."

He didn't smile. "That's not your name, not even your maiden name."

"I used it to honor the poet who built our house."

"What's wrong with Andrews? Have you written something you don't want anyone to know you wrote?"

I grabbed a copy of the poem from my desk and sailed it like a paper glider onto the table. He was not amused.

I heated a skillet, slapped cheese that was slightly greenish around the edges between buttered slices of bread and tossed the sandwiches into the frying pan.

"What does this mean? I don't get it." His stocky finger tapped at the words, "Love filled my skirt."

"Forget it, Dan," and before he could destroy my "masterpiece," I said, "Something else wonderful happened. I have a job."

Incredulous, he stared as I tore lettuce into odd sizes and shredded carrots into a skimpy salad. I explained about Neal and the booklet.

"Your salary?"

"I didn't ask," and when he clucked his tongue against the roof of his mouth, I knew he was thinking how naïve I was not to have immediately established wages. I scooped sandwiches onto plates and dumped dressing on the salad. "Dan, the important thing is that someone believes I can handle a writing assignment. The offer itself is the principle here. And rather than quibbling about what lines mean or what pen name I choose, can't you understand that having a poem published is unbelievably thrilling?"

He nodded, picked up his sandwich, and as a variant on apologizing said, "Am having a hard time accepting this stupid wedding."

It was my turn to nod.

But day's energy refused to slacken. Like a wind-up toy, I kept whirling. Without a list of what to take I flung clothes and cosmetics into a bag, vaguely recommended shirts and pants for Dan to pack and about nine, with restlessness still goading me, I said, "I must see Lorraine."

He regarded me strangely, and I studied him, trying to impose the figure of the young Dan I'd loved upon this middle-aged man. If I could catch a glimpse, even of the laughter we once shared, perhaps it would help, but before me was a disappointed near-stranger with a gaze that shifted toward the computer room.

Through the downtown section the Plymouth and I trailed a pickup loaded with teenagers. The noisy beat from their CDs whipped inside my opened windows. I envied their united dedication to the sound. Interesting, I mused for lack of a better word, how music defines decades.

Behind the truck I swung into the marina parking lot, full on this summer night. Squeals, young voices, beer cans hitting gravel bound them into a place, a time, denied me.

Finding the dock gate unlocked, I carried my letter from *New Poet* like a precious gift across the uneven pier. But *The Eden* bobbed in darkness. I called out a couple times but Lorraine didn't answer, so on the back of a deposit slip I wrote about the poem's acceptance. After wedging the note in the closed hatchway, I rested on the deck.

I'd miss moments like this, lulled by the sedation of water. No, tonight I wouldn't flirt with sadness. I'd listen to a fishing skiff chug through the break water and the burst of giggles from B pier.

Now in cool-silvered morning, Dan's every move reflected distress, which I'd not compound by admitting that mail and newspapers would accumulate next week.

We climbed into his car and rode without speaking until on the freeway, Dan cursed. "See that slow-up ahead? Every morning, same thing. Sometimes I think I'll have a heart attack fighting this commute traffic."

I could but answer, "I'm sorry."

In such non-communicative fashion we flew to Iowa, and when we landed in Des Moines, he stepped into the airplane aisle jam packed with other passengers. I took my time gathering up purse and book so that I, next-to-the-last person off the plane, wandered alone into the moist July heat. How rapidly I'd forgotten humidity. Mugginess clung as I put one foot before the other, intent on enduring this span of days until I could return to me.

CHAPTER ELEVEN

Once more I inhaled Molly's clean, good scent and felt her lovely suppleness, but this time I sensed a maturity. She released her hold on me and then Steve awkwardly hugged me before we piled into Steve's car. Molly draped a hand across his shoulder and with that intimate act I felt that without having witnessed a ceremony that they were married.

When her fingers flecked a stray black hair from Steve's forehead and his eyes locked with hers in some private interchange, a vein jerked in Dan's neck. Ah, it would be up to me to speak so I inquired about Steve's family, about Irma, Dexter, and about the bridal shower.

"Oh, that," Molly laughed. "Well, Julie—she's going to be my bridesmaid, or have I told you that? Anyway, she utterly surprised me. See, I got ready to go with Steve. We drove a few miles and then—" they laughed in tandem, "Steve said he must've left his wallet at the Hawkins. He wheels around and heads back. I say, 'But you never took your wallet out. Check your pockets.'"

Once more they roared.

"She began trying to feel in my pockets." Steve picked up the story. "I drove like a maniac before she could discover I had it and before she could get suspicious. When we walked into the Hawkins' living room, she about keeled over."

"Everyone had parked on side streets so I didn't suspect a thing. They jumped up yelling, 'surprise,' and I just bawled. Since we're having such a little wedding and not inviting kids from school, I didn't think it was right to have a shower and I'd told Julie not to. But we really had fun. Oh, sure, Irma had us play some stupid games and one girl made a dumb bouquet out of bows from the packages, but the cake tasted yummy and we laughed tons and I got, we got—" she flashed a smile at Steve, "some neat presents. Cookie sheets and a rolling pin, a clock, salad bowls. I can show you some, but most are stored at the Idersons. When Steve and I have our own place,

I can use them."

If mothering had died, caring certainly hadn't, for I winced at her yearning.

"By winter when things slow down on the farm we might be able to move to town," Steve said. "It'll be easier for Molly to get to her job, and I can drive out to help Dad."

"Her drugstore job." Dan's voice was flat.

"After Labor Day I'm on permanent and we'll have more income."

Before such news, Dan remained silent.

The "Welcome to Harding" sign appeared on the right. Slowing, we traveled by familiar houses along Main Street. With eyes shut I could have directed Steve, "Take a right at the next corner, slow for the dip, swing left in three blocks for the Hawkins."

As the car came to a standstill, Irma ran from her sentry post near the front door. "Look at you, Kate. Prettier than before." She spread her arms wide to include Dan and me. "What's your wife's secret? Steve, take their bags. . .Dexter, they're here. You must be exhausted. Dex-ter."

We lurched through welcomes, disjointed sentences and patches of noise. With false stops and starts we achieved the front room and then repeated the jerky greeting process with Dexter.

"Set your luggage back here." Irma pointed behind her. "'Course, you know that." And we shuffled toward the guest room where Dan closed the door.

"Live on that farm, work at that two-bit drugstore. Damn it, this whole thing's idiotic," he exploded.

Unzipping the suitcase, I tried to shake wrinkles from a bunched skirt.

"If she'd been with us this wouldn't have happened."

"For heaven's sakes, Dan—" but just then Molly tapped on the door.

"Want to see my dress?" she asked. "Uh, oh, this is a bad moment."

Bits from her letter where worry limned each phrase leaped into my mind, so I smiled. "Yesterday was an exciting day followed by a short night."

"Yeah, your mother's a poet, going to be published."

Molly's eyes widened. "Published? Like in a magazine?"

"*New Poet*, and the editor will look at more submissions."

"All right! Maybe you'll be on TV, on Oprah." So much for my daughter's congratulations. In her frame of reference, poetry came with the baggage of schoolrooms, difficult stanzas and sonnets penned by Shakespeare.

"For some reason your mother's writing under another name."

"Wow, Dad, you're sounding hostile."

"Then," and I piled my underwear on the bed and reached for my blouses, "I have a job, am going to help write Madison's history."

"For money?" She wrinkled her forehead, and I nodded.

"What's the problem?" she asked Dan. "I read this article in a magazine at the drugstore about men who are threatened by their wives. You changed your lifestyle and Mom went along with it. I think you'd be understanding about her changing hers."

Unnecessary for Molly to say more. Deftly she had introduced Sheila, deception, and the spectrum of hidden emotions, so I'd switch tactics and go see her dress.

I ushered Molly into the hallway and into the room she'd claimed for the last six months. Today it was almost as bare as when she'd carted in her belongings. Gone from walls were pictures and posters prominent in May. The bulletin board was denuded of thumb tacked notes, letters, clippings, and photos. Steve's graduation picture smiled from a clean dresser top where a hair dryer, brush and eye make up lay near the mirror Cardboard boxes stood opposite her bed.

"Stark, isn't it? But, as I said, nearly everything's at Steve's. Just three more days to go."

"Nervous?"

"No. Oh, Mother, I love him so much—" We cocked our heads hearing Irma's footsteps, and as Irma entered Molly brought from the closet a white gown sheathed in translucent plastic.

"Kate, you're going to love this. It has a touch of romance." And Molly lifted the wrapper on white tailored organdy with lace inserted at the neck, a detail duplicated on my green outfit.

"She's stunning in it," Irma said. "Wish you could have been here to shop with her, to attend the shower, but I did enjoy substituting for you."

Some part of me thirsted for the special magic in those events, ones I'd renounced for Franklin, permanently renounced, for although Molly might remarry, she'd never go through this particular experience again. As I fingered the cloudy soft material of her dress I remembered tension that colored my own wedding preparations.

On a "high" I glided through days oblivious of everything but gifts and details, of diplomatically persuading Aunt Jane to leave her undisciplined son at home, and of checking items off endless lists. Sleep hid the night before the ceremony. Without concern about the future, untroubled over promises, I worried instead about fainting at the altar. . .the organist striking a discord. . .the cake damaged in transit...a bridesmaid tripping. . .the photographer not showing. I wanted external loveliness, desired an untainted memory, a drop of romantic fiction to store against flawed reality.

The service fulfilled my expectations. Each candle shed purity. With feeling the soloist sang *The Lord's Prayer* and *I Love You Truly*. Attendants and pictures, refreshments and decorations, blessings and conversations were ideal.

"You approve, Mom?" Molly asked, and I was back in the Hawkins' bedroom.

"Absolutely. It's superb. I've brought two dresses. You'll have to help choose between them."

As she replaced her dress in the closet, she outlined the simple ceremony. Then, as if dinner were more essential than wedding plans, she guided Irma and me into the kitchen. Her guidance, too, channeled conversation toward the swimming pool's closure for repairs, Charlotte Gibston's twins, the history teacher's prostate surgery, rumors that the bi-weekly *Harding Gazette* was for sale. Irma and Dexter nibbled on the gossip and fed with such a diet, I gained temporary sustenance.

"Dan," Irma said, passing him a platter of steaming roasting ears, "I ran into Hank Rawlins last week, told him you'd be back for Molly's wedding, and he said he'd sure like to talk with you."

I felt Molly's inaudible gasp, felt her stare while I selected a hot roll and reached for the butter knife.

"Sounds fine, Irma."

"Think he's missed you. Business hasn't been so good from what I hear. Course there was something with his wife," Dexter said. "She just up and filed for divorce. Moved out of state."

"The divorce final?" I asked.

He dipped one shoulder, his version of a shrug. "She's not come back this summer, that's all I know. Heard her sons went to visit. Hank's been seeing one of the elementary school teachers."

Effortlessly sentences flowed into teachers and their three-month vacation that so victimized tax payers.

"I'll get it." Irma scooted back her chair at the phone's first ring; then called, "For you, Dan."

After he left the room Molly and I stacked plates. Dexter sought the television, and I re-enacted a scene so traditional that I could curve my hands to carry dishes if none were available. This "clearing the table," seemingly as involuntary as sneezing, required the same degree of aptitude.

With the skill of an experienced surgeon selecting a scalpel, Irma extracted dish pan and detergent from the cupboard below the sink. Automatically she tightened her grasp on the faucets, and when a stream of water she'd determined at some distant date to be the correct flow hit the plastic pan, she stirred detergent into bubbles.

One rain-spattered night Lorraine and I, relaxed on *The Eden's* bunks, discussed the need for tradition and constancy. I argued that I no longer required the stability of daily routines. Hadn't relinquishing my daughter proved my adaptability? Yet, on second thought, perhaps I'd traded a Midwestern housewife pattern for another as Franklin and I followed a schedule. There was a regularity to our/my writing, and I wanted to create a traditional home.

"Mom, you're tuning out."

I smiled and took a dish towel from the drawer to Irma's right as she asked, "Steve dropping by tonight?"

"Nope, tonight's my night with Mom."

"You can't guess who that was?" Pleasure lightened Dan's step and his manner. "Hank."

"And?" Although I watched him, my hand selected another rinsed glass to dry.

"Wants to see me. Isn't that something?" He paused, conscious of Molly and Irma. "Well, I'm meeting him for a beer."

"Give him my best."

After Dan left the house, whistling a pastiche of show tunes, and Irma settled with Dexter before a comedy re-run, I went to Molly's room made friendlier by the bed lamp's glow. What about a poem in which light cheered sterile—

"Doesn't it upset you," she asked, "his seeing Hank?"

I shook my head to answer her question and to clear away writing's grip. "What if they fight?"

I kicked off my shoes and as she scooted over, I curled up on the foot of her bed. "Hank's not a fighter, and if he has a new love, why battle about an old one?"

"Mom, how did you stand it? I mean last fall when Steve and I broke up for a while and he began hanging around with Janna, I got sick, I mean physically sick, like I wanted to puke. Even now when I see her, I can't like her."

I studied her serious face. How to reply? "Poorly. I handled it poorly. At first, I couldn't understand, forgive. . . anything. I was dead, didn't think I'd ever adjust to a move, separation from you," and I touched her calf, leaving my hand there as I continued, "your father's affair, but situations in California have opened doors for me."

"Yeah, writing, publishing, a job—but your feelings toward Dad?"

I examined the weave of the bedspread. "Are different. A decent man, he's conscientious, and—boring."

The term shimmered in the air. Never had I said, "boring" aloud although surely I'd implied it when I talked with Franklin and Lorraine.

"God," she readjusted her pillow, "I never thought of Dad as boring."

"He seems so to me because we have opposite interests. I want to write, want this job, want friends your father disapproves of. I want someone who's compatible, someone I can be close to and—"

"Neal? You want Teddy bear man?" Her eyes were big, scared, and I laughed.

"Man or woman," I equivocated.

"So what are you going to do?"

Around us the blank walls supplied nothing, gave no clues. I was, indeed, on my own. "I'm going to write, fix the house, and accept the job."

"But Dad? You aren't thinking of divorce?"

Once more I equivocated. "At the risk of sounding trite, things do have ways of working out."

She shifted her weight slightly, bent her legs, so that my hand slid to the bedspread, and turned to her most important issue. "What if Steve ever sleeps with another woman?"

I pursed my lips. "Doubt you can predict how you'd react. You might take it in stride, depending on the circumstances. You might never forget."

I could almost hear her thought progression. "How do we keep from being where you and Dad are?"

"Beats me," and I hoped I didn't sound, as Molly would put it, "smart ass."

"If we never leave the farm, do you think we'll be all right?"

I sat up, hearing a bed spring protest against my action. "You could argue that by staying in one place, sharing everything, you'd be closer, or you could argue that by doing so you'll grow tired of each other. Molly, I have no answers."

The mood had darkened. Should I have promised happiness? Insisted that she and Steve with their brand of love were immune? No, Molly deserved honesty. "Honey, there are no guarantees of anything, but you're starting out better than your dad and I did. You're already stronger and more confident than I've ever been—until recently."

When she hugged me a lump filled my throat. How proud I was of her. How I loved her, how much of my life was inextricably interwoven with hers. I cleared my throat. "Why don't you give me your opinion on the dresses I brought?"

As we neared the guest bedroom she said, "Oh, I promised to call Steve by ten. Wear whichever you'd rather, Mom, it makes no difference to me."

By eleven, when I closed my book, Dan hadn't returned, so I crawled under the sheet and slept, awakening to still heat. The window air conditioner was off, and as I jabbed buttons, he tiptoed in.

"Overheated," he said. "Let it alone. We can sit outside and I'll tell you about Hank."

I slipped on a robe, and we stole through the deserted living room onto the porch where, settled on the top step, we faced our former home. Across the lawn, across the driveway in that darkened rectangle, we'd lived for almost twenty years, and known what? Besides the heartache of dual miscarriages and the deaths of my parents, months and seasons coalesced. Only minor distractions—Molly's chicken pox, pipes freezing, Dan's trading cars, my collecting donations for the Heart Fund—emerged as minute peaks on a plateau.

"I'm not going to fool around with details and lead up to the big news. Bottom line: Hank wants me back."

"Here?"

"Where else? He said business went down hill fast after—after. Well, he doesn't blame me for Sheila. He said that at this point he sees their marriage had been rocky for years. What took place was like an accident waiting to happen, as he put it. Plus, he's mad about Gwen."

"The school teacher?"

As if eager to share information, he leaned toward me, his breath a yeasty cloud. "She's divorced, has two young daughters, and he's crazy about them. Said he'd always wanted a daughter. He asked me not to tell, but what the hell? They're getting married the end of August. In fact, if I could get back by then, he'd take off, would fly them all to Disneyland for a honeymoon."

I inched to the right and propped my head against the front porch column. "Some honeymoon."

"It's a fine idea. Shows he cares for the kids, is starting out on the right foot. Hank's younger sons are visiting Sheila and then will go to summer camp. Caleb leaves for college next month." Just as a persuasive speaker or a salesman might, Dan moved in my direction. "But he said his kids and Gwen's kids get along."

Frankly I didn't care to learn why Hank had custody, didn't care if the blended family succeeded or not. A light flicked on in my former house. I could trace the person's path to the main bathroom. Above the lavatory, lamp fixtures illumined a cream bathtub, matching toilet and cream-brown checked paper. Or had new tenants changed that? The light went out and the faceless form prowled back toward Molly's old room or the master bedroom. Master bedroom. Not mine/ours. That house, like a fading photograph, was pasted in an album rarely opened. I wished for my notebook.

"What do you think?"

"About their kids?"

He heaved an irritated sigh. "About Hank's idea."

"Not much. For one reason, I don't believe you can go back. You and Hank wouldn't work well together not only because of Sheila but because it's impossible to regain what you had."

"Just shows how wrong you are. Hank told me that if Sheila and I decided to marry that it wouldn't bother him. Says he feels absolutely nothing for her. She and I could live in Harding, he says. In that case it would be easier for them to share their sons."

I bit back my first incredulous, sarcastic reply as the full weight of his sentences struck me. Dan was talking about marrying Sheila. The "monster" topic we'd largely avoided had sneaked in on the Hawkins' porch where crickets with their summer song kept us company. "So you and Sheila might get married?"

He rubbed his palms along his trouser legs. I heard his tongue click against the roof of his mouth. "Only said that to show that Hank has no hard feelings. I figured you might want to move back to be close to Molly and Steve."

A lone car drove by. "I want to stay in Madison."

"What if I told Hank I'd come back?"

In the dark I tried to study him. "Did you?"

"No, promised, though, that I'd think about it. But it's what I want."

We were wandering into a boxed canyon, and although right before Molly's wedding was a bad time, perhaps there would never be a good time, so I said, "And you'd like to marry Sheila?"

In turn I heard him swallow and I smiled. At least he hadn't clucked his tongue. "I do love her, Kate, but I promised I'd stay with you and I will. It's simply that I can't stay in California. I'm a small town guy. I want to return here. I do think you could bend on this. You can write in Harding. Hell, maybe Harding has a historical society and you could land a job with them. Have an Adopt-A-Grave in this cemetery. Take care of your parents' plots. Fairly soon, I'd bet, Molly and Steve will have a baby. You'd be close by for a grandchild. You'd have everything."

Except for Franklin, I thought as I rose. "It's late, Dan. Let's sleep on it."

In the bedroom, he restarted the air conditioner, and we lay in the double bed beneath the sheet, letting cool air soothe us as we struggled for sleep.

CHAPTER TWELVE

*I*rma tapped her toe as she searched for diplomacy. "I do think a hat's in good taste at a wedding."

"Yours complements your outfit," I answered.

Once more she surveyed herself in the mirror where the large off-pink hat, a silk peony in the center, bobbed back at her. In a floating envelope of a dress splotched with red/pink, Irma straightened her shoulders, determined that at least one of us should go properly attired to this non-conventional affair. Decisively she clicked painted fingernails against the top of the crowded dresser. Here perfumes, colognes, powders, and music boxes competed for space. Actually everything in Irma's bedroom competed—floral bedspread, crocheted pillows, knitted dolls, bedside lamps and vases of artificial blossoms—even snapshots on the wall to our left overlapped each other forming a sea of perpetual smiles.

The door knob twirled in time with Dan's knock. Behind him stood a radiant Molly.

"Never fails," Irma said. "Brides are always transfigured on their wedding day."

Something precious and indescribable shone from Molly's eyes and face. Apart from its yoke, the gown personified her, as did the single pink rose she carried. No stephanotis and baby's breath, no orchids or nosegay, as I would have chosen. She wore tiny pearl earrings, Steve's gift.

Dexter yelled from the kitchen that we better take off, and as if afraid the ceremony might happen without us, we crowded and jostled each other in the constricted hallway. In a flurry of "excuse me," "sorry," "was that your foot?" we bumbled toward the Buick, glistening from Dexter's wax job.

Molly slid carefully into the back seat, between Dan and me. Dexter handed Irma his camera and backed quickly from the driveway. Then, either because he remembered the speed of funeral processions or because he believed this occasion begged dignity, he held the speedometer needle at ten miles per hour. I silently urged him to go faster, for there was everything to say and nothing to say. I prayed to have the service over and the wedding dinner finished.

Apparently mistaking our quiet for barely disguised hysteria, Irma assumed a tour guide role. "Kate, Dan, see the Hammonds have torn out their sidewalk. They'll use bricks, those old fashioned ones, you know, up to the steps.

"There, on the bike. That's the Gardener's youngest. Did well in Little League this year. Wasn't he pitcher, Dexter?"

"First base." He didn't turn his head, didn't alter his pace.

"Hi." Irma fluttered fingers at Blanche Terrison. "Her son got a paper route last week. Her mother's poorly. Arthritis?"

"Stroke."

"At this corner they're thinking of putting up a stop sign to cut down on speeding. The Lind's dog was killed right there by that man hole cover. You remember that little yipping mixed breed?"

"Poodle."

"Well, poodle and something else. Sure, I'm sorry the dog's dead because they grieved. But let me tell you, I never liked him. Dug up my zinnias."

"Peed on our lawn, left white patches."

Ahead lay the First Methodist Church and as Dexter parked before the parsonage, Molly took my hand. With fingers joined we walked to the front door, where without a word she headed for a small room off the hallway.

The four of us entered the living room, in hushed voices greeted the Idersons and Julie's parents—the only other guests. With our entrance the minister's wife, massive in a metallic formal, beamed and waddled toward the piano to pound out her version of "Jesu, Joy of Man's Desiring."

Daisies lined the mantel beside tarnished candelabra, and before that fireplace Reverend Ash posed with Steve and his brother Tim. Then Mrs. Ash beat out the expected melody, but since we were already standing in a lopsided semi-circle, we couldn't rise to honor the bride.

With an impish grin and that mincing gait which has introduced millions of bridal processions, Julie headed from the dining room toward the reverend. But when Molly set her own no-nonsense stride, Dan plunged his hands into suit pockets; then abruptly withdrew them to cross his arms. It hurt not to escort her down an aisle, but Molly said it was hypocritical for Dan to "give me away." She'd go to Steve alone.

As she walked toward him, she did not glance in our direction, and I swallowed against the force field of this couple's happiness. As she neared Steve and accepted his hand, Dexter, as self-appointed photographer, clicked the shutter.

Devoid of music and poetry, the ritual was brief. Steve pushed the thin band on her finger, kissed her, and laughing, they faced us for time-etched sentiments. Dexter reset his f-stops, tilted the camera, experimenting with artistic effects as I assured the Ashes that California was nice, told Julie's parents their daughter looked darling, and admired Mrs. Iderson's navy blue dress, aware that no one had commented on my green one.

"Bought this for my brother's funeral last month," Mrs. Iderson said. "The more wearings you can get from a dress, the less it costs."

I agreed and shook hands with her husband, compressed in a suit that predated the recent funeral. It was obvious, as well, from the way he rotated his head and tugged at the collar that this shirt hadn't been worn in years.

"Would you shake hands again? I didn't get it," Dexter said. So with terse smiles, Mr. Iderson and I, hands woodenly connected, listened for the click that would release us. *This is unimportant*, I reminded myself. *We're merely humming insects around the lighted couple, who now are emitting a subliminal command: let's go eat so we can go to bed.*

Again I invited Julie's parents and the Ashes to join us at Slim's Restaurant and again they declined. As our party edged from the parsonage into thickening heat, Mrs. Iderson pointed to mounting clouds and as if by leaving the state, I'd renounced any memory of local climate, she announced, "Thunderstorm building up."

Like an undamned river, we spilled down the sidewalk with the Idersons escaping first. Molly and Steve with Tim and Julie pulled away; then Irma, Dexter, Dan, and I sank into our seats in the Buick.

Because no one spoke, I wrapped the stillness around me and observed the darkening sky, aware that I missed these violent, explosive thunderstorms. At this odd mid-afternoon hour only a few cars claimed the restaurant parking lot. Set with gaps between them, they resembled uneven teeth.

With polite smiles, we six adults converged on Steve's car where Julie and Tim exchanged embarrassed grins as the newlyweds clung in an embrace.

Unsettled, Dan jingled keys and coins in his pocket, and as if seeking a theme far removed from sex and bridal nights, Irma, too, launched into a weather dissertation. With the Idersons peering at the ominous sky, Irma called out, "cirrus", cumulus", "barometric pressure," holdover terms from the natural science course she'd completed at adult ed.

Turning a deaf ear to the lecture I focused on Mrs. Iderson's reedy tone, one not fattened by emotions. If a voice defined a personality, did that one-dimensional pitch accurately represent her? Every fascinating individual I'd met spoke with resonance and depth. Could the idea of voice symbolizing a person be incorporated in a poem? Certainly voice was necessary for characterization, so perhaps. . . I unclasped my purse.

"Kate," Dan hissed, "for Christ's sake, don't haul out that notebook."

But any notebook opportunity took flight when Molly and Steve, breaking apart for air, regarded their parking lot audience, and, as leaders of this motley assortment, led us into the restaurant's chilly dimness. We passed through the bar to the banquet room where a table set for ten waited below the "Capacity 80" sign.

Metal chair legs scraped a flinty floor as we arranged ourselves around the table and its plastic flower centerpiece. Before I sensed Irma's outrage at fake flowers, I had wondered if she'd designed it. To my right, Dan's negativity roiled as a solid mass, and I could read some of his black thoughts. *If you'd been a proper mother, you'd have flown back early or at the very least have contacted Slim Jim's to ensure a tasteful wedding dinner.*

Molly giggled. "Talk about segregation, privacy. Wow. See, when I called I said that even though we only expected ten, we'd like a place apart."

"We're apart," Julie agreed, "but if you strain you can hear music from the bar. Anyone care to dance?" The teenagers laughed nervously; the adults didn't smile. I must play hostess and as if each syllable dragged chains, I dredged up questions and offered simplistic statements.

When the waitress appeared with menus, I muttered to Dan, "For heaven's sakes, order us some drinks."

And although the Idersons declined, I immediately drank a second glass of champagne after we toasted Molly and Steve. Dan refilled his glass and mine and as we raced each other to empty them, we were of one accord, ignoring Irma and Dexter's disapproval. But the champagne helped. More kindly, I spoke to Mrs. Iderson who tore the red plastic strips on cellophane packets around crackers. As she crumbled saltines into her chicken noodle soup, I nodded charitably when she said, "Don't know why they don't serve everything together. Who wants to eat a bowl of soup first?"

Through successive glasses of champagne I grew expansive in trying to convince Irma that a wedding cake was unnecessary.

"I know Molly said she didn't want one, that it was a waste, but it's not right," Irma grumbled.

"It's her day," and I grandly flung my arm in some fairy godmother gesture. "We'll do whatever she wants." I smiled at my daughter and son-in-law, their attendants, and at Mrs. Iderson for, miraculously, her nose had blurred and she looked less pinched. Even Irma's hat was stylish, and I winked at Mr. Iderson when he dropped his napkin and then his fork.

Through that gauzy screen I saw Molly and Steve rise. "We'll be taking off," he said, eliciting a barrage of advice. "It's raining. Drive carefully. Roads are slippery."

Molly circled the table, embracing the Idersons, the Hawkins, Dan and me. As we clutched each other, something within bent toward breaking, for when she and Steve returned from the Ozarks, I'd be in Madison, safe and ecstatic. However, at this instant anticipation of my future failed to cheer me.

Suddenly I sobbed and worried, she pulled back. "Mother, don't cry. *You've made it this far, Kate. Don't spoil it for her.*

I fought for control as Steve took her arm. Molly snuggled her face into his jacket sleeve and then said, "Mom, walk to the door with us."

Unsteadily I moved beside them, aware of Dan's loud footfalls, aware that at the table the remaining guests were debating who'd take Julie home. At the restaurant's steel door, its window framing a summer rainstorm, we hugged before the kids dashed across the parking lot to Steve's Ford. Their exit forced a residue of hot moistness inside.

"Never dreamed when she was little that I was raising her for a Steve." Dan's comment, the day, the champagne had conspired to usher in sadness. I took a step toward the banquet room, but I couldn't return to the Hawkins, couldn't ride back with them, sit in their living room, and listen to the rain accompany whatever sentiments Irma had stored for this moment.

"Let's stay here."

He half smiled. "Good thinking. I can't take Irma and Dexter right now."

"But how will you get back?" Irma asked when I said we'd stay at bit longer at Slim's.

"It's less than a mile. We'll walk."

"But it's raining," and as if the West Coast had erased some basic judgmental ability, she guided me to the window to prove that drops spattered the blacktop and windshields and deepened shallow pools on car hoods.

"It won't rain forever." Even to my ears, Dan's speech sounded slurred.

The Iderson's opinion of our decision and their take on our condition communicated itself through limp handshakes. With clown-like smiles, Dan and I waved to the six individuals as they drove away.

In the bar, a country western song about a cheating woman blared from a neon-lighted juke box, circa 1950. Three men hunkered down on stools, but the round tables were empty. Dan and I chose one against a paneled wall. While he downed a beer, I sipped wine, conscious that I was the sole woman in the bar and conscious that we were overdressed. Dan complained about the song's volume, but I welcomed it for we couldn't talk over it, couldn't speak about Molly, nor Dan's decision concerning Hank.

As I signaled for another drink, I closed my eyes, willing the north room to imprint itself, but I couldn't re-create it nor an image of Franklin. To a song about a truck driving S.O.B., I opened my eyes, drank my wine, and wove to the bathroom where an opaque bubbled window, raised a couple inches, furnished a peek hole into night. I swayed back to Dan.

"Before we get totally looped, we'd better leave. The rain's quit." But as if mind and body were disconnected, I missed the first step into sullen blackness. From a great distance I heard my high heels slam against damp concrete and felt storm-cooled air sweep goose pimples across my bare arms.

"Phone Dexter?"

"No," I said. "I need to walk."

He tucked his hand beneath my elbow, but our strides were not in sync.

"I feel let down," he said. "It was too—too nothing. It's like someone died and you feel rotten because you never said or did for them what you wanted, didn't properly bid them goodbye."

A remarkably astute remark, I decided, and tightened my grasp on his arm. "I understand," I answered. "If we'd given Molly the wedding we wanted at a time we thought right, to a man we'd liked, we'd undoubtedly feel sad but satisfied."

"Yeah." In a drinking buddy motion, he slung a companionable arm around my shoulder. "Yeah."

"Even our gift," I moaned.

"Money was best. They need it."

"But a check's so impersonal. I wish Molly had allowed us to buy a present."

Misjudging distance from curb to street we splashed into a puddle. Water flooded my open-toed shoes and slightly sobered me. I felt tired, drained, and nauseous. We plodded across irregular streets and sidewalks. With toes cold and feet throbbing, I longed for a dry burrow in which to creep. There I'd curl into a fetal position and close everything out.

We rounded a corner and neared Liston's Drugstore, where Molly worked. As we approached the building, a lighted display window trapped our images. Startled, I stared at Dan's paunch, the jowls redesigning portions of his face, but that—that woman beside him. . . .

"What?" he tugged at my arm.

"Is that how I look?" and I pointed at the reflection.

He squinted. "Yes."

Amazement registered in the face of the matron who wore a wilted green dress that was intended for a youthful figure. The hemline should reveal slim, shapely calves, and the skirt should fall across a concave stomach.

"Kate, it's okay," and Dan patted my shoulder as I suddenly sobbed. He continued to guide me the remaining distance to the Hawkins house where, like a replay, the same low wattage bulb in the living room cast our silhouettes against the opposite wall.

"We've lots to discuss," he abruptly said when he sat in the guest bedroom's one chair to remove his shoes. I steadied myself against the dresser and laid my silver earrings beside Irma's carrousel music box. Was it the effect of the drinks, or was there something bizarre in the fact that Dan was undressing as he'd done for thousands of nights while at the same time he was introducing areas that opposed normality? How, on the night of Molly's wedding, could we debate his decision to move to Harding? Wasn't it demeaning to unsnap and unbutton as we determined our future?

His second shoe clunked onto the floor. I heard him rise, heard him unzip his pants, heard him step from each leg. If I turned around he'd be standing in briefs and socks while he matched inseams. "Must we tonight?" I asked as I peeled off my Victorian gown.

In precise fashion he positioned his pants over a wire hanger and hung them in the closet. "I'm meeting Hank tomorrow. Last night you promised that you'd sleep on it, and today wasn't particularly conducive to discussion."

I pulled off my slip and while my head was entangled in white silk folds, I searched for an answer, because the notion had gathered ascendancy that Dan was the only person I had. After this emotional day with Molly, the knowledge that she would be near did tilt the scales toward Harding. I pictured her coming to our house on daily lunch breaks from the drugstore. I could. . .

The slip slithered to the floor and with my back to Dan, I unhooked my bra. Beneath the nightgown as it slowly descended, I wondered how I could be content in Harding. Franklin had changed me, and even when he went on after completing the poetry collection, mightn't he visit me? If that proved impossible, I still had exciting days with him. Plus there was my job and Neal, so as the nightgown in parachute fashion collapsed around me, I smiled.

In the mirror Dan noticed the smile. "Then your answer is yes," he said, but his eyes and his voice reflected no joy.

He's obligated to me, I thought, *and while life will be easier for him if we live in Harding, it won't necessarily be better. He no longer loves me.* Such surety weakened me, and I sat on the bedside to regard the pine floor boards that Irma had painted brown. To contrast with her handmade orange bedspread? Dan buttoned his pajamas and reached to pull back that bedspread Irma had crocheted because of a sale on orange thread.

"No, I won't move to Harding. It's tempting to be near Molly, and it's safe to stay in a town I've known forever." I breathed deeply. "There are more important things than security."

He lifted his hand from the spread and clucked his tongue before asking, "Such as?"

"A new life. Such as love," and I looked at his frown. I heard my own wild heartbeat as I added, "We've outgrown the old life."

Now he sat on the bed and as balance shifted, I wondered how many nights had I adjusted my position when he slipped into bed? When did unconscious adjusting become natural? How will it be to sleep alone?

"That line sounds like one from your buddy Lorraine. A pseudo-New Age concept. Cause I've not outgrown the old life. I want to re-enter it, live it, be near Molly, enjoy the same friends, shop at stores I know."

"But with a new companion, Dan, with Sheila. You've outgrown the old life of our marriage."

He chose to lay on the bed, to clasp his hands behind his head on the satin guest pillowcase and regard the stuccoed ceiling. Since he seemed disinclined to answer, I tied on my robe and padded down the hallway to the bathroom. I paused, though, at the entrance to Molly's room. Unable to see specifics, I knew the room was vacant, because it emitted nothing. She'd removed her vitality to a new life, just as I must do.

In the darkened bathroom I sat on the toilet battling such an array of thoughts and impressions that I questioned how I could ever unravel or explain the pain that still lingered when I thought of Dan with Sheila; countered by dreams of awakening each morning free to write, to work on poetry; weighed by the sexual euphoria of being with Franklin; contrasted by grief that my marriage was over; and complicated by the thrill of having a job.

As I washed my hands, I suddenly recalled a paragraph I'd once read. A woman fell in love with a man and took him to meet her friend. When man and friend shook hands, woman instinctively realized that they were meant for each other. Out of love for them, she relinquished the fellow. Isn't that what I should do for Dan?

I found him in the same spot, but he turned his head in my direction as I lay beside him. "So, is divorce the answer?"

"Not necessarily the answer I want, but perhaps it's what we need."

He scoffed. "Kate, don't play around with fancy, dancy language. You sound like something from a novel." And I laughed, appreciating that his laughter tagged mine. Laughter. Somehow, sometime, I must write about that. Why is it so much more difficult to describe positive emotions than negative ones?

"I'll not be fancy, dancy. Simply, I'm going to live in California. You're free to live here. Tonight, at least, I concede that Sheila is for you. We can separate and you can live with her, or we can divorce. Your call."

Surprisingly he moved his left arm allowing our forearms to touch before he cradled my right hand. At that point I felt tears. My god, on the night of

Molly's wedding, in a house next to the one that I'd loved for decades, in a place where my past was achingly close. . .

"Kate, if you mean it, if you really mean it, I sincerely thank you. I'll give as much spousal support as possible and Sheila plans to work. She's several options: at Jorgenson's Realty or as office manager for the Chamber of Commerce, and, eventually, as an only child, she'll inherit from her parents."

As hurt once more stung, I disengaged our hands. He and Sheila had fantasized about what they'd do when/if Dan were free. Had they pitied me? I turned on my side away from him, wondering if they'd said, "Oh, poor Kate. She's needy"? Or had they concluded that Dan was noble for honoring a promise to his wife?

"Kate, this isn't because of drinks. You do mean this?"

"Yes," I whispered.

"You're generous," he said, and then he slept. But I remained awake. Was I generous? If there hadn't been Franklin, Lorraine, and Neal, could I have released him?

CHAPTER THIRTEEN

*I*n the airport gift shop I bought a paperback that would fit Lorraine's definition of an "Oreo cookie book," with hopes that it might prove diverting on the flight West. Since creativity had shriveled, it was useless to open my notebook. However, en route to Denver, where we'd change planes, the story failed, as I felt pulled apart and not yet reassembled. Beside me, Dan pretended to read the in-flight magazine.

Pretense. We had pretended to Irma and Dexter and to the Bollingers, a couple who invited us for dinner. We pretended to Julie's parents when we met for cocktails, and when Molly phoned from the Ozarks, we again pretended with promises to contact her and Steve after we reached Madison. We even pretended to each other, keeping up a friendly façade, and only alluding to practicalities each night when closeted in the guest room. We whispered about finances, Dan assuring me that he would pay adequate support, and we whispered about division of the furniture. In a gesture fueled by magnanimity and delight, he said, "Keep everything, Kate. I just want my clothes and personal possessions." We whispered about the resignation he'd give Old Jer and about his meetings with Hank where they'd ironed out some details concerning their reconstructed business. We did not whisper about Sheila nor did we whisper about how we would co-exist until Old Jer released him.

As I gazed out the plane window, for Dan benevolently had insisted, "Sit where you can see out," I tried to determine our exact location over the Nebraska plains, and I though that I'd never read about divorcing spouses who lived together until they could live apart. When this was behind me, perhaps I could write about love in limbo or about loving two persons—or in my case, the memory of a person and an entity. Around me others were snared in similar situations. Peter, whom Lorraine loved, also loved his wife. Franklin loved me, but would go on to meet Amy. And Dan, who loved Sheila, still had feelings for me as did Hank for Gwen and Sheila.

At last we reclaimed our car at the San Francisco Airport parking lot, and as we headed across the Bay Bridge, I sensed the charm of my house on the hill and tension diminished. In my north room, Franklin waited. He would smile and—

"What do you think about a lawyer?" Dan unexpectedly asked.

"Don't know. Do we need one?"

He clucked his tongue and scratched at an invisible something on his nose. "With our living in two states. . . In the office building in the city a law firm's on the second floor and a paralegal's on the fourth. I'll check. Possibly we can use one lawyer if we even require one. And I can ask She—; ask Hank."

We said little more on the trip to Madison and when we found mail spilling from the box and newspapers scattered across bottom steps, he chuckled. As I unpacked and stuffed soiled laundry in the wicker hamper, he turned on the computer, and when he eventually came into the bedroom, Dan asked, "Shall I sleep on the couch?"

If he did, he might hear me in the night as I climbed the stairs, so I answered, "Up to you, but we managed in Iowa." He nodded, but for the first time in our married life he chose the bathroom to change into pajamas. Sheila must have said something. In my cotton nightie, I crawled into bed, feigning sleep, and after he settled onto the left side and after he gained the cadence of sleep, I hurried to the second level.

On the threshold I caught my breath at the wonder of my room. I closed the door, ran across the gray rug, and fumbled for the necklace on the closet shelf. In my eagerness and in the darkness, I bumped the shelf and the necklace fell to the floor. More cautiously I picked it up and secured the clasp.

"Katherine." Who could pronounce my name with such—such reverence? He pressed me against him, my arms encircled him, and I lifted my face for his cool lips. "Oh, Katherine, how I have missed you," and again he kissed me. I tightened my arms, but before I could repeat my news, he said, "We've nearly enough poems for a chapbook. Maybe three more will do it, and I've refined some ideas."

Naturally, it was grand that he was ready to work on poetry, but I longed for his touch, for him. Thus as he led me from the confining closet, I said, "On a personal note, I must tell you that Dan and I are divorcing. He's returning to Iowa, and I'll stay here in this house with you."

In the dark I couldn't see his expression, but his voice was as melodious as ever, "That is lovely for you."

For me, I thought. *What about us?*

"It's too late to work on our poems, and you're tired, but I look forward to the morning," and he raised my hand and kissed it.

In morning's light, after Dan had departed, I picked up the rosebud necklace from its shelf. That crack that occurred when I dropped it in the kitchen months ago had widened from the damage last night. Only a thread of bisque bridged the twin sections at the top. Could I repair it? How? But impatient to see Franklin, I couldn't risk harming the rosebud even more in an attempt to mend it, so gently I anchored it around my neck. When he extended his hands to bring me close to his chest I said, "It's cracking, the necklace."

For some moments he paced and then smiled. "It's a sign, Katherine, that we must work." I seated myself at the desk and listened to his footfalls as he continued around the rug's perimeter. In that fashion we worked until noon, and the lines I copied were a far cry from the poetry he'd published in *The Laurel Wreath.* We both had evolved in our writing, but if I allowed myself complete honesty, I would have to admit that his poetry was unexceptional and that his collection wouldn't interest a publisher.

Did Franklin realize that his verse would never be critically reviewed? Did he recognize his limitations? Was his hunger to publish based on ego, or did he truly regard himself as a talented writer with a duty to enrich the lives of future generations? How little I knew of him. In "real" life one observed how others reacted to an individual, picked up clues about another's inner world, but with Franklin I had solely our interaction, along with what he chose to tell me. The only "balance" was Emma's letter and those archival scraps courtesy of Neal.

By turning my head slightly I could watch him. Temporarily stopped, hand on chin, lips moving as if forming words, he presented a stereotypic portrait of a Romantic poet—a Shelley, a Keats, a Byron. Apparently he sensed my appraisal and with his smile managed to erase my silent questions. "Read back what we've done this morning, and then let's take a break."

Astonishing how much richer my voice sounded in this room. Astonishing, as well, how lines locked in my own brain begged for attention.

As I heated a can of soup—all I could find in the cupboard until I shopped at the market—Franklin stood at the open patio door. July's dry scent seeped into the kitchen. "Next to the north room, this back yard is what I will miss most."

My heart lurched. "Miss?"

He looked over his shoulder at me. "Katherine, we're virtually finished with the book."

"But if we got involved in another book, a sequel, or if we expanded this one—"

The phone's ring startled me, and I dropped my stirring spoon into the sauce pan, as I decreased the heat.

"Kate," Neal greeted my answer, "welcome home. Good trip and all that?"

"A decisive trip."

"Hmm," and he laughed. "Decisive can cover as much territory as interesting."

"I'll explain later, but what's new?"

"Was wondering when we could meet for some preliminary work on our project."

Project. Of course, Franklin could help with Madison's history. I'd convince him to stay, to take a sabbatical from the poetry book, so I answered, "I could come by the museum this afternoon."

By two o'clock, heat poured up the front steps as I opened the front door. I appreciated the dry heat, unlike Midwestern humidity, so hurried down the stairs, stopping only at the mail box. A business-sized envelope from *Myriad Magazine* contained the letter, "I am pleased to inform you that your poem, 'Love's Invitation,' will be published in our November issue. Upon publication you will receive contributor's copies and an honorarium."

I sat on the bottom step. Its heat seared through my khaki slacks and penetrated to my bones to merge with the fire of excitement. A second acceptance, plus money. The first acceptance wasn't a fluke. I'd read that some famous authors said that no subsequent sale ever equaled number one, but I disagreed. Surely the second, the third, the fourth, would prove one's talent.

I started back up the steps to Franklin, but halfway up reconsidered. I'd not told him nor Dan about writing/mailing "Love's Invitation." Alone, I'd composed this poem. Certainly Franklin would be pleased, but—

I jammed letter and envelope into my purse and walked to the museum, where fans in each room attempted to circulate air.

"Pretty stuffy, isn't it?" Neal called out. "Guess it's a good thing that museum hopping isn't a recreational priority on a summer afternoon," and his sweeping gesture indicated the people-empty rooms. "However, lemonade with ice waits in my office."

It was good to see him, and I felt so euphoric with my sale that it wasn't until I settled into the creaky folding chair and watched him grab the pitcher handle to pour drinks into paper cups that I was again conscious of his one arm. I steadied the cups he'd centered on his desk and when filled, we raised them in a mutual toast.

"So," and he rocked gently in his swivel chair. "What's decisive?"

"First, Neal, I must tell someone," and I unfolded my acceptance letter.

"I couldn't be more pleased," he said and lowered the letter to his lap. "Only wish I had something more appropriate than lemonade with which we could celebrate." He squeezed the back of my hand, leaving a warm imprint, and asked for details about the poem before he again inquired about "decisive." Briefly I described Molly's wedding and then delivered news of my pending divorce.

He didn't say he was sorry, suggest counseling, or hope that we'd reconcile. Instead he said, "You'll need a lawyer," and when I spoke of using the same attorney, he shook his head. He spun through a Roladex perched precariously on his desk corner. "Here's Sam's card. A long-time member of the historical society. Good guy. Make an appointment. Tell him I sent you."

"He'll give a discount?"

Neal grinned. "Promise him the first copy of our history book."

"Which is a grand segue into the reason I'm here."

Neal finished his lemonade, wadded his cup, and dropped it into an overflowing wastebasket. "Cheap cups. The rim around the lip mashes down when you drink."

"Next time, I'll bring straws," and when I said, "next time," I realized that I was already anticipating another session.

"Okay, I've been considering structure, not a straight chronology. Since history is story, what about a series of profiles? We could pick some of the most colorful, or most influential citizens, and write chapters about them, revealing Madison through their eyes. Maybe select one or two per decade and approach the town's progress from multiple angles. Various professions, religions, ethnic groups could be represented."

"I like that. Something with characters and problems."

He opened the top folder on the pile closest to his elbow. "The man for whom the town's named is a natural."

"Madison?"

"Madison V. Madison." He held up his hand. "I kid you not. His paternal family name was Madison, but his mother admired President Madison. At least, that's how the story goes. And Madison V. (for Vernon) Madison was a crook. Crafty, ingratiating, he swindled acres away from the Mexican don who owned the land grant, and he advertised lots for sale in eastern newspapers. Actually the lots were under water. In fact, a man who purchased a non-existent parcel, located in the Strait, is accused of killing him. The fellow boasted about it, but since no one ever located Madison's body, it's unclear how he died. So, we can bring in the Spanish, the topography, the wild life, the first church—"

I crushed my cup. "Why was the town named after someone that unscrupulous?"

"Most of his dealings weren't discovered until later. Plus, he did a great deal for the community, established lot lines, loaned money, and was charismatic. Married twice and fathered numerous illegitimate offspring. His oldest legal son, Thadderay Madison, entered the ministry and erected the Presbyterian Church that still stands on land he persuaded his father to donate, along with land on the opposite hill for the cemetery. Therefore, all Madisons, but missing Papa, are buried there."

"Other possibilities?" I asked as he edged the folder in my direction.

"First ferry boat captain and/or his wife. During the Gold Rush era, Lucas Hampton decided he could earn more money transporting passengers across the Strait than striking off for the Sierra Nevada. When the influx started he opened a hotel, conveniently adjacent to the bordello. Some four, no, maybe six years later, he married a 'lady of the night.' Ugly, poxed, she was most unusual. When proper women shunned her, she reacted by painting her home a vivid green. She took violin lessons and practiced at night, slept in a coffin after Lucas died (that way, assuredly, she could sleep alone) and operated a lucrative practice selling herbs to prevent pregnancies or end them."

Sunlight coated the window near his desk and flooded the room. The fan whirling atop the filing cabinet could not longer compete. Neal wiped his hand across his forehead. "It's a sweat box. Let's meet some morning."

We settled on next Wednesday and I headed home, but at the library I detoured up the concrete steps. In the dim interior where minimal lighting retained an illusion of coolness, I didn't see Lorraine.

"Know nothing about her," a new clerk told me, and for a second I considered going to *The Eden* for surely Lorraine was off this afternoon. She'd smile when I waved my acceptance letter, a smile that would lead into a wild whoop when I announced my second news. But I needed to see Franklin and needed to buy groceries, so I climbed our steep hill to place a weakened rosebud against my throat.

His cool cheek grazed mine and he murmured my name. When I told of the letter he said, "Congratulations. You're establishing contacts with editors who can give advice on printing my collection or ones we can contact for positive reviews."

While enchanting to be in his arms and to learn he wasn't upset that I'd written a poem, still I wished he'd ask me to read "Love's Invitation" and that he'd praise me. Instead I summarized Neal's concept. "You can help, Franklin."

"Well," and as he did when searching for a poetical strand, he paced the gray rug, "it is appealing, but——"

"But?" I prompted.

Wearily he ran his right hand through his black curls. "We're so close to the end of the collection. Can't we finish it first?"

I dropped down onto the rug, removed my sandals, and massaged feet still warm from the exterior world through which I'd recently traveled. "Yet when the collection's finished, you won't stay around, will you?"

He knelt beside me, inched his hand along my spine. "I'd like to stay with you, but I can't. For decades I've desired nothing more than to write my chapbook, and it's overwhelming to have that goal so very near. I never imagined that I would fall in love with the channel for my words. However, if I never finish the book, if I delay, and stay on with you, our life will always be a half-life."

I buried my face against that white, white shirt. "Would that be such a bad life? I could bring in stories from town."

"Katherine, my commitment to stay around until my book is completed has built a type of prison, one I asked for without ever thinking through its limitations."

"What if, what if I drove you places at night? Couldn't I expand the prison?"

And before he spoke I thought, *Once again I'm begging a man not to leave me.* I fought back tears and he increased his hold. As my nose and cheek mashed against him, I smelled my own sweaty, rancid odor. By contrast, Franklin had no scent. He never had a scent. I swallowed hard. "Forget my question. Let's work."

Too readily it seemed, he released me and I was back at the desk. He strode with a determined pace, and in tempo with his clipped action, his words were clipped and confident. When I read back, "And the night sung an anthem authored by the stars," he said. "I like it. We won't revise."

Shadows attacked the windows. "I must get downstairs," I said and he leaned over the chair to trail his lips along my cheek. "Thank you, my Katherine. Perhaps tonight?"

Not looking at him, I nodded, closed my notebook, and stacked it neatly on the desk, for he mustn't see how affected I was by the certainty that he would leave me. After painstakingly replacing the necklace, I stood in the lower hallway with its green floral wallpaper, its brass coat rack and a framed, tattered 1906 newspaper mounted on the southern wall. Franklin had given a cry of pleasure when he'd discovered the brittle pages wedged in a tool shed corner.

I was standing there, like one in shock, when I heard Dan's approach, and when he opened the screen door, we stared at each other as people do when meeting in an unfamiliar context. "You okay?" he spoke first.

"Sure, I—I was just going to the store. Have nothing for dinner."

As he passed me, turning left into the computer room, he said, "Want to grab a hamburger?"

"Why not?" and in the bathroom as I combed my hair, I lectured myself. "Kate/Katherine, you can do this. You can talk rationally with Dan. You can accept/face that Franklin must go on. As a reward, think about seeing Lorraine tomorrow." But then I thought, *What if she's already gone? She can't have.* No, I'd concentrate on my *Myriad Magazine* and on working with Neal.

At Zippy's Hamburger Palace with our knees bumping beneath the booth,

Dan smiled. "Old Jer's a peach. Said he'd accept a two-week notice, and if I can wrap up several pending cases, I can leave earlier."

I squirted ketchup on my fries and nodded.

"The Rivera fellows acted decently. Know they're not sad to see the last of me, but they presented a civil front. I didn't go into details. They don't know that you're not going along."

I sampled a french fry. "I needn't worry. Their wives won't be calling me."

"Then I talked with a paralegal. Divorce laws differ between California and Iowa."

I picked up my burger. The bun had sesame seeds. How upscale. When had the Zippy's chain added sesame seeds? "You want to file in Iowa?"

He paid sole attention to a thick onion slice he was removing from his sandwich. "Thought maybe you could file out here," and I realized he wanted to keep our divorce action out of the *Harding Gazette's* monthly vital statistics column.

"I'm going to consult an attorney," I answered. "I'll let you know. Never having done this I have no idea what to expect."

He clucked his tongue and stared at the menu board. "Kate, I am sorry."

Irrationally, tears pricked my eyelids. I sipped my milkshake and we ate without comment until Dan said, "I'd like to leave as soon as my cases get settled. Could happen in less than a week."

I nodded and laid the remainder of the Zippy Burger in its white wrapping onto the table.

"I'll leave you some cash. The checking account's yours."

Unable to speak, I once more nodded.

On the way home, Dan's monologue revolved around finances and income taxes, but as he shut off the motor, he re-iterated his willingness to provide assistance—long distance, of course—with any problem. "You can keep the computer and the—"

My laugh was curt. "The computer and I aren't friends. It's been your lifeline."

He didn't disagree and once in the house, he immediately tapped on the keyboard, doubtlessly informing Sheila of the quick, smooth progress. And because of his involvement with his computer, I answered the ringing phone.

"Mom, I'm in a dream world."

"You do sound ecstatic."

"I am. The honeymoon was super. It rained every day, so we stayed in our motel room. Then, since we got back, it's been heaven. Steve's parents are being extra neat, giving us privacy, and it's so wonderful to be together, to have our own bedroom. We've received more wedding presents. I can't believe it. I didn't mail out announcements—such a tacky bid for gifts—but here they came. Marcia gave us an iron; Sandy a vase."

I smiled at a rapture undiminished by a bleak room and a bleak farm.

"So what's with you guys?"

Rather than pursuing legal and financial concerns, I wished Dan and I had taken the time to co-author a script for Molly and others. No choice, now, but to plunge in. "Quite a bit. You dad and I have arrived at some major decisions. He's moving to Harding to re-establish a partnership with Hank."

"Dad as in by himself?"

"Dad as in probably living with Sheila until they can marry."

"Mom." Her wail was so loud that I held the receiver away from my ear. "Mom, you can't."

"I'll come visit you," I said but the words were hard to choke out.

Then as Molly began to babble on, tossing out juxtaposed sentences— "Where will they live?" "Are you having a nervous breakdown?" "Who have you told?"—I had a respite in which to compose myself.

"It's what we both want," I said. "I'm good with this. Really." And as if to underscore our accord, Dan at this instant walked into the kitchen and took his turn at the receiver.

I crossed to the patio door and stood where Franklin had this afternoon. Twilight retreated across the back yard, across the hydrangeas and giant geraniums, roses spilling petals upon trailing ferns. A healing scene, it deflected emotions that clouded the kitchen as Dan and Molly talked.

After he hung up, he neared me and took in the back yard. "It's a mess. Kate, who can you hire to get all that under control? If you're determined to live in Madison, why not rent an apartment?"

I smiled at the romantic, mysterious landscape and asked about Molly.

"Ahh. Upset, but she'll come around. Currently, I'm the bad guy, the unfaithful one."

The initial unfaithful one, I thought, *for I can't throw any stones. Had the man I loved been, well, human, I like to think I would have had the courage to admit my adultery to you and to Molly. The difference is that you have the opportunity until the far distant future to be with the woman you love.*

Such reflections were futile, so I'd be practical and grocery shop. By the time I returned from the market, night covered everything. As I carried bags up the front steps, I succumbed to night's spell. I remembered running through summer evenings, darkness triggering senses dulled by the sun.

Thus after Dan slept I took the necklace and Franklin into the back yard. We moved through a moon-kissed garden sensual and heavy with growth to the gazebo's splintered benches. Some nocturnal animal—a raccoon?—rustled in the bushes, a night bird warbled and I smelled the damp fragrance of buds closed against the night, of leaves and shrubbery receptive to secrets that find form only when day ends. Restful, the yard was also subtly passionate. In the overlapping of greening things, limbs and branches embraced and vines twisted in sinuous style. Yet in these hours charged with passion there existed the undertow of sadness. Another day had died. Summer was half-gone, my marriage had ended, and Franklin was destined to go. How long did we have left?

His breathing changed course. His hand pushed a nightgown strap from my shoulder. It fell in slow motion along my upper arm, kissing my skin. As if night had no morning, as if time were our servant, his fingers gradually eased each button of his shirt front. When, finally, he stood, moonlight dappled his chest. Carefully he folded the shirt and laid it on the bench as he whispered, "Tomorrow's poem will be entitled, 'Love in the Gazebo'."

Next morning I walked to the library where another woman—a substitute?—said, "Lorraine no longer works here."

I loped across the train tracks, the rails like hard sinews through my shoe soles, and rounded the dusty corner to spot *The Eden's* mast. But what if it were Adam and his lady aboard?

Grateful that someone had wired the gate open, I hurried across the dock calling, "Lorraine?" and felt relief when her head with its bandana popped up in the companionway.

"I was panicked that you'd gone."

With a grin she motioned me on deck. "Not without seeing you. How went the wedding? The trip?"

In the cockpit where I noticed varnish peeling and paint beginning to flake, I accepted a jelly glass of wine and summarized the ceremony, the visit, and the Decision.

She puckered her lips with the taste of wine and asked, "Can you afford to keep the house?"

"Dan's promised money, I have the job of writing with Neal, and I've sold a poem."

At that she raised her eyebrows.

"Okay, poetry sales won't buy food but maybe, eventually, I can sell others. Or, I'll hunt a job. I live frugally. I think I can make it."

"Sure you can," and then she looked toward the harbor entrance and flat water, where no wind teased the surface. "You've succeeded, I take it, in completely overcoming that—that delusion about Franklin Elliott?"

My pulse jumped, and I traced my tongue across lips flavored with salt and dead grapes before I answered, "I've come to terms with everything."

Now she smiled. "Oh, Kate, I'm so glad." As her concern poured out, I thought, *It's so easy to play with words.* But aloud I asked, "You're finished at the library?"

"Yep and have virtually everything packed. Adam's due to arrive tomorrow or the day after or—whenever he shows up. I'll have him drop me at the bus station."

"Bus!"

"I've never ridden the Greyhound. I'll start east and if it gets too bad, I'll catch the train or an airplane."

"You're headed?"

"For Chicago. If I can't get a job there, I'll go south. Have a friend in Asheville, North Carolina. Might try Atlanta and see a friend."

"Peter?"

Concealing her face in the jelly glass, she drained the dregs. "Last night I told him goodbye." Her voice was thick, so I went below for the wine jug, but paused at a skinned cabin: denuded book shelves, bunks stripped of everything but a rolled sleeping bag. The calendar was gone along with food supplies. In the forward cabin Lorraine's canvas bag with puffy cheeks rested against V-berths. Barrenness cut. She was leaving. I closed my eyes against this emptiness and pictured her riding away, across Nevada, across—

"Are you sitting down there enjoying that premium vintage by yourself?"

"Surely this is decadent," I answered as I took the jug topside, "wine before noon."

"This stuff's an exotic blend of east county vineyard rejects."

And then we were still. I could drink no more wine, couldn't linger any longer. As if sensing this, she depressed the life line with the toe of her sneaker and escorted me to the gate. "Was in Berkeley last week," she said, "telling The Colonel and his tribe goodbye. Remember them? Our sailing in the winter? Well, we went to a junk shop, The Returns, on Telegraph, and I spotted some lace curtains. Thought of you. Would be perfect for the front windows. They were saved from a demolished hotel. They're huge," and she extended her arms to indicate dimensions. "You could alter them, cut out the stains and the frayed parts."

"Thanks, would you—oh, damn, I almost invited you to go to Berkeley with me."

She stared ahead. "The address is easy to find."

"I'll check back with you tomorrow."

"No, get the address from the phone book or something, but don't see me. I'm lousy at farewells. Can't keep prolonging them."

"Then call me when you leave. I can drive you to the bus station."

"Would rather Adam did it."

At the propped open wire gate she grabbed me in a fierce hug. "I'll write. Scout's honor," she promised.

And in a voice like rust I answered, "Anytime. You want. To come. Stay."

"I know," and she turned away.

I watched the figure—its bandana handkerchief a red emblem—grow smaller. Before boarding the ketch she waved. Then there were only the dual masts, bare poles rising from a base decorated with bright blue sail covers.

CHAPTER FOURTEEN

*T*he sun exerted extra force as I retraced my dusty path. Footprints sank into bleached powder, ready when the wind blew to spin miniature cyclones. I'd think about objects—the roadway, railroad tracks, pebbles. I'd willed doors to close, but not this one. Not on Lorraine. Not on friendship. I kicked a cloud of dirt, watched the particles drift down wind to the salty Strait. Salt. I'd consider salt. It had multiple definitions like the saltiness of a character, the saltiness of Lorraine. Salt was essential for growth, for healing, for spicing bland food and bland lives.

As I wandered through the downtown section other nouns sprang to mind. For me Lorraine meant freedom, laughter, frankness and love. Love again, but in a different context, one I could explore in poetry.

By the museum I slowed, cheered by the thought of being in Neal's company. However, he and three older ladies were bent over a living room display case from which he raised his head to mouth, "Office."

On his desk he'd spread a spectrum of booklets, all histories of various communities and beside them brochures advertised printing options. Seated in his chair, I thumbed through "The History of Norland: A California Classic," and when Neal strode in, he squeezed my shoulder in welcome. "Unfortunately, I'm a captive of the Sorenson sisters, who've donated their father's tools. They're showing me the most advantageous spots to exhibit the collection. But, as you've brilliantly deduced, I've amassed a number of town histories we can study."

"Shall I take them along?"

"Great, and the printing options. See what you think. At first glance it appears that a pay-on-demand might work."

As I stacked booklets and brochures together Neal located a plastic bag in his bottom desk drawer. "Ne-al," called the Sorenson trio. At that he rolled his eyes, answered, "Coming," and quite skillfully shook out the wrinkled plastic bag, dropped in my stash and said , "Sorry. Would love to talk with you."

"We have our Wednesday appointment."

He nodded. "And Sam, the lawyer?"

"Nice of you to ask. I've not seen him but will soon. Dan's out of here in under a week."

"Good."

I continued home strangely cheered. The prospect of analyzing other histories, of comparing printing prices and promises offered something concrete in the midst of fluid emotions.

The house retained its coolness and after drinking a glass of water, I mounted the stairs intending to tell Franklin about Lorraine and the booklets before we commenced on "Love in the Gazebo." But at the doorway I reconsidered. Factual information could wait. I needed Franklin's touch, so I grabbed for the necklace with what must have been too much vigor. In the quiet I heard a rasp and simultaneously the rosebud gave. In my palm it lay shattered. Impossible. I couldn't be seeing correctly. That wasn't a leaf, a fragment of petal, or a chipped center. The miniscule metal holder which clipped the rosebud to the chain couldn't be all that remained of the necklace.

I laid pieces on the desk blotter. Glue them together? Yet such tiny pieces. I left them alone and snapped the chain around my neck. The room and I waited, for surely the chain could bring Franklin. The waiting lengthened. I selected the largest rosebud fragment, a pink petal, and pressed it against the chain. Nothing.

"Think," I commanded myself. "Think." As Franklin would, I paced the gray rug's edges. Concentrating on him wouldn't produce him, that I'd learned when I lost the necklace. Touching his favorite items had no effect either, but earlier he had directed me, had sent impressions of Dan in an effort to let me know that Dan had found the necklace. "All right," I said aloud, "Franklin, tell me what to do."

I attempted to clear my mind, tried not to think of anything, which, of course, meant extraneous strands flooded in: Molly's questions, Neal's smile, Lorraine's tears, booklets in the sack. . .

I scrutinized the splintered rosebud. I hadn't skill to repair it, but an expert could, or someone could assemble most of the pieces, enough that there would be sufficient power to summon Franklin. Gently I swept the bisque shards into an envelope, and in the computer room searched through the phone book. Jewelers worked with microscopic-sized instruments, and the yellow pages listed three. I chose the nearest, a downtown jeweler, and parked the Plymouth right before his door. An auspicious sign.

Probably disappointment is keener when so much is at stake, and when things originally go well, I later decided, for besides the lucky parking spot, the jeweler had no customers. He arranged the envelope's contents on a silver plate and examined them carefully. "My dear," he said at last, "I am sorry, but there's nothing I can do."

"You can't glue the bigger pieces together? I mean, it doesn't have to be complete or aesthetic looking, doesn't have to be a total rosebud."

"I take pride in everything that goes out my door. I wouldn't be proud of this."

With fragments in the envelope I tried the second jeweler, located in the mall. He pinned me with sharp eyes. "It's not worth fixing."

"I don't care. I need it in some form."

He arched an eyebrow as he waited for an explanation, but in my distraught state I could think of nothing, could only beg, "Please."

Whatever kind of glue or cement that he applied bound three sections together. But the rosebud was an oddity, disparate segments patched with a translucent fixative. He'd done what I requested and I rationalized that in whatever shape it was that it would work.

It didn't. When I encircled my throat with the necklace, the north room held only me. Maybe Franklin had to get accustomed to this new design. Maybe the glue needed to dry longer. I replaced it on the closet shelf, but my mind had atrophied. I couldn't think, nor examine the historical booklets. I was—bereft.

The house shrank around me, so I sought the back yard. Sunlight had heated the gazebo's grayed boards and the surrounding greenery. Nothing of last night was evident—no matted brush where bodies could have lain. It was as if it were a dream.

Dan found me there hours later when he came home. "Kate," he called from the patio. "Kate?"

I blinked. I had sat stone-like all afternoon, rather as I had when I'd experienced physical death: two miscarriages, Dad, Mom. Each time I had retreated to some far interior space beyond/below my mind. By huddling there, I had survived. I would this time. I would.

Dan neared and said, "What's wrong? Molly?"

I shook my head as he sank onto the opposite board.

When I didn't speak he tentatively asked, "It's not our—separation?"

"I guess," and I sounded close to normal, "it's Lorraine's leaving. The best friend I've ever had."

Since Dan couldn't approve of this aging hippie woman, he couldn't be sorry. Who knows she might have led his wife—soon to be former wife—into some illegal activity that would reflect poorly on him. However, he had the decency to say, "Must be hard for you."

As we ate dinner, as Dan discussed division of a savings account and wondered how best to handle a certificate of deposit, he would wait when I cried or when I grew distracted. I felt he wished he could smear his happiness onto me, for incredibly he'd wrapped up outstanding accounts that day (phenomenal what energies love can prompt) and Old Jer had released him.

Because we were roommates, ones thrown together on a final bumpy trip, we individually dressed in the bathroom; individually slipped into bed at varied times. Tonight Dan went first. At the kitchen table I regarded a back yard curtained by night. Some thirty minutes later I entered the north room. My heart raced, for I had such hopes. Perhaps the re-arranged parts had erected some temporary barrier that Franklin had cleared. Or maybe because he was nearing the completion of his book, the pathway between our dimensions was weakening and simply required more time for contact. Perhaps. . .

I switched on the desk light. Its glow crossed the notebook, folder with poems he had approved and the necklace. Even under kind light, the rosebud was pathetic. As I lifted it I thought, *Something must still exist and coupled with my desire and Franklin's surely it will be enough.*

I marked time's passage on a pocket watch. Franklin had groaned when I showed him the digital bedroom clock. "Numbers jump up? That's not right. You should see each second advance, hear the tick of time. And you should wind a clock. It makes you aware of your responsibility to time." So I had ordered a cheap pocket watch and if wound daily, it supplied the rhythm he needed.

At eleven-thirty I turned off the light, remembering that he appeared first during a power outage. I'd simulate that. I gazed out the windows onto the valley, vowing that it would become my valley. As I surveyed Madison and lights dotting the level streets and the opposite hill, I wondered about Amy. When she'd faced these windows, had there been lights, occasional ones? For the historical booklet, I could research electricity. Momentarily interest in that project rose, but it quickly deflated when I heard the tick tick of the watch's second hand.

At twelve-thirty, I opened the folder containing Franklin's poems and counted them. Sixty-nine. For a chapbook that number would be enough— if there were no more.

The following day I did not try to contact him. I focused on the now and on the future. I dumped the booklets and brochures onto the kitchen table. With pen and a pad, I outlined the text's structure, noted ratio of facts, anecdotes, quotations, and illustrations in each one. But that night I re-entered the north room and did so for seven succeeding nights. Franklin never reappeared.

After Dan left for Iowa and the house was solely mine, I opened the poetry folder and read each selection. But whether I read the work in the north room or on the first level the same questions plagued me. Do we think we're better or worse than we actually are? Does investing yourself deeply in any artistic endeavor, even if you're only adequate, somehow mean more in a cosmic sense than those who don't invest their natural gifts? Then I would sigh. And what of the audience, the common people—ones I didn't believe Franklin intended to address—but those that his poetry might affect? Would they like his love poetry? I smiled, recalling an English prof who'd said, "When you reduce most of the classics to their simplest denomination, they come off as soap operas. What makes them classics is the writing style and the lasting philosophical/humanistic questions they raise." Would Franklin's work evoke any deep discussion?

I closed the folder and hugged the collection to my chest. I had no answers. I only knew that in Franklin's house I had found myself.

EPILOGUE

In my north room I add the last line to my "Madison" poem; then hurry downstairs calling, "Neal." No answer. Must be in the back yard. I circle the boxes which contain the printed history books and the self-published chapbooks that I've entitled, "Love in a Secret Time," which we'll display and sell at the museum. I think Franklin would approve of this title, and believe he'd appreciate the note on the chapbook's first page which explains that I published his poetry just as I discovered it in his house.

Occasionally I wonder if he, wherever he is, finds any irony in the fact that the original lump sum of money Dan sent after he moved to Harding paid to publish the collection. Additionally, I hope that wherever Franklin is, that if he peers down, he will not be discouraged about the sales.

In our Madison History book we have included Franklin Elliott, and certainly he will be a secret part of my history forever.

Then I notice an envelope that Neal's laid on the end table.

"Hey Writer Lady,

If you seek material, try the bus. From Chicago to Florida a guy has read portions of the Old Testament to me (said he identified with Job, but don't we all) and I've signed a woman's petition. She's running for President of these United States on a platform of annexing Mexico. She promised it would solve the illegal immigration problem.

I've drunk anemic coffee and the stout bitters out of a Styrofoam cup, and I've coated veins and arteries with enough cholesterol that my innards— have always been confused about the location of interior organs—resemble some ninety-year olds. But I'm experiencing life and—"

"Kate," Neal calls from the computer room, which is now his study. "Molly's on the phone. Wants you to talk to Pierce."

I laugh. At eleven months of age, Pierce doesn't care if Granny Kate speaks to him or not, but into the mouthpiece I say, "Hi Honey."

And as I fall into a patter of baby talk, Neal wraps his arm around me, the pressure of his wedding ring against my upper arm a reminder of love and of jewelry. When Molly takes the phone from Pierce and before she gives her news, I turn my head to see into the living room. Over the fireplace hangs Amy's portrait, which Neal brought from the house he sold. Sometimes I imagine Amy's smiling, but I don't need to imagine the powerful beauty of the intact rosebud that glows around her neck.

End

ABOUT THE AUTHOR

*B*everly Lauderdale graduated from Simpson College (Iowa) and received her master's degree from Holy Names University (California). She has taught at the junior high and college level and has led "Craft of Writing" classes for Mt. Diablo Adult Education.

In love with writing since she could grasp a pencil, she has published poetry, short stories, and two novels, *Notes When Summer Ends* and *The Long Wind*. Her articles have appeared in a variety of publications: *Los Angeles Times, Travel & Leisure, The Writer, New York Post.* . . .

Lauderdale and her husband Bob divide their time between Martinez, California, and Cedarville, California. From both locations they explore the countryside via a vintage airplane.